Not All who wander Are

LOST

A Novel by
Phil Robinson

This novel, *Not All Who Wander Are Lost*, is fiction. Names, characters and events are a result of the author's imagination and not based on fact. Any similarity to an actual person or a real happening is a coincidence.

Printed in the United States of America

LitFire
PUBLISHING

LitFire LLC
1-800-511-9787
www.litfirepublishing.com
order@litfirepublishing.com

Contents

• • • • • • • • • • • •

I dedicate this novel to my sister, Patti, who always thought I could do anything, and to this day still drives a 1985 Volkswagen Westfalla.

I Acknowledge:

Debra Hamrick-Robinson is responsible for the artwork and design of the book cover.

Debra also edited the book, took out much of the foul language, and made the words I wrote sound better.

She is not only an artist and an editor, but a really good wife.

This book, which at times was very difficult for me to write, would have never been a live publication were it not for a few friends:

Roger Hall, Kim Valentine, David Burt, Heather Ramsay, Marie Simunvich, and Michael Levitt. All these people contributed to this book.

I also acknowledge all the soldiers, past and present who made it, but will never be the same, and those who didn't make it and will be forever in our memory.

PREFACE

· · · · · · · · · · · ·

"Now a days, seems like a gift when I wake up every mornin', and I like to just lie real still a minute and ponder the nature of things and how I came to be a real lucky man.

My name is Jimmy Johnson...you know, like the famous football coach, 'cept I ain't famous, and I sure ain't rich. Well, lemme say this: I am rich; I just don't have a whole lotta money. I am rich mostly because of the experiences I had late in my life.

I was born the son of a share-cropper who lived in Hog Mountain, Georgia. In the summer, when we weren't picking cotton, we would go swimming in the creek to cool off a bit before mama called us for supper. While I'm a-talking to you, I can still smell the aroma of collards and corn bread filling the air as we washed our hands on the front porch in an old wash basin that was beside the well. We thought we was real lucky to have a well right there on the front porch since most of our neighbors had to walk a ways and carry their water.

That all changed when I was 17 and joined the Army. It was the first time in my life I was around white people and before you know it, we were all shipped off to Vietnam where we all bled the same color. There was a few times in Nam I really did shine and was admired and respected...even got a couple of nice medals.

But, soon enough, my Army days were over and I wound up back home where I took the jobs that were available for someone like me: janitor, painter, garbage man, and washing cars at the Chevrolet place. I spent my life trying to do my best, and not cause no trouble; and I done decided long ago that my lot in life was gonna be not much better than that of a shoe shine boy in Atlanta. Just the same, I put one foot in front of the other every day so I could pay my own way.

Then one day, I ran into a man who helped me turn my whole life around. When I say I ran into him, I mean just that. I almost run him down in my garbage truck! Yep...that's right. I almost crashed into his Volkswagen Bus. Some say it was accident, some say destiny.

His name was Robert McLeod and his belief in me inspired a confidence and courage that had long been left behind. He managed to get this old man to see that I was really worth something and could succeed at any age. I went from driving a trash truck to the head of security for a large development firm. He even showed me the advantage of staying in shape and taught me how to invest some of my money.

All this happened because of a Volkswagen Microbus. A whole lot more happened too with that old VW, and I really should tell you the entire story of Robby and his Volkswagen. It's like he always said, "Everybody has a Volkswagen story."

His story goes beyond some tale of a man and his car. It's a story that only you can decide if it be true or not, because parts do seem unbelievable. I do know the whole story; I just don't know where to start.

Let me see...uh...I guess I'll just start from the very beginning... back in 1969 when Robby was 21 and just got out of the Marines."

Chapter 1

. . . .

"We met and talked"

Spring, 1969

As far as the eye could see, Robby observed a long line of naval ships tied to the dock in San Diego. He paused for a moment just to take in the quiet and the stillness of everything. It was hard to believe that less than a month ago he was surrounded by explosions, gunfire, yelling and screaming. The quiet was something he needed to get used to again.

Long gone is anything about him that looks military, except his buzz haircut...which was getting longer. He was now sporting a Hawaiian shirt, shorts and flip flops. He was about two degrees beyond cool, damn near chilly, but he didn't care. He had been hot, wet, and miserable enough for a lifetime. The cool breeze and the cool clothing were such a blessing.

Robby bellied up to the bar, one of many along the boardwalk. He looked at his new wrist watch and though, "Umm...1300. I'm gonna have to get used to saying 1 o'clock again." As usual, the bar was nearly empty that time of day. Someone put a dime in the juke box and played a Beach Boys song. After listening to the song for a minute, Robby turned to the bartender, "Roger that, I sure get around."

As he sat there, soaking up the quiet, he enjoyed the clean of everything he touched. Even   drinking real water with real ice was a good thing, as he recalled the green, slimy, filthy water in the village wells of Viet Nam, thinking about the immense difference... **BANG!!!** Robby dove to the floor, got behind his stool and yelled INCOMING!!! The bartender ran to him, bent down to look him in the eye and said, "Are you OK, sailor?"

"Sir, I am no sailor. I am a United States Marine. I apologize for what I did, sir – just reacting, or maybe over reacting as the case may be."

"Ah forget it. We get that in here at least once a day. Just so you'll know, you hit the dirt because a waitress dropped a glass."

"Well, as least I didn't shit in my pants...that would've been a revolting development..." he said as he pulled himself up and brushed off his knees.

"I tell you what, son, the next drink is on me. Whatcha drinkin'?"

Robby was a little ashamed to admit he had never drunk alcohol before and had told the waitress he wanted ice water while deciding what to have. He remembered one of his buddies from Arizona used to talk about tequila.

"I'll have some tequila with another drink of water. It seems I spilled mine all over your nice bar."

"Don't you worry about a thing, young man, you just sit at this table and Gretchen will be right over. Do you want lime with salt on the rim?"

"Sure."

Robby didn't know what in the hell the bartender was talking about with the lime and salt, but went along with it just so he wouldn't look so out of place. Robby took a sip of the tequila and, trying not to make a stink face, thought to himself, "Goddamn, this tastes like lighter fluid."

As he tryed to figure out how to get to the bathroom undetected and pour it down the sink, he heard a booming voice behind him, "FALL IN, MOTHER FUCKER!"

Robby, rotated slowly around, and right in front of him stood the best friend he ever had. It was Moose Forrester. Standing erect in the small bar, he looked larger than life, muscles on top of muscles. He was out of uniform, well, somewhat. He was wearing Marine issue boots with new jeans and an olive green tank top. Robby noticed a large white gauze patch on his arm.

"Well, I'll just be goddamn-go-to-hell. Moose!!" Look at you."

"Right on, man. I'm a P.F.C. now. That's Private Fucking Citizen."

"Sit, man, cool your heels and what's this, a tattoo?"

"Yeah, take a look"

"Moose, that's three naked women riding a rocket."

"No it ain't, they're riding a vibrator!"

"So, you took a half month's pay and spent it to get a tattoo of three naked women riding a vibrator?"

"Hell yeah. Ain't it great? Say, little bro, what are you drinking?"

"Tequila, it tastes like horse piss, you want it?"

"You just don't know how to drink it. Order two more and I'll show you what to do with the salt and lime."

As the two jar heads were engaged in a learning experience that involved shots of tequila, two more military men entered the bar looking very pissed off. One was a sailor, the other, from the Army – both still in uniform. The sailor was short like Robby but with a much smaller frame, weighting in at around 135, whereas Robby was about 160. The man from the Army was tall and slim, and carried himself in a distinguished way.

The two former Marines asked them to join the learning experience.

The sailor was the first to speak, blurting out, "Bat shit! Those goddamn hippies! We oughta take every fuckin' one of em, load em up in a ship and drop em off in the ocean. Our country would be better off if we took every one of them anti-war, liberal minded, cock sucking, bunny hugging mother fuckers and make them into shark bait; they're just a bunch of monkey twats."

The soldier from the Army stepped in, "Perhaps this is where we get the idea of 'cuss like a sailor'? I apologize. We have not been properly introduced. My name is Roger Hilton and my Navy friend is Kim Hernandez. I believe he is somewhat miffed about the service, or lack of service, of the taxi drivers here in San Diego. You see, we were trying to hail a cab to take us to the bus station, and this cab driver with long hair and little round glasses would not give us a ride because we were military and called us baby killers."

With eyes ablaze, Kim says, "And the hell of it all is neither of us has killed anybody...not a fuckin soul. I was a cook, and he expedited general supplies in the Army."

Moose looked down at the two, "Well then, thanks for the ride, sailor boy, and thank you, box kicker, for getting those boots to me on time. Nice boots are good to have while killing the enemy."

Robby glared at Moose and shook his head slightly 'no,' as if to say, "Don't start no shit."

Moose decided he had been in enough fights and backed off, and said, "So, youse still enlisted?"

Roger replied, "We have both been officially out of the military for about three days. I'm eternally grateful that it's all over and I can get back to my life."

"Oh yeah? What was your life?"

"I was in college, studied law for a while and transferred to a college closer to home and changed my major to marketing. I fell below the required grades and got drafted. I thought for sure I would be in Nam, right in the heat of the battle, but I was a quartermaster the whole time. The closest I ever got to Viet Nam was Okinawa, where I made ready supplies that were flown into Nam."

Kim chimed in, "I always wanted to be in the Navy. I was gonna be a lifer. When I first joined, they put me at Pearl Harbor pulling maintenance on a dry dock. I finally got on a battle ship and worked my way up to assistant to the officer on deck and assistant to the navigator. I was even scheduled to go to navigation school.

One day I was ordered to sand and varnish cabinets and book shelves in the Captain's quarters. I would varnish and wipe the excess off on a rag. I got to noticing that those fumes from the rag were making me high as a mother fucker. Before I'd finished the job, I had that rag pressed in my face, inhaling those fumes like it was the best thing on earth. I didn't finish the job. They found me high, in the Captain's closet with my pants down, stroking my wiener. After that, I was busted back to E-1 and never got off kitchen duty. So, that did it for me. Guess I'm not going to be a career Naval Officer after all."

Without a blink, Robby said, "Yeah, I can see that. You have to be the President or a Congressman to get away with something like that and I don't think you have much chance of becoming President."

"Nah, I don't think us Puerto Ricans have much chance of becoming President."

"Is that what you are? Puerto Rican?"

"My father is Puerto Rican from NYC, my mama's a sweet colored lady from Birmingham, Alabama."

And with a chuckle, Moose added, "...and colored folks don't have a snowball's chance in hell of being President either, so be more careful where you get high, and blop your baloney...."

"How about you, Roger, where are you from?"

"I'm from Canton, Texas. It's about 100 miles from the Dallas-Fort Worth area...somewhat rural, with many trees."

"Are you related to those Hiltons that own the hotels?"

"Yes, as a matter of fact, I am. That was why I was in college. I was going to work for my uncle who owns the Hilton hotels. I failed the first time, but now I have a second chance. And you Robby, what's your history?"

"I went to college in Atlanta for two years and joined the USMC."

"You left college to JOIN the military? Why? You had it made."

"With all the turmoil and anti-war demonstrations going on, I decided that we should back our country in its effort to stem the tide of Communism. I can always go back to school."

"And you, Moose, what's your story?"

"My daddy was a Marine, my uncle was a Marine, I'm a Marine...and that's all there is to it."

Kim took a gulp from his Budweiser can and looked across the table at the two Marines, "Where'd you guys serve?"

"We were all over the place. We were in a "bail 'em out" squad. We'd go in under fire, and rescue other outfits that were in trouble. They would drop us in and there we stayed until we either succeeded, or died trying."

"Fuck man, that must have been brutal."

Robby and Moose just stared at him...a long, blank, silent stare, no emotion. Robby finally broke the silence, "Well it wasn't exactly a John Wayne movie. And it damn sure wasn't like anything I was expecting."

All four of them became quiet, thinking their own private thoughts. Roger originally ordered a Manhattan; however, he had too much trouble explaining to Gretchen that it had to be Italian sweet vermouth with Canadian rye whiskey and nothing else would do. He settled for an imported beer with a frosted glass. He was pondering, rubbing his finger around the rim of the glass, making a high-pitched squeaking sound. He stared out the window, where all he could see were large ships, blue sky, smiling sailors, and pretty women.

Roger broke the silence, "You know, it is such a pity that after all we have done to serve our country and all the sacrifices we have made, we are still treated in such sub-standard fashion. There are still restaurants and hotels that Kim can't enter and enjoy. We are shunned and scorned because we wear the uniform of our country, by the very people in our country we are sworn to protect. I tell you right now, I am not looking forward to that long bus ride home, having to sit with people that I don't even know if they are for me or against me."

Kim nodded and said, "Yeah, I might even wind up on the back of the fuckin bus. Or at least be made to feel like I should be."

By now Robby had mastered the art of timing the salt, tequila, and lime. Each shot tasted a little better than the one before. In his altered state he piped up, "I gotta idea. It's brilliant...no... it's damn brilliant. We all live in the South, except Moose. Why don't we pool our money, buy some old car, maybe a '55 Chevy or something, and we can travel where we want, do what we want and see what we want. Hell, we can even just wander around for a while. It will just be us...the Fearsome Foursome! We can drop off Roger in Texas, Kim in Alabama, me in Atlanta, and Moose, you can drive it home to New Jersey."

Kim put down his beer can and said, "Well, what about the car we all put money into? If we get dropped off, and Moose drives home, does he keep the car for free, or what?"

Roger's face lit up, "I have it! We pool our money. We can get a '55 for about $500.00 or less. That would be $125.00 apiece. Moose can drive it home, sell it, and send us a money order for what he gets out of the car. That way, we can travel the whole country, or as Robby says, wander around for a while, and do it for free. Who knows? We may even end up making money on the deal."

Robby held up his shot glass in a toast, "Let's do it!! To the Fearsome Foursome!!!"

They toast one another, down their drinks, and are off to the experience of a lifetime.

Chapter 2

. . . .

"We made the purchase"

Robby had learned from Gretchen that there was a street not far from the bar that was block after block of car lots...both new and used, from a new Cadillac to an old Ford. So they hailed a cab, threw their belongings into the trunk, including a large duffle bag belonging to Kim, and piled in.

It didn't take long for the fearsome foursome to realize that $500.00 was not going to buy much car in San Diego. It seemed they were not the only servicemen in town wanting to make such a purchase. It was back to the law of supply and demand.

After visiting a few lots with no success, they entered a small lot that contained about 20 cars. The sales office was an old 1940's travel trailer. There was a 1954 Chevrolet with a sign on the windshield: "SPECIAL 695.00."

Robby looked carefully around the car, "This car is junk. Back in Atlanta, you could buy this car for $200.00. I mean...like... shit. The car is 15 years old, and has 90,000 miles with tires so bald you could puncture them with a marshmallow. It has that old 235 in-line six cylinder that's only good for 80,000 miles. We would have to buy tires and pray it don't blow up before we get home. And it's getting to where you can't even buy a good tire for less than $25.00!"

About this time a salesman came out of the little 8x12 foot trailer. He was wearing a big smile and a bow tie. Roger explained to him they were looking for something to ride home in, nothing special, just something that would make the trip across the USA.

The salesman smiled even bigger and gestured to the far end of the lot and said, "I have just what you need. Come with me. It's a 1962 Volkswagen Microbus. I just bought it from a man who was the second owner that used it as a work vehicle. He did home improvements and remodeling. The inside looks a little rough, but it runs like brand new."

The four stood there, at looked carefully at it. Kim called it tomato soup red. Not red, not orange, but somewhere in-between. Moose told the salesman that his daddy calls Volkswagens 'Nazi Bastards' and as far as he is concerned, you can give them back to Hilter. (They all think he really meant to say Hitler, but no one wanted to correct this huge hulk of a man). Roger just swallowed hard and dwelled on the prospect of driving across the country with strangers in something that looked like a turd someone tried to polish.

After a few more moments of staring at the Microbus, Robby asked for the keys and to borrow a long screwdriver. He got both and started a thorough examination the bus. The outside body was clean and waxed with a few small dents. He took out a penny and measured the tire tread, which was 1/8 inch deep... good tires. The motor started on the first try. He then went to the rear, opened the engine door, stuck the screwdriver handle to his ear and the other end on different parts of the engine.

Robby said aloud for all to hear, salesman included, "The number three intake valve is sticking. That's probably because it's been setting up for a while and nobody's been driving it. The worst thing you can do to a VW is not drive it. After it's driven for a while, it will either straighten out or we'll have to pull the number three jug. The trans and brakes check out. What are you asking for it?"

"I'll take $895.00."

"Let me talk to my buddies a minute."

The four guys walk a few steps away and huddled up to talk over what they were going to do.

"Hey Robby, how come you know so much about this Volkswagen?"

"From the time I was 14 to 18 years old, I worked in a Volkswagen repair shop. I owned a 1957 VW when I joined the Marines. It was triple black and had the little rear window. I used to drive 100 miles a day when I was in college, fifty miles each way. It cost me a penny a mile. Gas was 30 cents a gallon and it gave me 30 miles per gallon. I could put $2.00 worth in it and go 200 miles. What I saved driving that VW helped me meet college expenses. This van will get close to 20 mpg. We'll be driving about 2,400 miles. At 20 miles to the gallon, that's 120 gallons of gas. Even at 40 cents a gallon, it will cost us about $48.00 to cross the country. Now, here's what we do. Each of y'all give me $125.00. Moose, don't say a word, just play along."

Robby gathered their money, folded it in his pocket, then he took five one hundred dollar bills out of his own wallet, and walked to the van. He opened the side door and fanned the five one hundred dollar bills and placed them on the floorboard.

"Sir, it's like this. My buddy, Kim, has been called a spick and a nigger; we have been called baby killers, and war mongrels. People have spit at us, and flipped us off. All we have done for this treatment is that we tried to serve our country. Now, all we want to do is go home and start our life. We're poor soldiers who barely made $200.00 a month and now we don't even have that. Here's $500.00 cash in hundred dollar bills right here in front of you. Sir, we could use a break. Could you give us a break and accept this cash money for that van?"

"Son, you just bought a van."

Chapter 3

. . . .

"Our Journey begins"

As it turned out, Roger said the smartest thing anyone had said all day, "Let's take it to a service station, give it an oil change and lube, and then I think we should go to an Army/Navy surplus store and purchase some supplies. We may need to camp out sometime. Since Robby can fix anything on this bus, we should also purchase some basic tools."

Robby says, "Groovy."

"GROOVY? Did you say GROOVY? Shit, man, we gotta get you out of California. Next, you'll be growing long hair, smoking dope, and throwing up a peace sign. Fall in ladies, I'm sitting up front with my bro and you two guys sit in the back. Robby, you drive."

Moose didn't get an argument from anybody.

They stopped at a Goodyear tire store that serviced cars and sold appliances. Robby and Roger were looking in a glass display counter that was beside a large brass cash register. Moose was outside at the drink machine with Kim, cussing and fussing about how Coca-Cola and Pepsi now cost a quarter instead of a dime, as they did when he first joined up in 1965. Inside, behind the counter, there were shelves that contained several small black and white TVs, the store manager called these portable TVs and pointed to the fact they had a handle on the top. There were some 9 volt transistor radios that the salesman really tried to sell to Robby and Roger, telling them you can take them to the beach and the girls are crazy about a guy with a transistor

—
11

radio...cutting edge...only$7.95!

Robby stared at a metal box in the counter marked $109.95 and asked, "What is this thing for one hundred nine dollars?"

"Sonny, that is an 8-track tape player. You can play all kinds of music like you would hear on the radio but without the commercials and without the static noise. If you boys are traveling, it's a must to buy this to make the trip go by faster. You can pick your tunes as you drive along."

"How does it play the music?"

"Come with me to the demo model, and I'll show you."

The salesman plugged a plastic box in the tape player and, just like that, Robby heard his favorite Rolling Stones song. The song rocked throughout the entire store. By now, the Fearsome Foursome were all staring at this machine, opened-mouthed.

Roger said, "My roommate in college had an 8-track tape player in his 1965 Corvair. It worked great. In fact, it was more dependable than the Corvair."

Robby nodded at Roger, looked at the salesman and said, "But will it work on the VW 6 volt system?"

"It'll work fine as wine. All radios are still made to work on 6.8 volts. On 12 volt systems, the car manufacturers put in a resistor for the radios. That way the tubes don't get too hot. I tell you what I'll do for you. I bet you guys just got out of the service and I want to treat you right. The oil change is $5.00 , the 8-track player is $109.95, installation is $18.00 and speakers are $10.00 apiece extra. That's a total of $143.00. I'll throw in everything for $120.00: oil and lube, two new speakers, 8-track tape player, installation, and I'll even give you the Rolling Stones tape deck with my compliments. Is it a deal?"

In unison, the Fearsome Foursome yelled, "HELL YEAH!"

Robby went into the service bay and showed the manager where he wanted the tape player: under the metal dash to the right of the floor shifter, so putting in and taking out tapes wouldn't interfere with his shifting gears. The manager said, "We'll have to drill two 1/8 inch holes underneath the dash for the bracket that holds the tape player."

"No big deal," replied Robby.

They purchased enough supplies to sink a ship, and enough beer, scotch and tequila to make it float again. They had even caused a big smile to appear on a 55 year old lady who owned a music store, when they purchased over twenty 8-track tapes of all kinds of music. Robby noticed that against the wall there were two booths that looked like tiny closets that contained a small record player, where you could close the door and listen to a record you were thinking of buying. He told her it reminded him of Clark's Music Store back home.

She said, "Oh, nobody uses the booths any more. The public is going to 8-track tapes, and that's the future in music. I predict within ten years, there will be no more records, just 8-track tapes."

Robby thought for a moment and nodded, "This is definitely the wave of the future. They're so much better than records and so portable. I think you're right. By 1979, or 1985 at the latest, everything will be on 8-track tapes."

After climbing back into the van with enough music to last them the whole trip, the Fearsome Foursome decided the first stop on their way back home would be the Grand Canyon.

As they were headed north out of San Diego, Kim spoke up loudly above the sound of the music, "You know, guys, we're less than 30 miles from Tijuana, Mexico. I've been there once and let me tell you...that fuckin place is wide open. You can get anything there, and I mean anything. You can get anything from a small taco to a big tittied woman. Beer and tequila are dirt cheap, there's always a party going on in the street and you never seen prettier women. We'll never be closer. How 'bout it?"

Robby and Moose looked at one another, did a high five followed by a soul hand shake and yelled, "RIGHT ON...MEXICO!!!"

Robby made a quick U-turn right in the middle of the street and said, "One thing about a Volkswagen, it will turn on a dime and give you nine cents change."

So, in a blink, they changed direction from north to south, headed for Mexico.

"By the way, Kim, can you be our interpreter?"

"Si si, puto madre."

Chapter 4

• • • • • • • • • • • • • •

"Our Life In Mexico"

The Fearsome Foursome were aghast at all the sin and degradation that was being carried on in the streets of Tijuana, so they said a little prayer for theses drunks and extremely friendly women and started passing out Bibles...well ok, that's not exactly what happened.

Even though none of them could be said to have led a sheltered life, all four of them were behaving on the emotional level of middle school cheerleaders, laughing and pointing as if they had never seen a woman in a short skirt or a can of beer before. Someone had told them if they stayed on the main street, they wouldn't get in any trouble because that's where the souvenir shops and respectable cantinas were that catered to the tourists.

Kim said, "This reminds me of New York City with all the street vendors and shit. Instead of hot dogs and sidewalk sundaes, there's the smell of fresh tacos and burritos in the air; merchants coming up to you wanting to cut a deal...just like in NYC."

Suddenly, they realized they'd been living on a liquid diet all day with no solid food and the aroma of fresh beef and chicken sizzling on a small grill on the sidewalk was just too much. As they sat on a bench, four abreast, they wolfed down their fill of tacos and burritos and washed it down with a small glass bottle of Coca-Cola that was barely cool, having been in an ice chest on the sidewalk all day where most of the ice had melted.

A young Mexican boy with a wooden box strapped over his shoulder ran up to them, and with a serious Spanish accent, said, "I will clean up your boots and shine them for a quarter, senor."

Robby smiled, "Sure thing little fellow. I'll give you one American dollar for all four of us."

"Usted no está usando los zapatos."

"What did he say?"

"He said you are not wearing shoes."

"Tell him it's OK. I'll give him the dollar anyway."

They all sat back like they were kings. It was nice to be waited on, since for the past few years these guys had been busting their ass for everybody else.

As they sat there, the sun was setting behind the storefronts and the merchants were beginning to close their shops and the street vendors were pulling their carts off the sidewalk and heading home...all but the taco vendors. They stayed on the sidewalks 24/7. It was an old Tijuana tradition, as the shops died for the evening, the bars and cantinas came alive.

After the shoe shine, the Foursome first walked into a shop that sold sombreros and Mexican blankets. Kim stopped and purchased a blanket with an Aztec design that was maroon and grey and a solid white goatskin rug. The other three stared at him. "What... It's for my mama."

They were the sombrero shop's last customers for the day, and the first customers for the cantina next door. They sat right in front of a stage where two ladies in traditional Mexican dress were dancing around a large hat on the floor. Then someone removed the hat and two men in black suits came out and danced with the ladies in a traditional folk dance, their brightly colored skirts swirling around them.

Roger spoke up, "This looks a lot like square dancing like we have back home in Texas."

"Not quite what I expected according to what Kim said about this town...and another thing..."

—

Before Robby could finish his sentence, the folk dancers were replaced by a large mariachi band with guitars, accordion, two trumpets and a tuba.

Moose had been squirming in his seat and looking around for a while, much like a little boy who is forced to go to Sunday school. Speaking above the sound of the band, he said "It sounds like goddamn polka music like we get in Jersey, except I don't know what they're saying. Hey Kim, is this the best this town can do?"

"Fuck no, man. We finish these drinks and I'll show you a trick."

"Groovy, man"

"There you go with that groovy shit again. I would hate to have to beat that out of you after all we been through."

They followed Kim to a sign that read: "Zona Norte" and everything changed. The sidewalk was broken in places; the street was narrow and littered with trash; the buildings looked as though they were built by elementary school boys trying to make a hut out of daddy's scrap wood. Looking at the sidewalk, they saw a small stream of water headed toward them, and immediately looked to the right to see a man pissing in the alley. Robby had begun to think that wearing flip flops was not a very good idea.

Moose was the first to speak up, "Oh hell yeah, now this is more like it!! Lots of clubs, lots of women. It reminds me a little of R&R in Bangkok where I bought that shotgun. You remember, Robby?"

"Oh yes sir, indeed I do."

"Right on man, you can get any flavor of woman you want here. This is freaking swell," Moose said as he put his arm around Kim's shoulder and lifted him off the ground.

"I told you guys...anything from a small taco to a sexy mamasita."

Roger Hilton looked down the street at the scores of

prostitutes walking the sidewalk, there must have been a hundred or so; all wearing less than most women wear to the beach. He swallowed, turned a little pale, and hoped he would get out of here tonight alive and without a dose of the clap.

Before they made their first romantic encounter of the evening, and before they even had a chance to purchase a healthy beverage from anyone on the street, a young man wearing a sparkling white shirt came up to them and said, "Hey hombre, you wanna fuck my cousin? She never been fucked before.......by you. Just come with me and I show you heaven. She and my other cousins can do it all. You can stay all night, just 15 American dollars. You here for good time, no? We show you good time. Follow me, por favor."

As the guys were walking toward the gate to heaven, a beautiful lady who appeared to be very well-to-do approached them. She must have had some clout because as soon as she arrived and spoke two words to him, the man with all the friendly cousins left in a big hurry. They were all staring at a gold cross on her chest that was situated right between two very shapely breasts.

She broke the silence of the stare, "Is good thing I come along when I did, that man is no good. He will take your money and run."

"Thank you, ma'am, my name is Robert McLeod. We're just here for a little fun before we head for home. Can you recommend any good places?"

"Oh si. These places here are nothing but trash and will only bring you trouble. We are having a big party at my ranch tonight. Everything is free. You do not need to bring anything, not even your money. We have steaks, lobsters, plenty of good Mexican food, beer and tequila....all free. There are many young women there who love American soldiers. So, you want to come to my party, no?"

They all nodded yes in unison, still a little speechless and awestruck toward this beautiful lady standing right there in the not so beautiful surroundings... like a brilliant red rose blossoming from a garbage heap.

"Ma'am, since we don't know where you live, can we follow you in our car?"

"I must stay in town for some business. My assistant, Jose, can show you the way. Is OK he ride with you?"

She called out to a man across the street that was at a taco stand, who immediately ran across the street. He, too, was nicely dressed. He looked more like a butler or waiter, or even one of the dancers they saw in the cantina.

They all climbed into the bus with Jose sitting in the front beside Robby. He seemed very friendly with a ready smile, but did not talk very much. Perhaps he was shy, or maybe just knew very little English; whenever Robby needed to make a turn, Jose said, "Hey amigo," and would point left or right.

No one knew exactly how long they had been driving or where they were. Robby was positive they had driven at least 35 miles since they'd left town because he had been keeping up with the miles so he would know when it was time to get gas. This was a habit he formed with his '57, since it had no fuel gauge. He didn't trust the fuel gauge, since this was the first year VW had one. The rest of the Foursome were totally clueless as to their whereabouts. One thing for sure, they were in the middle of nowhere. The starlit road was flat, narrow and went on as far as the eye could see with nothing on either side but deep canyons and mesas covered in sage and chaparral. They only knew they had turned off the main highway a while ago.

Jose motioned for him to pull off the road, indicating he needed to pee. Robby turned his head to the rear of the van and with a half smile, says, "If any of you ladies need to use the powder room, now's the time." As he turned back toward the front, there was a .22 pistol staring him in the face, right on the side of his nose. Jose yells to Robby, "GET OUT!!!", and motions for the others to get out. Robby knew this is no time to argue or fight, but a time to plan and scheme.

"Oh fuck!! We're getting rolled."

"Quiet Kim, now is not the time for your mouth," said Robby, who is co-operating while deciding what to do.

Lined up beside the van with their hands folded on top of their heads, they stare at miles of wasteland while their thoughts race from fear and disbelieve, to anger, to some serious thinking about how they're going to get out of this.

"PONTE DE RODILLAS, PONTE DE ROILLAS," Jose yells at them, pointing to the ground with his empty hand.

"What did he just say, Kim"

"He said for us to get on our knees, I think."

With their hands still upon their heads, they all slowly kneeled on the sand. Jose went over to Robby first and placed the pistol about three inches from his forehead.

Robby looked up and calmly said to Jose, "I bet the reason you're doing this is because your mother was always too busy sucking dicks behind the liquor store to teach you how to do anything decent, you chili choking mother fucker."

Jose just grinned and nodded his head, pleased with himself that he so easily got the drop on this trusting bunch of gringos. Robby looked directly in Jose's eyes and said quietly, "OK, we know he doesn't understand English. If he did, he would've got pissed off and shot me. Kim, Roger, don't move, don't speak. Moose remember Dong Ha? Do it again."

Moose immediately dove forward into the sand yelling as loud as he could, rolled over, and was on his feet running full speed toward Jose, yelling as loud as thunder. Robby, who had never taken his eyes off Jose, watched him blink and turn his head. Between the blink and the head turn, Robby executed a perfect double windmill block and breaks Jose's wrist, sending the weapon to Roger's feet. Robby jumped to his feet as Jose reached to his back with his left hand and pulled out a butcher knife and started slashing at Robby, who grabbed his wrist, taking the arm over his shoulder, pulled down and breaking Jose's other arm.

BAM!!! Moose runs into Jose at full speed throwing him to the ground. Moose had him pinned to the ground with his knees and is beating him over and over in the head while yelling at the top of his lungs.

"YOU DON'T FUCK WITH MY FRIENDS. YOU FUCK WITH ONE OF US, YOU FUCK WITH ALL OF US...HERE YOU WANT SOME MORE? I GOT MORE! NOW YOU GOT A BROKE NOSE TO GO WITH THOSE BROKE ARMS."

Robby grabbed Moose's fist and said, "OK Moose, good job of kicking ass, but let's not kill him."

"Why the fuck not? He was gonna kill us. He needs to be tango uniform."

"Just stand down for now, and let's sort this out. If it's best to kill him, we'll kill him. If it's best not to, we won't." Then Robby looked over at Kim and Roger who are still on their knees, and said with raised eyebrows and the slightest smile, "So, how do you like Mexico so far?"

In a slightly high pitched voice and a look of near reverence, Kim spoke first, "Holy Jesus Christ on a wobbly crutch. I never saw anything like that. Did you learn to fight like that in the Marines?"

"No sir. We got eight hours training in hand to hand and that was it...and it wasn't enough. I started boxing when I was 8 and started karate a few years after that. I'm a black belt in Tang Soo Do, a Korean karate that I learned in Atlanta but it sure came in handy a few times in Nam."

"I have seen my share of goddamn fights, but I never saw anybody as fast as you. I bet you got the fastest hands in the whole fuckin' world!"

"There's always someone better. I fought in the Nationals in L.A. in 1967. I fought this guy who could kick faster than you could punch and punch faster than you could blink. He was Tang Soo Do, also. Anyway, he kicked my ass. I broke three ribs and two toes, and finished third place in the nation...this guy finished first place in the whole country. Goddamn, he was incredible."

"What was his name?"

"His name was Carlos, but they called him by his nickname, Chuck, I think. Yeah, that's it...Chuck Norris."

"Umm...never heard of him."

"Me either. All I remember about him is he had a Tang Soo Do school somewhere in California and was wickedly fast."

Roger had stood up during this conversation, and was brushing the sand from his knees when he noticed that it was wet in the crotch of his pants.

Robby saw it too, "Forget about it man. We all do that in battle sometime or another. You can't help it. On my first day out, I always either pissed or shit myself. Then you throw your underwear away and spend the rest of the time without any until you get back to base. You find yourself without underwear more than with. Huh, maybe that's why they call it going commando."

"Well," Roger said, quickly recovering his dignity, "My congratulations to both of you. You saved our lives and it took you less than 20 seconds to defuse the whole situation."

"The situation isn't totally defused yet, Roger. We still need to decide what to do with old Jose here."

Roger looked down at the sand for a second, and directed his attention to Robby, "It's like this: We are on foreign soil and subject to the laws of Mexico. It is doubtful the U.S. would get involved, so we are on our own. If he gets loose and informs the authorities, we are looking at 20 to life in a Mexican prison. It would be our word against Jose's, who, by the way is pretty beat up. We are talking major assault with intent to kill. We would have all the cards stacked against us. That woman he works for has money and is feared. She probably owns half the police and judges in the area. I am thinking she runs a sting operation...

robbing military men all night long. If we kill him and get caught, Mexico does not have the death penalty. But for what we did, the banditos in prison will take care of us. We would not last five weeks in one of those prisons. I recommend we tie him up really well and hide him in the desert. Let God make the decision if he lives or dies. His lady boss will be on that street in Tijuana all night and will not miss him until sunrise. It's midnight now."

Robby nodded in approval, and before anyone could say anything, he said, "Alright, all we have to do is keep him from getting to anybody until we cross the border. I'm banking on the fact that he's a known criminal and they won't pay much attention to him anyway. His boss may not even allow him to go to the authorities. Once we get to America, we'll be OK. Here's what we do, 50 yards out at 10 o'clock there's a large cactus that looks like a tree. Moose and Roger pick him up and make him walk to that cactus. Take off his shoes and hog tie him with some of that survival cord we bought. Then tie him to the cactus on the back side where he can't be seen from the road. Tie him up right and tight...no mistakes. Kim, take his shoes about 100 yards from the cactus and throw them away, in opposite directions. Take the pistol apart; throw the rounds north, the cylinder east and the barrel west another 50 yards out. Wipe it clean...no fingerprints. I'll stay here and pull sentry on the van."

Moose, who had been sitting on Jose during all this, asked a good question, "How in the hell are we going to get back to the border. We're at the end of a road that is at the end of a road that is at the end of another road. None of us know where we are. We may as well be in Bumblefuck Egypt."

Kim broke out in a big smile, "I bought a Rand-McNally map and an Army issued compass. I can get us back to the border. I was the navigator's assistant, remember? Getting back to the good ole USA will be as simple as fallin' in a well."

"OK fall in, we all know what to do."

Moose stood up, placed his giant foot on Jose's chest, and

reached into his back pocket to pull out a bag of Levi Garrett chewing tobacco, took some and offered some to the rest. Robby took a small wad while the other two lit cigarettes.

With the sound of authority, Moose said, "No smoking, ladies! Out here, you can see the fire on the tip of that cigarette for miles. That's why we chew. One of our buds got hit by a sniper 'cause he was smoking at night and we sure as hell don't want nobody to see us out here."

"Moose is right, guys. Put out the smokes and do without, or take a chew. Wait until we get down the road...no, wait until we're across the border. And don't leave those mashed cigarettes in the sand. Put 'em on the floorboard of the bus. Now, let's get busy and let's get to hell outta Dodge."

Chapter 5

· · · · · · · · · · · · · · ·

Here We Go Again

"WOOOO!!! It's zero two hundred and we are back in the USA!!! WOOOO WEEEE!!! Pull over, Robby, I wanna kiss the ground."

And sure enough, Robby pulled over and they all got out and kissed the ground. Roger looked southward, "I think it would be a good idea to stay out of Tijuana for a while."

Kim looked up from the ground, stood up straight and looked Roger right in the eyes, "For a while? For a while? I got a better idea. I'm gonna stay out of Mexico....forever! You can have the whole enchilada. If I get rolled, it's gonna be in the NYC, not in some half assed border town where I find myself toes up in the middle of the desert. For a while? Oh hell no. Not for a while, but forever."

They all decided that the farther from Mexico they were, the better. So they headed north. Kim thought that San Bernardino would be a good place to stop for the evening. According to the map, it was about 120 miles north, northeast of San Diego. That would make it about 150 miles from Tijuana. He calculated their ETA to be about 5:00 in the morning.

Robby leaned back in his seat and half yelled, half yawned, "I'll be glad to get to San Bernardino and get a nice room with a shower. I don't know about y'all, but I'm good and ready for the three S's."

"Right on! And something to eat, too. Killin' that piece of crap Mexican asshole worked up an appetite."

—

Roger had almost fallen asleep. The constant hum of the engine right behind him was lulling him into a dreamlike state. Plus, he had been awake for 25 hours, and it had been a rather busy day. But this statement jolted him back to wide awake, "Hey Moose, we have not killed any Mexicans; and you had better never say that again anywhere, anytime, if you want to stay out of prison."

Robby stretched again and before Moose could say something else stupid he added, "Roger's right. This is something we should never tell anyone. That whole trip to TJ was something that should have never happened. If fact, it never happened. Isn't that right, Kim?"

"What trip? We ain't took no fuckin' trip to TJ. We met in a bar in San Diego, bought some supplies and are traveling together in this fine bus to do some sightseeing before we go home. And that's it. We ain't been to Mexico. Never happened."

"You ain't wrong, Kim. It never happened. Are you with me on that, Roger?"

"Yes sir."

"Kim?"

"Yes sir"

"Moose?"

"Sir, yes sir!"

"Hell yeah. The Fearsome Foursome rides again. We are the dream team. Now, let's find a nice motel."

According to Kim's schedule, they pulled into a Holiday Inn at 5:00AM. Or, as Moose would say, zero five hundred. They decided they would get two rooms instead of all sharing one room. It just seemed that sleeping in the same bed with another man in a Holiday Inn was...awkward.

Robby was in the shower and Moose was sitting on the edge of the bed watching a 19 inch black and white TV. He was sitting there so it would be easy to get up and turn the channels. Robby said the more expensive rooms had color TV, but they were a bunch of trouble because you had to keep getting up to adjust the color. But for $12.00 they have a nice room with a real bed for the first time in a long time, hot shower, air conditioning, and free ice. And best of all, they didn't have to clean up the room. Is this heaven, or what? Just then, a knock on the door and in walked Kim and Roger with big smiles on their faces. Kim had his duffle bag over his shoulder.

Moose broke out in a big grin, "Damn. You guys are like a turd that won't flush. You just keep popping up. What's going on? You miss me already? You damn sure aren't moving into this room with us!"

"No. We don't miss you; I made an incredible discovery as to what's in Kim's duffle bag and we thought you might want to see what's in it."

Just then, Robby came around the corner wearing a pair of 4-F underwear, "I'll bite, what's in the bag?"

Grinning like a mule eating briars, Kim said, "Mary Jane."

"You have a woman in that bag?"

"No, Robby, Mary Jane means marijuana."

Kim throws it on the bed, unzips it for all to see the 50 pounds of high grade pot.

"Hey Kim, is that what's in all the sailors' duffle bags? Where did you get this stuff, in Mexico?"

"No, I picked it up in Jamaica just a couple of weeks ago. You know, in NYC, I can get $35.00 dollars an ounce for this. That means there's close to $30,000 in this bag."

"I don't even want to know how you acquired it. You aren't a druggie are you?"

"Oh hell no, I'm gonna take this shit and sell it to my uncle in New York when I get home. It'll give me a head start. But until then, we can have all the free pot we want...you want to twist one now?

Robby, not knowing if he should be embarrassed or proud, says, "I've never smoked marijuana before."

Moose looked at Robby in surprise and then looked over at Roger, and as he closed the curtains said, "Well just fuck me to tears. Let me get this straight: Saturday at 1300, you had your first drink of hard liquor, which I taught you how to drink. And now, I'm gonna have to show you how to roll a doobie?? You never drank or smoked until today? Man, where have you been?"

"I never had time for drinking and smoking pot. I was in Nam trying to stay alive and back home I was always training for a karate competition, busy working at the Volkswagen shop, or going to school. I always wanted to stay straight and stay out of trouble."

"Well, little bro, I'm gonna lead you astray. But first, somebody's gotta make a food run. How 'bout you, Roger. You're good at gathering supplies...say you go get us some snacks for the munchies."

Robby looked at the chest of drawers and saw his VW key with his wallet, then he looked down and for the first time he realized he'd been standing there in his underwear and even though he suddenly felt a bit silly, he's distracted, trying to reason out why they need food. "We just ate at the diner, why do we need more food?"

"Trust me, little bro, we're gonna need plenty of munchies."

"OK. Roger, the keys are beside the TV. The papers are in the glove box."

By the time Roger returned, the motel room was so full of smoke, that when he opened the door, a large billow of familiar aroma came out and engulfed him as if it were a fog in the marshlands. He stepped in to see his three friends staring at an old movie on TV. The sound had been turned off and music was playing from a small transistor radio. Roger, for the first time, seemed to loosen up a bit and was acting more like one of the guys.

As he tossed the key to Robby, he said, "Hey Robby, glad to see you found something to cover up those 4-F britches you were wearing."

At this, the stoned three started laughing like crazy. Roger continued, "Are you the only Marine that wears those white briefs with the little hole in the front?" They all find this incredibly funny and laugh even harder.

Moose joined in, "Yeah, he is the only one. He started wearing them when somebody told him that 4-F stood for Find me, Feel me, Fuck me Fast." This made them laugh even harder still, their eyes started to water and they're nearly rolling on the floor.

Robby tried to take a deep breath and said in as straight a face as he could muster, "I bought these because they were not Marine issue, and I really wanted to get away from the Marine look for a while. Hey Roger, fall in, you need to catch up. You can have a puff of my pot cigarette."

"It's called a toke, little bro. He can take a toke off your doobie."

"Oh, yeah, right," and he started cracking up all over again.

Roger took a hit and said it reminded him of his college days, at a time when he and his friends would get stoned and listen to Bob Dylan for hours on end.

Kim's eyes got very large as he said, "I got something for Bob Dylan and your college buddies," and he lifted his leg and.... fff....t, he farted.

Now everyone was literally rolling in laughter.

Moose said, "I see your one, and raise you two...fart poker." And farted twice.

"Anyone gonna raise my two?.......Well then, I win!!!" Moose continued, "Hey, check out this bad tattoo. It's naked babes riding a vibrator. And look! When I flex my bicep, the vibrator wiggles."

Everyone pointed at the tattoo and laughed so hard and loud you would have thought they were just the funniest bunch on the planet...they just kept laughing until tears were rolling down their faces and could barely catch their breath.

By now the Fearsome Foursome did not look so fearsome.

They looked more like little eight year old boys at a spend-the-night party who were giggling, laughing, rolling all over the bed while staying up late. Looking at them now, no one would ever guess that just a few weeks ago, these silly boys were disciplined military men who were willing to kill or die for the cause.

For a moment, there was complete silence in the room. Kim pointed at the TV and said, "Look guys, there's our van on the television. Except you can't tell if it's tomato soup red or pumpkin orange."

They all looked at the black and white with no sound and see a VW commercial playing. There was a happy father and mother all dressed up in their Sunday best with two children, all getting in the van with bright, smiley faces, waving as they pulled out of the driveway.

At that very moment, while the ever so happy guys were staring at a Microbus on TV, a song came on the radio. It was a new song by Steppenwolf about traveling down the highway. Robby looked at the TV, and then looked at the transistor radio.

"Oh man, totally cool. At the same time the van is on the television that really great song is playing on the radio about traveling down the highway. That's us, man, looking for adventure, while traveling down the highway...oh hell yeah. That song and commercial was meant to be at the same time right here in the same room with us. Man... that is so...so...uh... so spiritual. That Microbus is spiritual and will not let us down."

No one said a word, no one laughed. They all just sat and pondered on what Robby had just said, and kept staring at the silent TV.

* * *

Robby was awakened by a knock on the door followed by a loud announcement, "CLEANING SERVICE."

Robby jumped up and got to the door just as he heard a key turning on the other side, making it just in time to block the maid's view of the room. "Oh ma'am, I am soooo sorry. We drove all night and we overslept. We'll be out of here in no time."

"That's OK, sweetie, checkout time isn't until 2:00 and it's noon right now. You have time. I'll come back later."

He closed the door, turned and looked around. On the counter and on both sides of the TV there were empty bags of potato chips and corn chips. Broken chips and crumbs could be found all around the TV and on the table between the beds. On the floor, between the window and the first bed, was an empty box of Velveeta cheese and crackers that had been spread on the floor and walked on a few times. On the floor in front of the TV there were empty packages of Slim Jim ready-to-eat meat. He was surrounded by empty bottles of Coke, Pepsi and Orange Crush. Moose was on his bed, diagonally, face down, holding a bottle opener. Kim and Roger were on the floor between the beds, still sound asleep. He stepped over the duffle bag on his way to the bathroom and splashed some water in his face. It was quite cool in the room since someone had turned the air conditioner all the way to the lowest temperature and had the fan on constant.

He opened the curtains, and with one of his flip flops he banged on the front of the A/C unit and yelled, "OK GUYS, WE'RE BURNING DAYLIGHT. EVERYBODY UP AND AT 'EM. WE HAVE A ROOM TO CLEAN AND PLACES TO GO!!!"

Chapter 6

· · · · · · · · · · · · · ·

Pure Fun

All agreed that they had met their quota on drinking, smoking, fighting, and partying for a day or two, so they decided to go to the Grand Canyon and camp outside for a few days.

"Navigator, set our course for the Grand Canyon. And, don't forget your duffle bag."

"Aye aye, sir," replies Kim with a winning smile.

Kim figured it to be an easy trip compared to what they went through Saturday night and Sunday morning. All they had to do was stay on the highway that went from San Bernardino to Flagstaff, Arizona, and go north into the park. It should take eight hours. As he guided Robby to the highway, he gave him an ETA of 9:00PM. All they had to do to make it on time was stay out of trouble...that's all...how hard could that be?

Robby had the bus wide open, as fast as it could go, almost 60MPH. He looked in the rear view mirror and said, "You know, I really liked that song last night about traveling down the highway. I'd like to stop somewhere and see if I can buy that 8-track tape and play it on the road."

Kim was the first to speak, "Hell no, we ain't stopping for a damn thing. Every time we stop, we either spend too much money, or somebody tries to fuckin' kill us. Let's just stay the course, see the Grand Canyon, camp a few days and get to hell home."

Moose grinned, "What's the matter, sailor boy, lost your spirit of adventure? What happened to 'join the Navy and see the world'?"

"See the world? See the world?" I mostly saw the inside of a ship and lots of buckets of grease and goddamn grey paint on the dry docks of Pearl Harbor. You can take those leaflets and poster boards about joining the Navy for adventure and wipe your ass with them. And if what we went through in TJ was adventure.... well...fuck that. I just want to get back home to Birmingham and see my mama and my cousins."

"Alright already. Damn, don't get your panties all in a wad!"

Robby chimed in, "Hey Moose, Kim makes a good point. We all want to get home and start our life again. Seems we just keep getting side-tracked."

"My granddaddy called it chasing rabbits," said Roger, who had been very quiet all afternoon, and didn't want to admit he was getting homesick, too.

Robby had put a Ventures tape in the 8-track player about two hours ago and it had been playing non-stop over and over again. By now, he was sick of guitar music and pulled out the tape. Moose was in his seat, sitting up perfectly straight with his head tilted back, sound asleep, snoring, about as quiet as a chain saw. Kim was sipping on a beer while Roger was staring out the window at the flat, desert-like landscape that seemed to go on forever.

Roger's thoughts had drifted to a girlfriend he had in high school and that night at the drive-in movies when he had first stroked her breasts while *To Kill A Mockingbird* was playing on the big screen that had swing sets and a sliding board in the foreground. The very thought of the first time he had ever gone so far with a girl was getting him aroused and he couldn't help but notice he was getting an erection. Since there was nothing much to do about this enlarged creation, he lit a cigarette and kept looking out the window.

By now the sun was setting and was putting on a display of natural beauty that this band of travelers had never seen before.

The clouds seemed to be close enough to touch and were spread out in a way that made them appear like brush strokes of carroty orange, pale pink, and lavender. The vivid colors were reflected in the rock formations and the sand, making the desert floor take on different shades of dark crimson, ginger, and a deep purple that was almost black in the shadows.

Robby was taken in by the sheer beauty of it all and noticed that Kim and Roger were equally astounded. He was thinking how the sunset, coupled with the various rock formations, looked as though they were on some distant planet. It was certainly different from where he grew up, in the inner city of Atlanta, Georgia, and it was damn sure different from the scenery in Viet Nam.

This silence was interrupted by Moose waking up, and after an all-too-loud yawn, he said, "Man! I'm so hungry I could eat a skunk. Let's stop and get something to eat."

Robby nodded and asked, "Kim, how's our time look?"

"Not too good, sir. Our ETA is about 11:00PM."

"That settles it then, we'll stop and get something to eat, and if we can find a store, we'll buy some supplies to make sandwiches and stuff so we won't be stopping so often to eat."

The bright vivid colors were giving way to darker shadows and hues as nighttime approached. Robby's attention was drawn to a bright blue sign blinking in the distance. As they got closer, they could see that the blue neon sign belonged to a bar and grill that, in days gone by, was a Pure service station. The old Pure sign was still hanging on a pole by the road. The neon sign in the window said "Pure Fun." As they turned and left the highway, there was a two inch drop from the pavement to a gravel parking lot that jolted everyone back to reality. The old service station had bathrooms in the rear, so before they went inside they walked around the building and found three doors that were labeled, "Men" "Women" "Colored."

Moose chuckled, and says, "Hey lookie here Kim. You have

your own private latrine. This way to the boudoir, ladies."

By now, Kim kneww that Moose meant no harm or disrespect and his way of showing fondness and friendship was by teasing. So, Kim retorted, "Oh hell, you just jealous 'cause they don't have private bathrooms for you pencil-dick pollocks."

"Pencil-dick, my ass! Why do you think they call me moose? It's because I'm hung like a god damn moose."

By now, Robby has grown impatient, and said in a commanding voice, "OK guys, let's stop talking about our dicks and wash up and get some chow."

As they entered the front door, they noticed a jukebox on the left playing an old Chuck Berry song about four measures beyond loud...so loud you couldn't hear someone talking to you unless they leaned across the table and yelled right into your ear. In the front of the café were white Formica tables with gold flakes that seat four. Each table had plastic chairs in an assortment of colors. Toward the rear, there was a bar that went the length of the building with barstools that had chrome legs and vinyl seats. Behind the bar was the grill and stove. A cook wearing a white apron had his back to the customers, flipping about a dozen burgers on the hot griddle.

They were greeted by the only waitress in the place, who pointed to the ceiling and yelled, "There's the menu. You order there, go sit down and I'll bring it to you." The menu was a homemade sign that was hand written and hanging from the ceiling: Hamburgers, Hamburger Basket, Chili Hamburger, Hot Dogs, Slaw Dogs, Chili Dogs French Fries, Breakfast Anytime. Coffee, Tea, Soft Drinks, Beer.

After placing their order at the counter, they found a table to sit and wait. Robby insisted on sitting in the chair that faced the door...old habits die hard and you can't be too careful. While waiting for their order, they couldn't help but notice the decor. The pine-paneled walls were covered with amateur photographs enclosed in black picture frames: an old picture in black and white of a cowboy holding the bridle of a large, white horse; four Native Americans in full dress, including their feathered headdress, mounted on their ponies with a stoic stare on their faces; pictures of the desert, including the Grand Canyon; a man, woman and child standing in front of a '55 Chevy that is two-toned, grey and pink; two pictures of little league baseball teams, and a Coca-Cola poster that said, "Delicious and Refreshing."

Roger loudly remarked, "The pine paneling reminds me of my father's den. Except my father doesn't have so many pictures, and a lot less grease on the wall."

As they all leaned in to hear better, Robby said, "My grandfather had a '55 like that, but it wasn't that god-awful pink and grey. His was a two-toned black and white. It was kinda funny because people would mistake it for a police car, and pull over and jump the curb and shit."

Kim chimed in, shaking his head, "So this is the kind of place they been trying to keep us colored folks out of all these years? Holy geese, that's just fucked up."

They noticed on the side of the room opposite the juke box was a small area that had been cleared of tables so people could dance...a very few people, perhaps four or six. By now, the rockin' and rollin' of Chuck Berry has been replaced by a soft, slow tune called "This guy's in love with you." As the mood seemed to change with the music, a petite and pretty lady approached the table of the fearsome foursome and said, "Hi. My name is Joan. Would any of you good-looking men like to dance?"

In less than a blink, Moose jumped up and said, "I would be honored to share this dance with you." This, to the amazement of the other three, who had no idea Moose could carry on a civilized conversation.

Moose and his new-found love share the dance floor with one other couple; he held her hand in his and had his arm around her waist as they shuffled their feet to the music. Since she is utterly shorter than him, Moose had to bend and slouch just to reach her waist. He was smiling and laughing while little Joan could not keep her eyes off this hunk. Moose showed her his best smile and whispered in her ear, "You know, my Aunt Grace never made it to five feet tall. You remind me a little of her. She was four feet, eleven inches, and she always said that tall women are loved, but short women are adored. That's the way I think of you. I think you're adorable."

"Oh thank you very much. I'm glad you think so. Uh...are you guys soldiers?"

"No, I'm not a soldier, I'm a Marine. My buddy over there in the Hawaiian shirt is a Marine, too. The other two aren't Marines. The short one is a sailor, the tall one is a soldier in the Army. We all just got out of the military and we're traveling around a little before we go home."

"Oh, that sounds so exiting. I've never even been out of my home town and you've been all over the world. What kind of car are you driving?"

"Uh...it's not exactly a car. It's a Volkswagen bus."

They danced in silence, and the longer they danced, the more Joan rubbed herself against Moose. The more she rubbed against him, the more aroused he became, to the point where he had a full-blown hard on... a hard on so big, he didn't have enough skin left to close his eyes. Cute little Joan buried her head in his chest, and where she could gently inhale the scent of a real man. This scent had not been covered up by cheap cologne and clean clothes with perfumed detergent, it was the real thing. With her nose pressed against his shirt, she breathed in a musk-type aroma that emitted a primal, almost prehistoric, bouquet; one that spoke to a hard-core strength not found in all men. She started breathing heavily, and, as her eyes looked up and met his, Moose said, "Would you like to see the inside of our van?" Joan smiled and nodded yes.

The two walked arm in arm, right by his three friends at the table, who were completely and totally dumbfounded.

Kim grinned and said, "Holy crap, do you think he's headed toward the van?"

"Not sure. Maybe we should go outside in about twenty minutes and check on things. You know...see if the bus needs a good cleaning," Roger drolly stated.

Robby chuckled, "Yeah, well, Moose is over-due. He's been fighting in the jungle for 39 weeks. He volunteered three hitches in a row."

Their musings were interrupted by food being placed on the table. All but Kim had ordered the hamburger basket. He had ordered a foot-long hot dog even though he was sure it couldn't compare to the ones at Coney Island.

Out at the bus, as Joan stepped into the van, she slipped off her sandals, sat on the back seat, and unbuttoned the two top buttons on her bell-bottom jeans. Moose reached down to pull the laces on his boots as he followed her into the bus and while kissing her, tried to take the boots off by placing his left foot at the heel of the right boot, struggling to pull them off using nothing but his feet. His kiss came hard and passionate as he placed his left arm around her shoulder, and his right arm around her waist, pulling her as close to him as possible, his lips never leaving hers. Joan allowed her lower lip to protrude slightly, causing Moose's mouth to barely open. She rubbed the tip of her tongue back and forth until their tongues touch and begin to stroke each other.

Moose took his hand, and gave a quick pinch to the center of her back.

"OUCH!!! What are you doing?"

"I'm trying to unfasten your bra. I want to feel those beautiful breasts of yours."

"I'm not wearing a bra."

"You're not?"

"No, hip chicks don't wear bras, didn't you know that?"

"Guess not. I've been in the jungle for way too long...ain't seen a decent woman like you in all that time. Geez, things have sure changed."

With nothing more to say on the subject, Moose again placed his lips next to hers and unbuttoned her blouse to expose two beautiful breasts the size of lusciously ripe oranges. Her heavy breathing and the sight of her erect nipples were driving Moose into a wild and crazy frenzy. He lowered his mouth to her neck and ran his tongue down until he was nestled between her breasts, opening his mouth wide as he took into his mouth all he possibly could of her breast on the right side, then to the left. As he began to pull away he gave her nipple a long, slow bite that gently stretched her nipple before his teeth and then let go. The same hand that tried to unsnap a bra that wasn't there, unfastened the last two buttons on her jeans. His lips and tongue never left her body, as he delivered powerful kisses and gentle licks to her stomach, around her naval, swabbing his tongue inside her belly button as he felt Joan tensing up as her hips rise to meet him and then release with a moan. As he arrived at the top of her jeans, his nose stroked her public hair right below her panty line. He grabbed both hands around her hips and began to tug at the very tight jeans. Joan helped him by raising up from the seat just enough to wiggle her butt, allowing the jeans and panties to fall to the floorboard. Before her pants find their way in a pile on the floor, Moose unzipped his to allow more room for an erection that was becoming a little painful inside his new jeans. He looked at Joan, who winks and shifts her eyes downward as if to say in body language she really wanted him to go down on her.

He buried his nose deep into her dark public hair and placed his tongue on her clitoris, and with a strong stroke, he licked upward back into her thick hair and then to the clit...up and down he went. With his teeth, he gave a gentle tug on her hair. As Joan moaned once again in delight, Moose noticed something was caught in his throat. Oh Shit. A pubic hair is lodged deep in his throat and it won't go up or down...just hangs there, like a fish hook.

Meanwhile, back inside the grill, the other three had finished their sandwiches and were wondering how long it was going to be until they could get in the van, since it was...occupied. Roger excused himself to go outside to the restroom. Shortly he returned and asked, "Could anyone tell me why Moose is leaning against our van with his pants around his ankles, gagging and trying to throw up?"

Robby starts to grin, "He probably swallowed a pubic hair; he's kinda bad about that. He's got more than one story...you'd think he would of learned by now."

Kim's face lit up as he said, "Oh hell no...I gotta see this."

Kim stepped onto the parking lot just in time to see Joan pulling up her pants and buttoning her blouse as she headed toward her car, holding her sandals in her hand. She caught a glimpse of Kim and said, "I just don't believe this shit...you guys..."

Joan made her way across the gravel parking lot to her car, a shiny black1963 Ford Falcon Futura with a red accent stripe. She stopped at the car, looked back at the van where Moose was still trying to clear his throat and catch his breath as the other three are standing around him, at first trying to look sympathetic, but not having much luck keeping it together. She finished tightening the straps on her sandals and sat for a moment with her hands grasped ever so tightly on the steering wheel. With white knuckled hands on the steering wheel, she banged her forehead a few times on the top of the wheel, pushed in the clutch, and backed up right beside the same van she just exited. She watched as Kim, Roger, and Robby could barely stay on their feet as they roll with laughter, while Moose is looking a little dazed by the whole experience. She took one last look at the fearsome foursome, put the car in first gear, raced the engine and popped out the clutch, spraying gravel as she went. As the spinning tires met the pavement of the highway, there was a screech and a four foot long tire mark left behind.

As her tail lights went out of sight, Robby wiped his eyes and said, "Hey Moose, do you want your hamburger basket? It seems that fur burger you went after didn't work out so well."

Moose knew it would be a while before they let him off the hook for this one, if ever. He turned from watching the fast disappearing Falcon and said, "Aww fuck it. Let's get back on the highway."

Chapter 7

· · · · · · · · · · · · · ·

Rolling Away

As Robby slid under the steering wheel, Moose had changed his mind and ran back inside to grab his hamburger basket and got a Coke to go. The burger was no longer hot, but it was better than nothing, and his little jaunt in the van had worked up an appetite.

As Robby went into fourth gear, at a blistering speed of 50 MPH, he couldn't help but notice how vast and empty his surroundings appeared. The highway in front of him was long, straight and lonesome. The next mile looked like the previous one...flat desert land, for miles and miles. The headlights, which he learned only worked on low beam, did a great job of lighting the long stretch for about 15 yards, if that. As he gazed over the vast emptiness, his mind drifted. He wondered if this is the way the surface of the moon looked, and then dismissed this thought, thinking we'll never know for sure what the moon's surface was really like. Landing on the moon would be impossible, at least for a long while. They had discussed this in physics class in college back in 1967, where the professor said it was mathematically impossible to go to the moon and back. The hard part would be getting back. If the timing and angle of entry was just a few degrees off, the spacecraft would bounce off the earth's atmosphere and forever be propelled into space.

Another glance at the terrain made him think back about their experience in the desert in Mexico just a few days ago, and he wondered how long it took Jose to get loose...if he got loose at all. Then, his mind drifted back to Dong Ha and a similar experience he and Moose had shared just a few months ago. Inside his head, he could hear screams of pain and loud shouts of NO! He began to tremble and hold his left side, as if there was a sharp pain. As he looked down where he had placed his hand, he saw no blood. All he saw was a clean hand that was touching a red Hawaiian shirt with large white flowers. Robby wiped his eyes because they had started to swell up with tears, shook his head and looked for a place to pull over for a minute. He crossed a bridge and pulled over, jumped out of the van leaving the door open and ran to the stream running beneath the bridge. He began splashing his face and rubbing his entire head and neck with the arctic-cold, clear liquid.

Moose was on it. He was right behind Robby. "Hey man, what the hell? You OK?"

"Yes sir. Everything's cool. Just my mind fucking with me, that's all. I'm fine. Uh...I was just thinking, this would be a good place for us to camp out...plenty of good water, nobody around for miles to tell us what to do."

"You don't have to call me sir, little bro. We ain't Marines anymore."

"You don't get it, Moose? I know we're former Marines. I called you sir because I respect you as a person, not as a Marine, but as a man and a friend. Respect is a way of life inside or outside the USMC. And I respect you more than anyone I ever met."

"Thank you....uh...sir!"

This unexpected moment was interrupted by the sound of footsteps running down the hill to the creek side to make sure everything was OK. Moose saw Kim and Roger first, and trying to sound light hearted, called out, "Everything is cool, guys. We decided to camp here tonight."

Roger looked around the campsite, assessing the situation. "This time of year, it can get down to 30 degrees at night in this desert. We need to gather up a whole bunch of sage brush and whatever kind of wood is available to keep a fire going all night."

By now, Robby had pulled it together to the point where no one could tell he was about to lose all his marbles just a few minutes ago, and he chimed in, "I was thinking the same thing. We can also use our lanterns and camp stove for heat if we need to. I think the van will be OK without anyone pulling sentry on it. We're close enough if somebody starts messing with it, we'd be on them like stink on shit."

"Yeah, Robby's right...stink on shit, that's us. We are bad mother fuckers," said Kim as he did a little dance, bouncing left and right, throwing left and right jabs.

While Kim fired up the camp stove and filled up all the canteens with fresh water from the creek, the other three started gathering anything they could find in the desert that would burn. By the time they returned, Kim had cooked up a pot of baked beans and made hard-tack biscuits from flour, water and salt.

"Hey Kim, these biscuits are pretty good. Did you learn to cook these in the Navy?" Roger asked.

"No man, I learned this from my mama. Sometimes all she had was two bucks to feed the four of us for a whole week. We ate a shit load of biscuits."

"Two dollars and that's all? What did your father do about this?"

"Oh, that bastard left by the time I was eight. I saw him three times from then until I joined the Navy. I know where he lives and I know his brothers and where they live, but that's about it. We ain't what you'd call a close family."

Robby joined in with a sly grin, "Yeah, these are good. Did you make sure that Moose got biscuits without any hair in 'em?"

They all broke out in laughter again as Moose jumped up and charged toward Robby full force. As he reached out to take hold of him, Robby grabbed his finger tips and pulled straight into the ground, bringing Moose to Robby's feet, face down in the coarse sand.

"I'm still faster than you...you cocky bastard. You didn't think you were really gonna get me, did you?"

"No sir. But you can't blame a man for trying."

Robby reached a hand down to pull Moose up. Moose came up smiling as they high-fived and slapped each other on the back.

Kim, who had now seen two different demonstrations of Robby's fighting skills, took a sip of water and said, "The last time I saw you guys fight, it was in Mexico and you said, 'Remember Dong Ha.' What happened at Dong Ha?"

Robby turned his head and stared into the peaceful, babbling creek for a moment. He looked back at Kim and said, "Ah, nothing much. We bailed out some Screaming Eagles, had heavy casualties, made it out with three. That's it."

Moose, who had been stirring the fire and adding more sagebrush and tumbleweed, looked around and said, "Well, there's a little more to it than that, but Robby's just a little shy about things. Hey Kim, go get some 'Kool-Aid' out of the van and I'll tell you what happened...well, at least some of it."

Kim turned off the stove, walked to the van, gathered up the scotch, beer, and tequila and returned to the fire. By now everyone was sitting on the ground, legs crossed, the burning embers reflecting in their faces, making them look eerie and indistinct.

Moose took a swig from the scotch bottle and began, "We were ordered to rescue some of the Screaming Eagles who got themselves surrounded by the enemy. They didn't have a snowball's chance and neither did we. We got inside the perimeter after about four hours of heavy-duty fighting only to get captured by those goddamn gooks where they took our clothes and held us at gunpoint. I broke loose and charged right toward the guys that had Robby. Robby got loose and killed two of 'em with nothing but his bare hands and bare feet. I picked up an A-K that they didn't need any more, and took out the rest. I still can't figure out how we fuckin' survived that mess, but we did. We managed to save only one of the Screaming Eagles and he was a nephew of some big shot in Washington D.C. Some senator, and he wrote Robby a letter, thanking him for pulling little Billy bad ass out of the fire."

"No way! Hey, Robby, you still have the letter?"

"No. But I kept a business card he sent me. It's in my wallet. You wanna see it?"

And sure enough, he pulled out of his wallet a card with the United States seal which had the name, address and phone number of Senator Ronald B. Richland.

"Holy shit. I've heard of him," said Kim, who looked at the card as if he were a child gazing at a Mickey Mantle baseball card for the first time.

"Impressive," said Roger as he took another sip of the water from his canteen.

"I appreciate that, Roger. But we were just a bunch of grunts doing our job. All we did was what we were asked to do. It's a goddamn miracle any of us survived. I will always wonder why I was spared and others died," Robby sadly stated and took another gulp of tequila straight from the bottle.

"Oh, I'm sure Robby. And I completely understand how you feel, and there are many who are proud and thankful for what you and Moose have done. However, that's not what I was talking about. The water...it's the water that is so impressive. It is cold, clear, has no chemicals, and it's better than any water I have ever tasted. I am thinking you could bottle this water, mass market it, and make millions of dollars."

Kim's eyes opened wide as he said, "Man, I thought you were a little fucked in the head, but now I'm positive you're way off kilter. You're saying take plain water, put it in a bottle, like a Coke or Pepsi, and sell it in machines? Why would anybody buy water when they could buy a Pepsi or an Orange Crush? There ain't a damn soul that would pay a quarter for plain water when they could buy a soda. Goddamn...there's a water fountain everywhere you look and you can get it free. In Birmingham, they have water fountains for colored and white...and it's all free."

Moose laid the bottle of scotch on the ground and took a gulp from his canteen. Without thinking, said, "Yeah, it's good water, but who in the hell would buy water in a bottle when you can get free from a hose? When we're outside and get thirsty, we just find the nearest neighbor's garden hose and help ourselves. If we're inside, we just turn on the tap. Shit...it's even free in restaurants. That's about as dumb as charging money for air at a service station. Air and water should be free."

Kim and Moose seemed to have forgotten they were talking to a man who was a marketing major in college and didn't notice the look in his eyes, the little wheels of innovation spinning around. Roger looked down at his canteen, placed his nose at the opening and gave it a deep sniff.

"Sorry guys. I smell money here. It's like this: there are 150,000,000 people in this country. If only 5 per cent of them buy a bottle of water each week, that would be 7,500,000 people buying water. If you made a profit of .02 cents per bottle, you would make a profit of $150,000 per week, that's $600,000 per month. And that's only if 5% of the population buys it. It could be more people, or they could drink more than one bottle. I'm telling you guys...this is a conservative estimate. It could be bigger. Robby, you've been quiet, what do you think?"

Robby looked down inside his half-empty canteen, shook it back and forth, watching it splash inside. "I'm thinking with a great big pile of money for advertising and marketing, and with a whole lot of work and pounding the pavement, it might fly. But you're wrong about this Arizona water. The best water you will ever taste is in the North Georgia Mountains."

"Really? Why do you say that?"

"Have you ever heard of Stone Mountain? It's in Georgia."

Kim chimed in, "I have. When I was sixteen, we went there and rode the train around the base of that mountain. Fuck man, that's one big-ass rock. I climbed it with my brother and cousins. You can see Atlanta from the top."

Roger said, "I know it's the largest piece of exposed granite in the world...like Kim says, one big-ass rock."

Robby nodded, and continued, "Well that enormous rock is like a little pimple on your ass. That mountain is not even a percentage point of the granite that is underground. There's a slab of granite miles wide and hundreds of feet deep that runs underground from North Georgia to Chattanooga, Tennessee. It pops up everywhere and really pisses off farmers and builders. Anyway, all the water that's in the water table underneath the surface happens to be filtered through this granite. I'm saying if you're crazy enough to think you can sell water to the American public, at least market the best water. And that would be in North Georgia. And that's my opinion."

Moose, who had been drinking more scotch than spring water, blurted out, "Opinions are like buttholes. Everybody's got one and yours stinks. Mau ha ha ha!!"

Robby and Roger just shook their heads as Robby said, "Time for more firewood, then I'm turning in. Tomorrow, the Grand Canyon."

Chapter 8

. . . .

Finally, We Have Arrived

The guys didn't sleep very well that night. Moose kept having bad dreams and nightmares. Robby didn't sleep at all; he just sat and stared at the fire all night and added fuel as it burned low... lying down for a few minutes, sitting up again, getting up and walking around, then repeating. Kim, who was not accustomed to sleeping outside, finally gave up the idea of camping beside a fire, went to the van and fell asleep on the back seat, taking the camp stove in case he needed heat. Roger rolled himself inside a woolen army blanket and curled up beside the fire, using a pair of pants and a shirt rolled up as his pillow. Of the four, Roger slept the most sound...totally motionless, lightly snoring with slow, heavy breathing.

Robby looked up at a sky that was so vividly lit by billions of stars and a half moon. He thought about how clear the sky was and was somewhat taken away by the fact that the stars were so numerous and the air so pure. Until that night, he had never been anywhere but in the inner city and in the jungle of Viet Nam and had never really looked heavenward. For the first time in his life he felt connected to the universe, somehow very small and insignificant and yet very powerful. At that brief second in the long ribbon of time in his life, he made a solemn vow: One day he'd have a place of his own where he could gaze at the stars all night. He'd have a home in the city that's above the trees and the other buildings, where he'd go on the roof to enjoy these very same stars anytime he wanted. He also vowed to find a good woman to share it with.

Robby's vision of the future was interrupted by the snorting sounds of Moose coming awake. Loudly yawning, stretching, and farting, he rolled over, sat up and asked, "What time is it?"

"Zero five-hundred."

"Why are you up so damn early?"

"It isn't early; it's still late last night."

"You still can't sleep? Fuck man, you never sleep. How do you do that shit?"

"I just can't shut off the voices in my mind. I'm either thinking about the past or worried about the future...just can't shut down, you know...always wired, always pumped."

"I can dig it. Every time I close my eyes I see things, I hear things that drive me outta my tree. Oh well, what the fuck. We made it this far, we can make it through anything."

"Yeah, or die trying."

"Well, you wanna wake up the ladies, or let them get their beauty sleep?"

"Let's get them up at zero five-thirty. Five-thirty is a good time to get up. Not too early, not too late."

Roger rolled over and said, "I heard that. This lady is awake. All I need to do is powder my nose and I'll be ready to get going."

Robby smiled, "Well, just don't piss in the stream. It would be bad for your business."

It took only a few minutes to break up camp and get in the van. Since they didn't have much, they didn't have much to pack. Roger poured water on the fire while the others picked up their belongings and climbed into the bus. Roger turned around and took one last look at the totally transparent water as it shimmered and sparkled under the starlit sky.

In the back of the van, Kim sat up, scratched his head and looked around. "It's coffee and biscuit time, and I ain't cooking for you mother fuckers."

"OK, we'll make a quick stop before we head out to the

Grand Canyon. Let's make it fast in and fast out ...no fighting, no fucking, just eat and run."

"Oh please, Robby, we haven't got in a good fight in about four days...mau ha ha ha. And...we still haven't fucked any little ladies. I'm ready for some real fun."

"Oh come on, Moose. Is that all you think about is fightin' and screwin'?"

"Uh...yeah. Can you think of anything better to think about?

Roger interrupted the priceless dialogue between Moose and Robby and said, "I can think of one thing better...getting home. I'm all for seeing the Grand Canyon and getting home."

Kim perked up, "It would be cool to get back home...I got some dope to sell!"

Robby plugged in a Little Richard tape, cranked up the volume and headed north, with Kim navigating.

Not long into the journey, Robby saw a glimpse of a road sign that said "Last chance for gas before the Grand Canyon – Parker's Gas and Grocery." He could see a very small building a few miles ahead on the right. From a distance, it looked to be no bigger than his thumb, but as he got closer, he saw an old building that looked more like a shack than the grocery stores and gas stations he was accustomed to in Atlanta. He spotted a familiar Texaco sign as he pulled off the road and drove up to the only two gas pumps – one regular, one ethyl – both pumps accented with the famous big red star. The pumps were situated in the parking lot just a few feet from the grocery store that had been weather-beaten with age to a pale shade of grey. Before Robby could turn off the motor and get out, a young man in a plaid shirt and bib overalls came out of the store and ran up to Robby asking, " Yes sir, fill it up?"

"Sure," Robby told him as he got out, stretched and yawned a little, wishing now he had slept last night. As he walked toward the screen door to the store, he heard a voice from behind say, "Hey mister, where's the gas cap and how do I check the oil?"

Robby showed him how the motor is in the back, the gas cap in the front, and then had a Volkswagen conversation he would have rather skipped so he could go inside and get something to eat...maybe even some hot coffee.

He stepped over the pump station and walked across the gravel driveway toward the old country store and noticed an elderly man sitting on a homemade bench to the left of the door next to the steps that led inside. The man had weathered with age much the same way as the store. He sat slumped over as if time had beaten him down to the point he no longer cared about sitting up straight. His legs were crossed the same way a woman crossed her legs, which was no effort for him because he was very slim and bony...almost skeletal. Robby noticed his face was thin and hollow. The space between his cheek bone and jaw line was sunken in such a manner that testifies to a hardscrabble life. He shaved his white, soft whiskers about once a week and it looked like tomorrow will be the day for his weekly shave. They looked briefly at one another and nodded. Robby wondered if that was the grandfather of the young man who's servicing the van.

The steps into the small store were two boulders, a smaller one stacked atop of a larger one. He grabbed the handle to the screen door, which was nothing more than a large empty spool that at one time was on a sewing machine but was now nailed to the weather beaten screen door. There were enough holes in the screen to allow access to an entire battalion of swarming insects. It seemed the owner solved the insect problem by hanging two pest strips from the ceiling. They fell in curls and swayed in front of the door, reminding you of the blonde ringlets on a Southern belle (well, a very dirty Southern belle). Robby wondered if the fly paper was keeping the flies out, or keeping them in the store. It seemed Robby had been in the store all of 30 seconds when the screen door produced a loud bang, bounced back, and was followed by two softer bangs. Robby jolted as if he had stuck his finger in a light socket and turned around to see the elderly gent who had been sitting on the bench had stepped into the store and was coming toward him.

"Howdy, can I help ya?"

Robby really didn't like anyone startling him or looking over his shoulder, and being followed around a store made him feel like he was a prime suspect for a major shoplifting ring. Trying to be polite, Robby tempered his tone, "Do you have any fresh coffee?"

"Well...don't have no coffee, but there's a diner a few miles down the road...good coffee, good biscuits, and cute little honeys that bring them to the table," the old man said with a big smile, displaying the few teeth that had stood the test of time. "Look around all you want. I'll be right here if you need something." He slowly made his way back out the door and very carefully led himself down the steps, hanging on to a hand rail made of galvanized pipe.

The first thing that caught Robby's eye was a large cooler about three feet high, two feet wide and four feet long, in the center of the room...sky blue with a Pepsi logo on the side. He peered over the top and saw a very strange apparatus designed to dispense the bottles of soda. The bottles were standing upright, where you can see only the bottle cap, and the neck of the bottle is held in place by this rail, so you could slide the bottles to an ultimate destination which was a little turn-style door that opened when you put a quarter in the slot. And therein, a smorgasbord of soda, indeed: Coca Cola, Pepsi, Yoo Hoo Chocolate Drink, Red Rock Ginger Ale, Frosty Root Beer, Upper 10, Bireley's Non-Carbonated Orange Drink, Nehi Grape, Tab, and one he never heard of: Mountain Dew. Ten rails, ten different drinks. As he was trying to decide which poison to choose instead of coffee, he heard the door slam again and the loud clomping of boots on the hardwood floor. Moose had made it inside.

"Hey, Moose, which of these drinks would be best to take the place of a cup of coffee?"

"Well, for you, nothing takes the place of a cup of coffee, but you oughta try the Mountain Dew. It looks like horse piss, but it tastes pretty good and it'll jack you up. I used to down 'em by the dozen in Jersey when I worked third shift."

So, Robby looked down at the drink machine and saw it would cost a quarter to find out if he liked Mountain Dew. He saw a large galvanized wash tub full of ice with Check Cola, Topp Cola, and Jug's Root Beer. Just when Robby was about to go outside to ask the old man a question, the door slammed again but Robby doesn't jump this time. Instead, he turned to look at the young man who came in from filling up the Microbus and asked him, "How much for the drinks in the tub?"

"Oh, they're a dime."

He noticed Topp Cola is larger, and comes in cola, strawberry and orange flavor. So he purchased a standard cola.

"Hey man, you know you are so tight with your money, the Indian yells because you squeeze a nickel so hard. Are all you Scotsmen so tight with your money?" asked Moose in his most charming voice.

Kim chimed in, laughing, "Yeah, you can tell his house in the neighborhood. It's the one with the toilet paper hanging out on the clothes line."

Robby gave a quick retort, "Well, it's not what you make, it's what you save that makes a difference."

As Moose was looking around, Robby saw on the wall at the rear a collection of fan belts lined up like a timeline of school portraits, with the short ones on the left and gradually getting longer as they ran down the length of the wall. The proper length for a VW bus is exactly from his wrist to his elbow and even though these belts are no doubt for farm equipment and American cars, he picked one and knew the one in his hand would fit the bus.

He turned his head to Moose and said, "All you need to keep a VW going is one belt. Check the belt; check the oil, that's it...no radiator, no water, no power steering fluid...no bullshit...just a belt and oil. Just in case we need a belt, I got one."

"This place may have a belt, but it don't got no beer, or whiskey. What kind of fuckin' place is this?"

"It's a dry goods store you dumb Pollock, not a bar."

The young man who had been servicing the bus finally spoke to Robby in a very quiet, shy manner, "That'll be $3.90. It held almost 10 gallons."

Robby's eyes widened in surprise, "Damn, gas is getting outrageous. Back home, it was 27 cents a gallon, but then I guess that was a couple of years ago. I'll get this moon pie and can of Vienna sausage and a pack of your Beemans gum."

"I'll go get granddaddy, he handles the money."

The old man didn't have a cash register, he used a black, heavy, adding machine with a pull handle on the right side. The wooden knob on the handle wobbled and had been stripped of all black lacquer, leaving it polished and smooth from the old man pulling on it for years. Underneath the hand-operated adding machine was a cash box that opened with a distinct ring when you pulled the handle twice.

"Well let's see here young man, you got $3.90 on gas, $1.49 on the belt, 10 cents on the moon pie, a nickel on the gum and 15 cents on the Vienna sausage. That's $5.69 plus....uh... plus...uh... oh hell, I never could figure out sales tax on these confounded machines. Let's just make it an even $5.70."

"OK, here's $6.00. By the way, you didn't charge for the Topp Cola, and I'm leaving the bottle here, so there will be no deposit," Robby said, as he pointed to a yellow wooden crate in the corner three fourths full of an assortment of soda bottles of many different colors and shapes...an artist's collection that nobody wanted... like a stained glass window that had run amok.

"Well now, I appreciate your honesty, young man. Say, are

you boys just outta the service?"

"Yes sir."

"I fought in World War I, all over France. I fought the Germans and seen it all; one thing for sure, I don't want to fight them sons of bitches again." He paused, and as his eyes swelled up with tears, he looked out the door into the scenery that stretched for miles. Then he turned back to Robby and said, "You know, you'll never be the same. I mean after being in war, you are never the same."

"Yes sir."

"By the way, my name is Frank Walton, Frank James Walton. My brother's name is Jesse James Walton. Our grandfather rode with the James gang for a while and the names kinda got stuck on us."

"My name is Robert McLeod, from Atlanta, Georgia...just got out of the Marines and headed home. We wanted to stop by the Grand Canyon. What did you think of the Grand Canyon?"

"Uh... never been. Can you believe it, I've lived around here all my life and never been," he said, shaking his head.

Robby thought this to be a bit strange until he realized there was a lot of Atlanta he had never seen and people came from all over the country to visit parts of Atlanta he cared nothing about. It seemed that familiarity breeds complacency.

Chapter 9

•••••••••••••

How Great Thou Art

After stocking up on such healthy snacks as moon pies and cola, the idea of stopping at the diner for coffee and a biscuit was not as appealing as before. They voted unanimously to bypass the diner and go directly to the canyon. The plan was to view the canyon, hike, spend the night, get up in the morning and head home. If they stayed to plan, it would be the first time since they met that they didn't go astray in some manner or another. Mr. Walton told them to go to the southern rim. Not only was it much closer, but this time of year the northern rim had ice and snow... maybe even impassable roads. Since the microbus was lacking for any decent heat, they opted to stay south. Upon arriving, they also discovered they didn't have to walk the trail to the bottom of the canyon, but could ride in style on the back of a mule. That is, until they discovered Moose would have to lose 40 pounds before he could straddle the jackass.

From the Grand Canyon visitor's center, they walked to an overlook and all came to a dead stop, with absolutely nothing to say...motionless, speechless...totally caught up in the awe and majesty of it all.

Kim broke the silence with a whisper, "Fuck man, that's one big-ass hole. It goes on forever. It's the most amazing thing I've ever seen in my life. How was this all made?"

Roger cleared his throat as if he were the valedictorian about to speak on behalf of his classmates and send them off to cure all the ills in the world. "Well, the Grand Canyon is not as old as the earth itself; they say the Colorado River has been carving the Grand Canyon for 6 million years, but the canyons themselves date back about 70 million years. More than 5,000 feet down you can see the Colorado River and from up here it looks small and quite harmless, but once you see it up close, you will find it to be very large and powerful...powerful enough to eat through this rock. It's the erosion caused by the river that formed this canyon."

Not to be ignored, Moose said, "I heard it different, I heard a Jew dropped a quarter and started digging...mau ha ha ha ."

Slightly irritated, Robby firmly states, "Hey bro, watch it. Is that the best you can do? A Jew dropped a quarter and started digging? That's so fucked up, it's plain out of sight, man. Those different layers of rock, with all those vivid colors represent a monumental record of how the earth was formed millions of years ago and is a testimony of survival up to today. This "big-ass hole" is about 250 miles long, 16 miles wide and one mile deep. We once had a theory in physics class that proved mathematically you could put every man, woman and child alive today in a huge box and throw them into the Grand Canyon and still have room left over. This is Mother Nature at its best and we are damn lucky to see it."

"OK, OK, little bro, I was just cuttin' a funny. Geez, I think somebody needs a nap. You always get whacked off and start running at the mouth after you've been up for about three days. No need to get all touchy and show off your education."

"Showing off my education? How do you show off your education? By reading the funny papers?"

Robby, realizing he'd gone a little overboard, punched Moose on the arm and pivoted away from Moose's return swing. Robby returned to the business at hand, "We need to gather up everything and start hiking to the bottom. The sun will set sooner in the canyon than it will in the desert."

By now, Kim and Roger had grown accustomed to the little

spats between Robby and Moose. They knew they meant no harm, and they were positive there could never be a greater love or deeper respect than these two had for each other.

While Moose and Robby were discussing the pros and cons of higher education, Roger had been gathering up their backpacks and supplies needed for the hike. "OK, let's do this. We need to drop the cotton if we expect to reach the bottom before dark," said Roger, who was getting a little impatient about how everything had been going since he agreed to travel the country with a bunch of fuck-ups.

The guys had not walked fifteen minutes when they heard Moose bellow a thundering "GOD DAMN."

"I just stepped in a piled of donkey shit. And these are my good boots...just God Damn!"

"Those aren't donkeys, they're mules."

"Well, their shit smells the same, I'll betcha. And I never seen so many freakin' flies in one place in my life, and big black birds everywhere!"

As they started on the trail, they were too awestruck at the beauty and magnitude of it all to keep up any grumbling. Many times the foursome would stop and look around at the incredible beauty of rock formations, the Colorado River snaking through the bottom of the canyon, topped by a brilliant blue sky. The immenseness of it all was almost more than they could comprehend or describe.

After they had hiked a couple of miles, Robby broke the silence and said, "Roger was right. The sun will set early since we're down in this canyon. By the time we get to the bottom, it'll be dark...maybe before we arrive at our campsite."

For sure, by the time they had walked the trail to the bottom of the canyon, they could barely see each other's faces. However, the darkness brought on yet more beauty within the canyon. The countless stars with the moonlight provided an eerie feeling as the night light cast shadows on everything at the floor of the canyon. If anyone had been watching, it would have been quite remarkable and surprising to see these young men who were so full of mischief, energy, and authentic bullshit...to see them stand in stunned silence and wonder.

As they walked the trail, Roger kept looking toward the sound of the Colorado River, while Robby was looking for the campsite. Moose and Kim were just looking around in general for a place to pee.

When they settled down at the campsite around a blazing fire, a strange silence fell over the fearsome foursome. It was as if a dark fog had surrounded them and caused them to suddenly behave like mature adults. Gone were the silly dances, holding their balls, and telling middle school jokes. There was no drinking, no smoking pot, no farting contests accompanied by giggles. They simply sat very still, within their own thoughts, saying nothing to one another.

There was a palpable change among the band of brothers. Perhaps it was the idea that they had reached their destination and realized that as soon as they left the Grand Canyon, real life would begin again. Maybe it was the thought of transition, of going from a warrior in the jungle to getting a common, ordinary job and leading a mediocre life with the possibility of a mountain of debt and obligations that never went away. Maybe they were worried about getting married...or worried about getting divorced...forever enslaved to alimony and child support. It could have been a little fear of the unknown. In spite of how fearless these men had been, both on and off the battlefield, they were a little anxious about tomorrow, as they transitioned back to civilian and, hopefully, productive citizen. Or, it could have been the dread of going home.

Robby was thinking of purchasing a tall apartment building so he could see the stars and enjoy the best of city life. He didn't know how he was going to do it, but somehow, he would make it happen. Maybe he would start his own karate business, or look for a job with a big firm. He might have to go back to school, but he would do whatever necessary to achieve his dream.

Roger couldn't stop thinking about marketing bottled water, and even though it seemed a fantasy, he was determined to make this dream come true. He was tired of being the poor little rich boy who had everything handed to him and had his path paved for him before he even set foot on it. He couldn't help but wonder if he was assigned to expediting supplies in Okinawa because of the powerful influence his uncle and father had on their congressman. This, too, would haunt him all his days to think he was alive because he had a rich uncle, while others of less means perished. The very thought of it made Roger angry and sick toward his entitled world of high class everything. More than anything, he wanted to make it on his own without the help of his wealthy family. First, he needed to go back to college and get his degree.

Kim was thinking of selling his duffle bag full of dope and how he would spend the money wisely. He wasn't sure how he wanted to spend it, but knew this was his chance to get ahead if he would just think it through and do the smart thing. He was determined to never be poor again.

Moose was thinking about women.

Without so much as a "goodnight" they all closed their eyes and became very still in their sleeping bags...with the sound of the river to the left, the shadows of the canyon all around them, and the stars and moon above them. For this moment, they were not rowdy and wild guys just out of the service. They were a small part of nature, a tiny speck in a large, timeless canyon. In no time they were all sound asleep and snoring in tandem, sounding like bull frogs at the lake in the summertime.

Chapter 10

· · · · · · · · · · · · · · · ·

Let's Go Home!

OH SHIT...HELL...AND DAMN!!! It's10:20! How in the hell did we sleep so late?" shouted Robby as he front rolled across the ground and leapt straight up.

"Well, little bro, I'm thinking you needed the sleep since you have not slept in a fuckin' week," snapped Moose, as he adjusted himself between the legs before trying to get up off the ground.

"...and the canyon shields the sun for most of the day, so we were not privileged to see a sunrise this morning, thereby allowing the warmth of the sun to awaken us. I need some coffee and a cigarette," said Roger, as he patted his shirt pocket only to find it empty.

"Oh well, we're fucked...again. It will take us an hour to have coffee and pick up the campsite, and then it'll take six or eight hours just to hike back to our car," complained Kim.

"Why so long?"

"Well, it took about four hours to get down here, going downhill. It's gonna take much longer to take the same trail uphill...at least six hours. If we leave camp by 11:30, it will be somewhere between 5 and 6 o'clock before we can ever hope to see the Nazi Bastard. By then, we'll be starving and it'll be dark as a mother fucker."

"What's done is done, nothing we can do about it. Let's just make like horse droppings, and hit the trail," Robby joked, hoping to turn the mood around boost morale. He added, "Kim, as soon as we get back to the bus, plot us a course from here to

Canton, Texas. We are homeward bound, guys! Roger, you'll be the first to break up the fearsome foursome."

"That's cool with me."

As it turned out, Kim was right on target with the logistics of getting to the top of the canyon. It was 6:08 when they put their camping equipment in the microbus, and, sure as shootin', the sun was on its way down. The four of them stood and looked one more time at the magnificence that was the Grand Canyon.

Kim interrupted the silence, "You know, seeing a place this big with all this power and beauty really makes me think of how great and all-powerful God is."

Robby jumped in total shock and surprise. "What? I thought all you knew about God is that his last name is damn. No, man, this canyon came about due to millions of years of erosion, and if there is a God, I seriously doubt he cares whether or not this canyon reminds you of Him."

"Hey Robby, don't you believe in God?"

"No. If you had seen all the shit I've seen, neither would you. There is no way any god would allow children to get raped while their mothers were burned alive. And where does He get off allowing cancer to kill good churchgoing people? None of it makes sense, so, if you want a good fight on your hands, just keep on bringing up God. I got no use for him or any of these half assed religions."

"OK, man, it's cool...everything be everything."

Kim didn't say another word; he simply got in the van and stayed quiet while staring out the window in the direction of the canyon. This was the time to be quiet and not argue. He had never seen Robby get so upset and didn't want to see it again. So, instead of acting like one of the guys, Kim behaved more like a little colored boy on a city bus...just sit back and keep your mouth shut...he really didn't want any trouble.

After a few minutes, Kim pulled out from under the seat his map, found a pencil that writes in red, and a plastic 12 inch ruler.

"Well, just fuck me to tears, it's gonna be better than a thousand miles from here to Canton. Hey Robby, I think we need to plot our course from Highway 180 to the expressway...I-40."

"Shit man, you know I don't like the expressway; with this bus peaking out at 60 MPH, I feel like there's a little boy on a tricycle trying to pass me...gives a new meaning to slow-poke."

"Sir, it's the best way to get there, and just about the only way to get there. So we can go this route, or learn how to fly."

"All right, plot the course and we'll not stop until we get into New Mexico. At least it's getting dark and it'll be cool and not much traffic on the expressway...not too bad a ride, maybe. Hey Moose, you drive for a while. I haven't rode shotgun since we bought this bastard."

"Uh....Uh...Uh I can't"

"What? Why the hell not?"

"Uh...I can't drive a stick shift."

"Oh hell no. You mean it? Where I come from, all my friends could drive a stick. We had to; only rich people had an automatic transmission. And you mean to tell me with all you been through, you never drove a three on the tree?"

"Shit no, man, my uncle and father both had an Oldsmobile 88, and my car was a '55 Ford with a Ford-O-Matic transmission. We weren't rich, but we didn't drive no candy ass stick shift, either."

"Ok, Moose. I guess it never crossed your mind that you'd be driving this bus on the last leg of this journey...by yourself. Sometimes you just plain scare me. I tell you what, you'll not learn any younger. Get in...time to learn how to grind 'em 'til you find 'em."

For the next hour Kim, Roger, and Robby wondered if the Nazi Bastard was going to survive the long learning curve that Moose was giving it. He either stalled the engine so many times the battery was almost dead, or he popped the clutch so fast it jerked and jarred until it stalled. They had to wonder if the clutch was going to hold up when Moose floor-boarded the gas pedal and just let the clutch fly. It was a comfort to know that the Volkswagen was so forgiving. About the time Robby had ran out of patience with his best friend, Moose caught on. Smooth sailing...finally.

About an hour into the ride, Robby noticed two farmers in bib overalls throwing fire wood in their pickup truck on the side of the road. There was a manual jack and tire tool beside the truck... one of those jacks that you push on a handle as hard as you can, and the truck rises one little click at a time. These jacks were not only good for raising a vehicle, but excelled in making some pretty lady a widow, or making sure you were called nubs the rest of your life if the jack slipped of its stand and the car crushed your fingers. He figured what happened was the truck had a flat tire, but with all the wood in it, was too heavy for such a small, portable jack, so they unloaded the heavy wood, jacked up the truck, changed the tire, put it back on the ground, and were now throwing the wood back in the truck as darkness overtook them.

As he drew his next breath, Robby was reminded of a time he saw the dead bodies of his buddies, stacked like cords of firewood, being thrown into the back of a refrigerated trailer. With this vision in his mind, as vivid as a large movie screen, he once again asked himself why he was the one that survived while better men perished for no good reason. He shifted his weight in his seat, looked around at Kim and Roger to see they were napping, looked up at the sky, and did whatever he could to get that image out of his mind. He convinced himself that this long ride home in this slow-moving microbus was the best thing to rid himself of his demons.

Robby began to notice that about every mile or so there was a marker alongside the road, so he occupied his mind by counting these markers and trying to memorize the Burma Shave signs:

DON'T LOSE

YOUR HEAD
TO GAIN
A MINUTE
YOU NEED YOUR HEAD
BURMA SHAVE

IF A GIFT
YOU MUST CHOOSE
GIVE HIM ONE
HE'LL LIKE
TO USE
BURMA SHAVE

WE'VE MADE GRANDPA
LOOK SO YOUTHFUL
HIS PENSION BOARD
THINKS
HE'S UNTRUTHFUL
BURMA SHAVE

None of it was working. Not the counting, not looking at the stars, not reading and memorizing the Burma Shave ads. So, he decided to just listen to the hum of the engine in the rear. Maybe if he just thought of that and nothing else and closed his eyes, some of the demons would go away.

Robby sat in the seat with his hands folded in his lap, eyes shut, looking very much like a statue of Buddha. But, in time he fell asleep and went back in time through a dream:

Master Sergeant Roberts yells, "OK, ladies, the Screaming Eagles are in deep shit again and we gotta bail 'em out. Let's go!!! Assholes and elbows! Move it!"

Robby takes a seat in the Huey and he can barely think

because of the incredibly loud wop wop wop of the blades spinning overhead. It doesn't help matters that the ear-piercing turbine engine is right above him. The deafening noise could be heard for miles as it penetrated the jungle. He's thinking, "Great! Couldn't they make these bastards any louder? I mean, like, a deaf VC could hear us coming for 30 minutes before we arrived. Yeah that's it! Let's give them plenty of time so they can draw a bead on us as we come in.

A little voice tells him not to think about this ear-splitting problem anymore, but to get focused on the business at hand.

He sits back and closes his eyes, breathing deeply. He remembers back when he was nine years old and he had stolen a quarter from granddaddy Bob's red coin holder. He was amazed by the way you squeezed the ends and the center popped open, and, as he opened it, there was a quarter he couldn't live without. Just then, he heard granddaddy coming down the hallway, saying, "Did you take any money?" as he took the coin purse back. Robby shook his head no. Little Robby was encased in fear and was trying not to tremble. He shook his head because he couldn't speak, since he had quickly placed the quarter in his mouth, hiding all the evidence. Although he was scared to death, he didn't get in any trouble, but after granddaddy left and he took the quarter out of his mouth, there was still a metallic taste in his mouth.

This same taste was in his mouth as he stepped into the Huey...a dry taste of dirty metal that brought back the feeling of loathing and dread that he had that day long ago. Since it was too loud to talk and no one wanted to talk anyway, he opened his eyes again and just looked around. Some new guy was tapping his toe. A buddy, named Johnny Spears held his M-16 as tight as possible, white-knuckling the stock and *barrel, then releasing his grip, tighten up, release, repeat over and over. To his left, Robby saw the blank stares of young Marines, and to the right he caught glimpses of tree tops that whistled by at a blinding speed.*

He knew he would have to double-time it getting out of the helicopter because the landing field was small and there was just enough room for them to land one at a time. So the choppers came in lined up one behind the other at a slight angle to the left, looking much like kids standing at a water fountain at school.

Corporal Forrester was the first to exit, placing both feet on the skid and jumping before they had landed, hitting the ground at a dead run, bent at the waist. Robby was next, stepping down onto the ground with his left, foot while the other foot was about 10 inches high on the skid. Before he could move his right foot, the Huey landed, which made him feel the springing action of the skid.

He runs behind the Corporal, and thinks to himself: "mmmm... solid ground; the last time I jumped into a goddamn rice patty I was wet as a water buffalo all day." By now, everyone was present and all were experiencing mass confusion. The gunships were circling, firing hundreds of rounds a minute as a suppressing fire... rockets exploding all around, orange smoke that marked the landing site had not yet dispersed. After about ten minutes of circling, the gunships left under heavy fire, as one crashed and exploded...adding to the deafening noise. Above all the noise and confusion, Robby could hear the familiar sound of the enemy's bullets whistling by.

"It's the ones that don't whistle you worry about," calls out a

red-headed Marine named Johnson. He had no soo...
words from his mouth when Robby saw blood gus...
fire hose from both of Johnson's legs. Robby knew J...
dead before he hit the ground and kept running toward the
enemy, changing clips as he ran.

He follows as Corporal Forrester (aka Moose) finds a place
behind some fallen trees and elephant grass to get cover and
re-group, and hopefully make a game plan.

"Those mother fuckers have 'em surrounded. All we can do is
break through at the closest point and 69. We'll go in butt to
butt and leave butt to butt."

The bail 'em out squad lost half their men by the time they
had broken through the line. Robby yells, "We made it to the
party, now let's dance!" As he's changing out another clip, he
noticed Moose and the others had stopped what they were
doing and dropped their weapons.

"OH FUCK!! We've been captured."

Robby counts only three Screaming Eagles and five from his
outfit are left. It felt like a movie in slow motion, as they were
forced to take off all their clothes except their underwear,
and then get on both knees with their hands on top of their
head. Those who weren't wearing underwear kneeled there
bare-assed naked. He watches two of the enemy grab one
of the Screaming Eagles by his arms lifting him up and
dragging him in front of him and Moose, while a third one
took a machete and began to hack away at him as if he were
a small tree; first hacking at the legs, then arms...slowly one
little hack at a time until both arms and legs looked like raw
hamburger. Robby couldn't watch anymore, but refused to

close his eyes or look afraid. He looked away for a split second into the jungle and thought of a pretty girlfriend he had in Atlanta and realized he would never see her again. This brief thought was overcome by the thumps of the machete hitting the soldier's bone, and the screams of pain echoed in his mind more loudly than all the gunfire and rockets they just experienced.

His fear and trembling began to diminish as anger took its place. What a moment ago was the dread for what was going to happen to him and pure apprehension of how it would feel and how long the torture would last was replaced by a strong resolve to beat these debased bastards at their own game. Still trembling on his knees, and trying to come up with a game plan, Robby watched them finish the soldier with a long slash across the abdomen, his intestines falling to his knees. As he hits the ground beside Robby, he made one last gurgling sound and with his right hand, pointed his middle finger at the enemy.

When Robby saw him flip the bird, everything went silent... no gunfire, no screaming, no popping, no overhead...nothing. He no longer heard the laughter of the Vietnamese soldiers, nor the outcries of his own men. It was just Moose and Robby against twelve.

Robby looked over at Moose and said, "Give me a diversion."

"What's a diversion?"

"Oh goddammit Moose, do something to get their attention."

"Why didn't you just say that, college boy?"

Moose jumped up from his kneeling position, threw up both arms and started to dance and sing: "Euuu...I feel good."

As the VC stare in dumbfounded wonder at Moose, Robby grabs the end of the AK that was pointed at his forehead, steps to the side, pulls the rifle straight down into the ground and executes a perfect axe kick to the back of the neck of a man who would no longer need his weapon. He looks toward Moose to find he too had grabbed an AK-47, and they pray and spray. Only one left of the twelve now, and he takes dead aim at Robby only to learn he has no rounds left...empty gun...no good for him. All Robby has to do is take aim and pull the trigger. Holy shit!!! His weapon jams. Robby steps forward and plants a heel deep into his chest with a perfect spinning back kick, and for a split second he hears the snap of the enemy's breast plate as he falls to the ground, gasping for air because of the broken rib piercing his lung.

He looks around and sees that besides him and Moose, only one Screaming Eagle is still alive. The other one had tried to help Moose and stopped a stray bullet. The others of the bail 'em out squad had also been caught up in the gun fire.

"Let's haul ass. What's your name?"

"Lt. Richland, what's yours?"

"Robby McLeod, 9ᵗʰ division, USMC welcome to Dong Ha, Lt. Richland. Let's get the fuck outta here!"

All three took off back in the direction they had come when yet another VC jumped from the elephant grass and sliced Robby across his entire mid-section. He looks down to see lots of red and pink and as he looks back up, POW POW POW, he sees Moose shoot the son of a bitch in the head with the AK's he had brought along just for fun. Robby felt a thump as Moose grabbed him and threw him on his shoulder, running for safety.

* * *

The microbus almost went off the road when Robby bolted upright yelling NOOOOO!!!! It was so loud and unexpected that the others immediately jerked to attention, hearts pounding.

Moose found a spot to pull over, and Kim grabbed a Pepsi and some Ritz crackers in an effort to soothe Robby's agitation. Kim had no idea what the problem was but he had to do something; and being a cook and having a mama from the South, he was brought up to believe that food solves every problem.

Robby took a sip of Pepsi, slumped back in his seat and apologized, "Sorry guys...bad dream."

Roger, who has always been the quiet one throughout the trip, and also the wisest, said, "Robby, we've seen you stay up for two days without sleep, and when you do sleep, it's only for an hour or two, and not without jerking and moaning while asleep. We have seen you fly mad over nothing; we've seen you almost kill a man with your bare hands. Now, we are not moving this van another inch until you tell us why. Tell us what happened to you that has made you borderline psycho."

He looked at Moose, who very slightly nodded yes and Robby told them the story of the events that haunt his sleep. Dead silence falls on the fearsome foursome.

Finally, Kim was the first to speak, "Hey man, you were just a guy doing what he was ordered...no need to feel bad about what you did or why you did it. It's all in the past, man. Somehow you gotta learn to keep it in the past. Me and Roger can only try to understand how you must feel about being one of the few that survived. I know you think that God is only so much bull shit, but there has to be some kinda reason your life was spared. So make this life count...make it count."

"Gee whizz, Kim, you shoulda been a chaplain or something," Robby responded, being a bit of a smart ass, trying hard to shake off the distress caused by his dream.

"No, really man, to hell with the military, and the war, fuck it all and go from here, from right this minute. My mama used to say that there ain't no sense worrying about crossin' no bridge that might not even be there tomorrow, or done burnt up yesterday.

I figure she was saying we should live for right this minute and forget the past and not worry about the future."

The quiet one responded, "Kim, in spite of himself, has given some good advice that we all would do well to heed. We are lucky to be alive and now it's up to us to do something with that life."

Roger can't help but think the biggest battle is ahead for him too. Robby's not the only one who has a problem with still being alive.

Robby took a slow breath, held back the tears and said, "I copy."

Without a word, Moose pushed the clutch to the floor, found first gear on the second try and eased back on the road. He was thinking that the wiry little sailor made a lot of sense. He was also glad it was in the middle of the night, in the middle of nowhere in black-as-tar surroundings, so nobody saw the tears running down his cheek. He had his share of demons as well.

Chapter 11

· · · · · · · · · · · · · ·

Here we go Again

After this troubling episode, Robby came up with a plan: he was going to stay focused on the sound of the little engine in the rear and think of nothing else. When he wasn't driving, he would stay centered by thinking of nothing but the sound of the engine. This was a little trick he learned as a karate student. He'd been trained by his *Sah Bah Nihm* to empty the mind and pay attention to only one thing for a long time, such as a flame on the tip of a candle. He suddenly realized it was that kind of mental attentiveness that saved their life in Dong Ha. That's why all sound went away...extreme concentration and the power of focus. All he had to do was to direct this martial art style of focus and concentration to making the memory of war go away...too easy, right?

Putting plan to action, he relaxed into his seat and closed his eyes, focusing on the sound of the engine until he had fallen into a deep sleep, only to be jolted back when Moose roared, "OH HELL YEAH!!! WELCOME TO NEW MEXICO, LADIES!!!"

Robby wasn't the only one. With a voice that had all the gentle finesse of a baritone fog horn, Moose had jolted everyone back to the land of the living.

Amidst all the yawning and stretching, Roger spoke up, "I don't know about you guys, but I'm about done with the camping out and sleeping in the bus. I could use a soft bed, cold beer and hot shower. Anyone else?"

"Sounds good to me."

"Sure thing."

"Excellent. The next place we see, let's stop. Moose, you and Kim look on the left and Robby and I will look on the right."

It wasn't ten minutes after this conversation that they entered Rehoboth, New Mexico. Lady luck was smiling upon them with favor because right at the entrance of town was the Rehoboth Inn.

"Let's check and see if they have a laundry. I've been wearing this same sailor suit way too long and I can barely stand it myself."

"Yes, we're all getting a little ripe. A good laundering is definitely in order," said Roger with a smile that emitted from the corner of his mouth.

Moose was thinking about the times when they were dropped off into battle and left for three days without a clean anything: clothes, shirt, socks, or underwear. If they were in the field more than three days, a Huey would drop all new clothes from the skin out along with necessary supplies. Meanwhile, his clothes would smell of sweat, pee, poop, vomit, and assorted blood and flesh from nearby casualties. Sometimes the blood would be his; sometimes it would belong to somebody else. Out loud he said, "Well, you ladies ain't smelled nasty until you get a whiff of the smell of death and a Marine's clothes after three days in combat. Now that's goddamn ripe."

"Sir, although it's true we haven't seen the horror and aroma of battle like you have, we know when we are on the verge of filth and squalor. We are not overseas any more, and clean is in fashion and easy to obtain." Roger replied, getting a little miffed about the superior attitude that Moose seemed to continually display.

Realizing that Moose as getting on everybody's nerves, Robby changed the subject by saying, "Hey look, guys. There's a laundry, an ice machine, and a bar next door. We can eat, drink, and be merry! There are even picnic tables and a swing set in the back."

Oh boy! Here we go again.

Being the frugal one of the bunch, Robby asked if they had a room without a TV, where he could get a discount... not happening. He was informed that all the rooms had been recently renovated and there was a new color TV in every room and all rooms cost the same – $17.00. After looking at Roger and mumbling something about how damn expensive things were these days, they all decided to each get their own room. As soon as they crossed the threshold, Kim wanted to go to the bar next door and Moose thought he should accompany him to make sure he didn't get into any trouble. Robby and Roger were feeling a little road weary and wanted no part of it, deciding they just wanted to stay in and watch some color TV.

Moose and Kim read the sign over the door, "The Blue Acorn," and Moose wondered what kind of name was that for a bar. Inside, the bar was very dark and cold. Now, they got the part where a bar is supposed to be dark...so it covers up a lot of ugly, well, that along with plenty of alcohol, but damn, they had to stand there for a minute for their eyes to adjust just so they could take a step and not run into anything. With just the one dim light in the middle of the room they managed to bump into an empty table and slid into the seats. As soon as their butts hit the chair, a very lovely lady with exotic features appeared from the darkness. Smiling, she asked, "What can I get you gentlemen?"

By now, their eyes had become more accustomed to the dark and as they ordered a beer, they got a better look at the bar maid. In fact, Kim couldn't keep his eyes off her. She was dark...raven black hair with a slight curl that fell almost to her butt with an olive complexion that was smooth as marshmallow cream sauce strained through an old brazier. She was wearing a black sheer blouse with a white mini-skirt. He looked down and saw she was wearing go go boots...one white and one black. There was something about the fact she wore different color boots that just tore him up. This was just too cool and way too sexy.

They both ordered the burger plate and a couple of beers. By now, Kim was grinning like an idiot and following her every move, beginning to fantasize about being with her tonight. Every time she came to the table to check on them, Kim would stare at her with big puppy dog eyes and his heart would skip a beat every time she favored him with a look.

When they had finished their burgers, she approached them once again and asked, "Would you like anything else? We'll be closing soon and this'll be last chance for alcohol."

With his biggest smile Kim said, "What I would like is to buy you a drink and after the bar closes, we could go outside and sit at the picnic table and get better acquainted. Would you like to do that?"

Without a yes or no, she says, "So, are you in the Navy? You know, my father was in the Navy during World War II."

"I was in the Navy for eight years...just got out."

"Oh, ok. I think that would be groovy to talk to a sailor. I get outta here in 30 minutes. I don't want a cocktail, but you can get me a Coke to go and I'll meet you out at the picnic tables."

Moose shook his head and sighed, "There's that groovy shit again. Don't anybody just talk plain English anymore? I'm having another shot of scotch and I'm turning in. You're on your own, sailor boy."

As the Blue Acorn closed, Kim ordered two Cokes to go and waited at the picnic tables. As the ice began to melt in the Dixie cups, Kim spotted her walking across the parking lot toward the tables. Her legs were long and lean and looked like a dancer's legs...shaped by muscle tone and not an ounce of fat. He began to breathe heavily and his palms began to sweat. He wiped his hands on his pants and got ready to jump up to greet her when she got closer to the table. A slight breeze caused her hair to sway in time with her hips, and as she approached he could feel his heart trying to fight its way out of his chest.

Kim, the one of the foursome who was the most vocal, who

had the most to say about anything, was all of a sudden struck speechless by the thought of an encounter with this beautiful girl. As she drew almost close enough to touch, he gathered his courage, jumped to his feet and nervously said, "Hi! I'm Kim Hernandez, what's your name?"

"Karen...Karen Butler."

"Hey Karen, have a seat. Here's your coke."

Karen settled onto the bench across from Kim and leaned in towards. "May I ask you a question?"

"Sure."

"What are you?"

"Uh, I'm a guy who just got out of the Navy and me and my buddies are headed home."

"No, I don't mean it that way. I'm Hopi Indian; my mom was full-blooded, my dad, half Indian. So, what are you? I can't quite place you?"

"Oh, I get it, now. I'm half Puerto Rican and half colored. My mother is from Alabama and my father is a Puerto Rican from New York City."

They talked in a way that Kim had never spoken with someone else before. It was just so easy to talk to her. He was completely under her spell and felt he could just fall into those gorgeous dark eyes and be happy for the rest of his life. He learned they shared many of the same dreams as well as many of the same fears and frustrations. They were both from a small town and both had had their share of people teasing them, spitting at them, making low-class, uncalled-for remarks about them just because their skin was brown instead of white. She told him once she tried to put white shoe polish all over her body when she was in the 4th grade because none of the boys wanted to dance with her because she wasn't white. They shared with each other the strong desire to break away from the mold that had been cast for them and do something really special, to live a truly meaningful life.

Kim could not keep his eyes off her and for a moment would lose concentration on what she was saying and simply look at her from head to toe. Her long raven hair with a slight curl, her soft skin which covered a petite body with a slim build, those dark eyes, so dark they were black and seemed to sparkle in the moonlight captivated him. Her lips were a little pouty and a shade darker than her skin. He watched her lips move and tried to focus on her words as she talked to him about how much she admired people like Martin Luther King and Richland Means, men who fought for the rights of their people, but he would lose focus once again, mesmerized by the movement of her lips, those soft, puffy lips that he wanted to kiss with all his heart and soul. Abruptly, he interrupted her and said, "This is a great conversation, but, would you mind if I gave you a kiss?"

At first startled, Karen smiled at him and said, "Yes, actually, I would love a kiss from you. And I want you to know that I don't go out with just any guy after work. In fact, I don't even date much at all, but there's something special about you."

Kim quickly took off his big black horn-rimmed glasses and placed them on the table as he rounded the picnic table to sit next to her. He gently pressed his lips to hers and she immediately responded by slightly opening her lips to allow more warmth and moisture to fall on his. This incredible kiss made him only want more and he pressed harder and wrapped his arms around her, holding her tight to his body as they both became lost in the moment to each other.

Kim broke away and stood to take off his neckerchief and pull off the top of his Navy uniform. It was now her turn to become mesmerized by the sight of Kim's chiseled chest and hard as steel arms and shoulders that seemed to shine in the moonlight. Karen stood up next to him and allowed her finger tips to glide up and down his chest as she felt every ripple of his lean muscles. She glanced down, noticing an erection. They began to kiss again and her left hand gradually slid down his chest, to his stomach and then to the bulge in his pants. As she felt him, her heart raced and her eyes opened wide...he was enormous. To be a rather short man, he was certainly packing a heavy load.

Kissing down her neck, Kim unbuttoned the shear blouse enough to see her beautiful breasts. He slowly kissed from top to bottom, ending with her hard, tasty nipples. He placed both hands on her tiny waist and in one easy motion, lifted her onto the picnic table. With one hand still around her waist, he placed the other hand under her skirt and instead of touching silk or cotton, he touched something soft and moist.

She let out a deep, throaty moan and slowly spread her legs, so taken with passion that she didn't even register that they were on a picnic table out under the stars. He gently stroked and massaged her and she pulled him closer to her so she could feel him inside her.

He gradually inserted only an inch or so, slowly going in and out, going in a little deeper with each thrust as he quickened the pace. With a long, deep moan, Karen had a celestial orgasm just as did Kim, and in a complete state of euphoria, they totally let go of all tension and collapsed together, side by side, on the table.

After his heart slowed to a manageable rhythm and he was able to breathe again, Kim whispered in her ear, "I so hate to get up and leave you....you have no idea how much I hate to get up and leave you, but we have to leave around 7:00, and it's gotta be around 3:00 now. Oh...never mind. I'm not leaving you. We have the rest of the night or at least until 7:00 and I want to stay with you until the very last minute. I have a room at the hotel and I would be honored if you would stay with me for the rest of the night."

So she did. Talking, making love, more talking, more making love until the morning sun was streaming through the curtain.

Kim said, "I really want to see you again. As soon as I get

home, I will call you and we can make plans to see each other again. Is that OK with you?"

"Oh yes, I would love to see you again. There should be a pen and some stationery in the room. Let's exchange phone numbers and addresses."

As Kim walked her back to her car that morning, he began to wonder how soon he could see her again. He had only taken 20 steps toward the motel when he stopped and looked back to see her one more time, only to find her looking at him. And in this bittersweet moment, they waved and he sadly watched as she bent down to get in her white Mustang and leave the bar's parking lot.

As he walked back to his room, he glanced at the picnic table where they had their first romantic encounter, and the thrill of it all came back in a rush. Taking a few more steps, he wondered about someone eating lunch there today, and for a brief moment pondered if they should've wiped it down. Oh well, it's not like they left big spots on it or anything. And besides, everybody does it on a picnic table, right?

Chapter 12

· · · · · · · · · · · · · ·

You Never Know

The New Mexico sun had risen and it was already getting hot as Kim crossed the parking lot to meet up with Roger and the two Marines. About half way across the parking lot, he was contemplating the thrill of wearing his uniform another day, and saw two men approaching out of the corner of his left eye. Kim sensed trouble because they were walking swiftly in his direction and they weren't exactly smiling. They appeared to be cowboys, or at least cowboy wannabes, dressed in tight jeans, boots, cheap cowboy hats, and the obligatory big belt buckle. These guys didn't know that real cowboys wear tennis shoes... they wear tennis shoes so people won't mistake them for truck drivers, Kim thought to himself, trying to keep a straight face and not let on to how goofy he thought they looked.

One was large and the other small. Kim was too far from the motel room to make a run for it. Instead, he thought of two things: Number one: If they tried to attack, he'd go after the big one first, and Number two: Now would be a good time for Moose to show up. Ooooh Shiiit! Here we go again!

The smaller one spoke first. "Where you think you're going, you little four eyed freak?" he asked with a sneer that showed his green teeth.

"Look, I don't want no trouble, we're gonna be leaving before the hour's out, and we'll be outta your town forever. Please sir, just let me get to my room so we can leave," Kim said trying to defuse the situation, not wanting to spoil what had been an

—

incomparable experience for the past few hours.

With a balled up fist the huge one says, "What's this WE shit? You got a mouse in your pocket? Or maybe a turd? 'Cause I don't see nobody but you...you sawed off little bitch,' giving Kim a shove that pushed him back six feet.

Kim was almost amused thinking about the several things these two morons didn't consider. First of all, it's best not to mess with a black man who had been raised in a rough neighborhood, who from childhood was told to avoid a fight at all cost, but if you must fight, fight to win...no rules. Second, they didn't know who he was or that he'd been in the Navy for a while, and this is by no means his first confrontation. And the third and most important thing these bullies neglected to realize...when you see a sailor grab the knot of his neckerchief and bend over rapidly, it's time to run. Like all good sailors, Kim had a $10 roll of quarters in the base of that neckerchief that was now in his hand swinging back and forth in a figure eight pattern. A very effective weapon...one that is capable of knocking out your teeth and rendering you unconscious in a heartbeat.

WHAM!!! Kim takes two steps forward and quickly strikes big boy in the shin, and as he drops his hands to grab his shin, WHAM!!! Kim strikes him across the bridge of the nose...instant broken nose with blood splattered all over his fancy blue and white cowboy shirt. The smaller man in the cheap cowboy hat had scooted behind Kim and grabbed him from behind in a bear hug, rendering his arms useless.

"You broke my nose you little mother fucker. Now I'm a gonna bust you up real good."

At this point, two things happened at the same time...Kim, with all his might, lifted his left knee as high as he could and stomped the foot of the man who had his arms confined. As the short, little tormenter was thinking about the pain in his foot and letting go his grip on Kim's arms, they heard a voice say, "I don't think so, gentlemen."

It was Roger, wearing nothing but his combat boots and boxer shorts. Roger was standing right behind the man who was larger than Moose, with blood on his shirt, and very pissed off. Roger assumed the stance of a boxer, his back straight, knees slightly bent, all his weight on the balls of his feet with the heels off the ground just enough to slide a piece of paper under them, and his hands up in a guarded position. Big man just laughed as he threw his very best hay-maker punch at Roger, who ducked the punch and countered with a double hook to the ribs, a hook to the jaw with his left hand, followed up by an over-hand-right that connected with a loud thud to the point of the chin...all in less than two seconds...right "on the button." This giant of a man looked like an inflatable clown that someone let the air out of. He melted into the pavement, unconscious. Score a knockout for Roger.

Kim had been busy getting loose from his attacker and didn't see everything, but he did see a man bleeding all over his nice new cowboy outfit lying on the ground with Roger standing over him, rubbing his knuckles.

As he broke free from the grip of the man behind him, he spun around, hit him between the legs with his roll of quarters and then across the mouth. As the man was falling to the ground, holding his balls, Kim was sure he saw a tooth spew from his mouth.

This morning's exercise was broken up with the sound of applause and whooping and hollering...Moose and Robby propped against the van as casual observers, where they had stood there, doing nothing, watching the whole thing.

In total amazement, Moose says, "Youse did a hell of a job of kickin' ass. Hey Roger, I thought you were nothing but a pansy-assed box kicker. Where'd that come from?"

Still rubbing his knuckles, Roger replied, "Well, I boxed Golden Gloves from the time I was eight to eighteen. My father even hired a personal trainer for me because he wanted me to go to the Olympics. In 1964, I was fourth in the nation and went to Tokyo as an alternate. I didn't fight in the Olympics; I just was there in case the main competitor was injured. I boxed in college, too."

"Well, just damn. And you Kim, remind me not to fuck with you...you're bad ass!"

Robby stood there calmly and said, "You never know...you really never know what's inside a man... How soon before we leave? Or would you two rather hang around for a while and go for round two?"

Kim speaks up, "Oh no, let's saddle up and hit the trail."

"Saddle up and hit the trail? Is that what you just said? You kick ass one time and already you start sounding like John Wayne."

Three days ago, Kim would have been offended by Moose's remark, but now he considers it a compliment, pleased that he's gained the respect of one tough Marine.

Robby poured some cold water on the two wannabe intimidators in western attire, who came around, got a good look at the fearsome foursome ...and ran.

Kim adjusted his glasses and yelled, "You forgot your tooth. Who's the bitch now?"

"OK Kim, calm down, and let's plot a course to Canton, Texas. We need to get Roger home before he gets in any more trouble."

"Right on. Consider it done, sir!"

After consulting the map and making calculations, Kim decided the best thing to do was to take I-40 to Amarillo and then decide if they wanted to travel any farther, although he recommended spending the night in Amarillo. It would be about a seven hour drive to there and still nobody had any clean clothes. An argument ensued about the pro and cons of just driving through all the way to Canton, Texas, which would be about a 12 to 13 hour trek, in the heat of the day.

Robby said, "Well, one thing's for damn sure, we aren't

making any miles standing in the parking lot, arguing about logistics. Let's get in the bus and go. We can work out the details as we travel. But at least let's do that...TRAVEL."

Robby always had this manner about him that when he spoke, they all knew he meant it and there was no point in any further discussion...just get with the program and do what he said, and that's all.

Chapter 13

· · · · · · · · · · · · · ·

Good Bye to Roger

As they piled into the van, Roger looked around and said, "We are low on supplies. No beer in the cooler, hardly any scotch or tequila, no ice, and no cokes and the water jug is empty." Roger once again thinks to himself that a bottle of water would be nice, but the only bottled water is very expensive and comes in little glass bottles.

"Fine, we'll stop and get supplies and then hit the road," Robby answered impatiently, wanting to get going.

The only place open this early is a little 7-Eleven store across the street from the motel. Robby scowls a bit and says, "You know, the little stores like this...I hate the high prices. I'm surprised the store owner isn't walking around with a gun on his hip. I mean...these prices are highway robbery!"

Roger taking a different approach, "Just view it as paying for convenience. If we didn't have this store, we would have to wait until 9:00 or 10:00 just to get a Pepsi."

"Oh, so then we should call these "Convenience Stores"? Well, it's not convenient to my wallet."

After they listened to Robby bitch and moan about the outrageous prices in these small stores, the foursome purchased all they needed for the trip, including an ample supply of beer, but no whiskey from this store. As Robby shifted through the gears, little by little getting to top speed, he thought he would rather just drive straight through to Canton. At this rate, the motel bills were going to break him.

—

As they got on I-40, eastbound to Texas, Robby plugged in the 8-track tape, Steppenwolf, and listened to his theme song about getting out on the highway. As always, he cranked up the sound to the point that the people in the car next to them could sing along if they so desired. It struck no one funny to see these four young men sporting military haircuts, barely out of their teens, in an old van barely going 50 miles per hour, in clothes barely fit to wear, singing at the top of their voices how they were born to be wild. They really didn't look all that wild although they were an odd assortment. As far as being wild...well those days were fast approaching their end and they all knew it deep in their soul.

After five hours of driving, drinking beer, eating cheese and crackers, and listening to Little Richard, The Turtles, Chuck Berry, James Brown, and The Beatles, they stopped for gasoline where Robby once more got a little annoyed with people making Volkswagen comments.

He surmised that you could put these people in two categories: 1) those who think the VW is a bit of a novelty with a lot of practical and basic mixed in, and 2) people who still harbor ill feelings about the Germans and the atrocities they committed during World War II, and have no use for a Volkswagen regardless of how economical it was or how long ago that war had ended.

While an attendant was filling up the bus, Robby had a conversation with one of these tax-paying citizens who represented those in group number 2. Robby's feet had just landed on the ground, and as he reached in his Levi Garrett pouch for a pinch of tobacco, a man in his mid-40's walked up to him and said, "I don't understand how we spent four years of crawling in the mud to defeat Hitler, and now here we are kissing his ass by buying the very car he invented. It ain't right. They shoulda never let them in the country. Do you have any idea what those damn Nazis did to our boys?"

Robby spit tobacco juice about two inches from the man's

shoes, took in a deep breath, and responded as calmly as he could, "I was in recon and rescue in the United States Marine Corps, sir, and I know QUITE WELL what the enemy is capable of doing. And... the VW, although the brain child of Hitler, was designed by engineers who hated Hitler as much as you do... maybe even more. This van is cheap, dependable transportation. Maybe Chevrolet or Ford should make something like this. And besides, World War II was over 20 years ago...time to put it behind you and move on, mister, and don't be insulting me or my van."

"OK, OK, son. Didn't mean no harm."

Robby realized at that moment he needed to heed the very advice he just gave the WWII veteran, put it all behind you and move on. Maybe in a small sense, the van represented that. People who bought these German cars had to put behind them the anti-German thoughts that were spawned by the horrors of Nazi warfare. As such, so should he. So now, when he looked at this dented, dull van with all the windows open, he thought now it's his turn to scatter those bad thoughts out to the entire universe.

As the man turned and walked away, Robby's eye caught the building across the street. It was a laundry mat with a liquor store beside it. There is a God after all.

"Let's go across the street, get some Kool-Aid, do our laundry and then go straight through to Canton."

Roger agreed, "Sounds fine with me."

Moose and Kim nod yes and prepare for another seven hours of travel.

After an uneventful thirteen hour trek to Roger's home, they finally arrived in Canton, Texas. Roger directed Robby to turn off the main road at the driveway coming up on the left. At the entrance of the driveway was an extra large white mail box sitting on a pedestal which looked more like a column for a porch than it did a pedestal for a mail box and had the Hilton name on top written in a wrought iron plaque.

As he approached the driveway, Robby shifted into second gear and wondered why Roger hadn't even moved to get his gear bag behind the back seat and soon discovered that the reason was because it was not even close to time to get out of the van. The driveway twisted and turned through large pasture land where horses ran free, then crossed a small river and circled its way around a 10 acre lake that was surrounded on two sides by forest and the other two sides surrounded by sand for a beach. The guys were silent as they took in this sparkling clear lake that shimmered in the moonlight, and had a dock about 100 feet long with a boat tied to each side. The driveway started to twist and turn as it passed the lake, since it was now climbing a hill that would end at Roger's house.

"Oh my God, this ain't a house...it's a hotel!!!" said an astonished Kim. Rob and Moose were still silent, almost the same way they were a few days ago when they saw the Grand Canyon.

Robby had no trouble finding a place to park in this enormous circular driveway, but he did feel quite underdressed as he parked the '62 microbus behind a new 1969 Lincoln stretch limousine that was behind a black Jaguar luxury sedan. Roger calmly stated his mother was home because the Jaguar was her car.

"So, this is how rich fuckers live...a little different from our four room house in Birmingham."

"Well, Kim. I guess that's the way it goes. Y'all come on inside, and I'll introduce you to my family and show you around. If you want to, you can spend the night here; we have several guest rooms."

By now, three Rottweilers had done an excellent job of announcing their arrival and it turned out they were more like big babies than dangerous attack dogs...much to the relief of Kim, who wasn't the biggest fan of dogs. The dogs went totally insane when they saw Roger, and Kim thought he would be licked to death by these very exceptional pets. Finally, Roger managed to pry himself away from the dogs long enough to introduce them to the others, "These are my dogs. Their names are Moe, Hairy, and Curly. When I was a kid, my favorite show was The Three Stooges."

As Moose leaned over to scratch Moe's head, he said, "Oh hell, it's STILL my favorite show!!!"

Over the sound of the howling and barking came a very loud voice full of excitement, "OH...MY...GOD!!! ROGER, IT'S YOU!!!"

Down the porch steps ran a trim, attractive lady wearing dark slacks and a white silk blouse. She was in such a hurry, she skipped the bottom step and ran directly into Roger's arms. With tears of joy streaming down her face, she took his face into her hands, then held him tight for as long as she could, then looked back at his face, and finally managed to say, "I had no idea you would be here today. Couldn't you have called? Oh never mind. I'm just so glad to see you!!! Are you OK? Are you hungry? Who are your friends? What kind of car is that?"

"MOM!! MOM!! One question at a time! I'm fine...just fine. I apologize for not calling. I never thought about it when we were close to a pay phone and when I did think to call, we were on the road. To be honest, I didn't know we would be here today, either, but we decided to drive straight through from New Mexico. These are my friends. This is Kim, this is Moose, and this is Robby."

"So nice to meet y'all. I bet you boys haven't had a good meal in a long time. Well, now, y'all come on in, make yourselves at home and I'll get Lula Mae to make us a big supper. In the meantime, you can tell me about your trip in that interesting little car."

Roger took his mother's arm in his as they walked toward the house, up the steps and through the side door leading from the driveway. "Thanks momma, we are quite hungry and truly can't remember when our last decent meal was. As for the trip, we started in San Diego a couple of days ago and made it to here, and that's about all there is to say about it. Nothing happened along the way. We just kept driving day and night until we arrived."

He looked at his buddies for a little support and Robby added, "Yes ma'am, it was a pleasant trip. We had good weather and no problems. By the way, how many horses do y'all have? I was raised in the city and never saw so many horses in one spot in my life." Robby really didn't care one bit how many horses they had. He was not even particularly impressed by horses. As far as he was concerned, they were something you had to feed and then clean up their crap later. He asked about the horses in an effort to change the subject.

In a few moments, the conversation went from the Microbus and the trip experience to horses as she led them all into the mammoth foyer that would rival any old plantation in the South. Robby was thinking how the stairway reminded him of the stairway in the movie, *Gone With the Wind.* He saw that movie in Atlanta when he was twelve, then it came again four years later at sixteen and he always thought it was all make-believe and no one really lived like that, but here they were in Roger's house and it looked even better than the house in the movie.

These thoughts were interrupted by Mrs. Hilton saying, "Y'all are going to spend the night, aren't you? We just wouldn't have it any other way, now. So while supper is being prepared, Roger can show you to your rooms so you can freshen up."

Something told these guys that "freshen up" meant more than wash your hands and check your hair. They were all given their own private room with their own private bath and no one needed to tell them they were in a very elegant and stylish place and it was time to act respectable. Without a word, they showered, washed their hair and put on their freshly cleaned uniforms.

They all looked their best for dinner, although Moose had a

hard time fastening his pants. He blamed the dryer for making his heavy-duty military pants shrink. He was positive it could have never been all that beer and junk food he consumed along this voyage.

Robby, Moose and Kim weren't sure what the next step would be, according to protocol, so they stood in the foyer at the landing in front of the steps, and waited for Roger and his mom to show them what to do next. The two Marines stood as if they were in a dress parade, as did the sailor...motionless, speechless, standing tall. Roger appeared in a white shirt with tan pleated pants and wing-tip shoes. It seemed he had found his closet and everything he had left behind still fit perfectly. Just as Kim was about to say something really stupid about Roger's attire, his mom made her approach to the foyer, wearing a maroon cocktail dress that made her look more like a movie star than a soldier's mother.

Her face lit up once more as she said, "Oh my, don't we look nice! Would one of you gentlemen escort me to dining room?"

Moose, to their surprise, again, stepped forward, and in a clear, baritone voice, said, "Ma'am, it would be my honor."

Mrs. Hilton slid her arm in his, a bit surprised by the size of his biceps, understanding why they called him Moose. As they took their first step, Moose realized he had no idea where the formal dining area was, so he walked toward the aroma, with the notion in his head that Mrs. Hilton will steer him in the right direction if he got too far off course.

The dining area was by no means a disappointment and neither was the food presented on the table. Lula Mae, their cook and all-about-everything with the house, stood in the corner beside the door that entered the kitchen. She was a middle-aged, slightly overweight black lady with a shiny glow of joy in her face as she delighted in witnessing this reunion. She had helped take care of Roger from the day of his birth and loved him as her own. Roger immediately ran to her and bent down to give her a long, loving hug and a peck on the cheek.

"Oh Lula Mae, I so missed your cooking; and look at you... you haven't changed a bit...just the way I saw you the day I left. And just look at this spread you made for us. You are truly a wonder."

"Boy, I need to fatten you up...you be skinny as a tooth pick! I sees they don't feed you right in the Army. You ain't been eatin' right, have you?"

"No ma'am, not since I left this table have I had a meal like this. There is nobody, nowhere quite like you, Lula Mae."

Robby, Kim and Moose just stood there staring at the table: sliced roast beef with gravy, creamy white mashed potatoes, green beans, squash, okra, beets, turnip green and pork chops all lined up in the center of the table like a delicious food parade, with the beef taking the lead and the pork at the end, and all the vegetables in the middle. There were five place settings of the finest china and cutlery, lending an air of importance to this meaningful occasion.

Mrs. Hilton broke the silence with a slight clap of the hand and said, "Well, ya'll find a seat. Let's not just stand here and let the food get cold."

And eat they did...like never before or since did they eat such a feast.

Thankfully, the conversation was held to small talk and polite, casual experiences...nothing about the war, the military, or the trip. After the meal, Lula Mae and her daughter, Hatti Ruth, cleared the table and served homemade peach cobbler and vanilla ice cream.

The group lingered over coffee and conversation for a bit more, and as each of them found it harder not to yawn out loud, Roger thankfully suggested they all retire for the night.

In his room, Robby stripped down to nothing but his underwear and stretched across the bed, took in a deep breath and exhaled a great sigh of relief before suddenly jumping up and heading to his private bathroom to pee, having drank too much coffee with the cobbler. Before returning to bed, he went to the window, opened the curtains, raised the shades and opened the window about two inches. He plopped back on the bed, turned out the lead crystal light on the antique night stand, and looked at the bright stars that shone so brightly in the clear night. He took in a deep breath of the pine-scented fresh air coming through the window. His ears searched for sound, but he heard nothing...absolutely nothing. He fell asleep less than a minute...soundly sleeping on top of the covers.

Chapter 14

· · · · · · · · · · · · · · ·

After breakfast, what?

Robby was awakened by the bright sunlight pouring through the window, making the dust particles that were in the air look like so many UFO ships hovering in outer space. His first conscious thought was the heavenly aroma of coffee brewing and bacon being cooked. He bounded out of bed and prepared to go down for breakfast. It appeared that Kim and Moose shared the same experience since they all converged in the hallway the same time.

The boys were met by Lula Mae at the entrance to the dining room with a bright smile that would brighten anyone's heart and made it impossible not to smile back. With her dark eyes sparkling, she said, "Y'all youngens are just in time for my cat heads. Just seat yoself and they'll be right out."

With a slightly panicked look on his face, Moose says, "It ain't a real cat is it?"

"No, you moron – excuse my language Miss Lula – but a cat head is a large biscuit...big as a cat's head. My mama in Alabama learned from her granny who cooked them up on a wood stove."

"Dat's right, Kim, I know dat's right. The best cat head you ever ate is five minutes away."

As it turned out, the cat head biscuits would have been a meal all to themselves, but that would never do in the South for company. The table was loaded once again, this time with biscuits with red eye gravy, a mound of scrambled eggs, grits, fried potatoes, sliced tomatoes, bacon and sausage, coffee, orange juice, and "if you don't see it, ask for it. If we ain't got it, we'll order it."

Kim, Robby and Moose ate without Roger and Mrs. Hilton, who had already eaten and moved out to the front porch. They were slowly swaying back and forth in large white rocking chairs with coffee in one hand and a cigarette in the other...a kindred spirit, indeed. They sat in companionable silence as they watched the horses play and frolic in the early morning where the temperature was still low enough to see the steam rise from the backs of the beautiful, thoroughbred animals.

They had sat there many times before in days gone by; when he was a little boy playing with his toys on the hardwood floor of the porch, as a teenager they had talked of sadness and heartbreak when he had lost his first girlfriend, and as a young man going off to college only to return in shame and sorrow because he flunked out and knew he would be drafted, the fear of going to war palpable in the air. Throughout the years this old porch had seen more joy and heartache that could even be recalled.

But today, there was no conversation. There was only a mother and her son, rocking in silent tandem, soaking up the moment for all it's worth. The mother had wondered in fear if she would ever see him again alive; often she had dreamed at night about his coming home and sitting with her just one more time, and here he was, by her side once more.

The two looked into the distance as if in a dream until Roger turned to her and said, "Mother, shall we walk together for a while?"

They put out their cigarettes in the astray on the table between them and stood, coffee cups in hand.

They had not even noticed that the three who just finished breakfast had also come out on the porch. Roger took his mother's arm as they stepped down onto the driveway and turned left, heading towards the lake.

After they had gotten a little ways away, Robby pointed in the other direction on the porch to a large wicker table with matching chairs and quietly said, "Kim, go get the map and spread it on the table so we can plot the course to Birmingham."

Kim didn't take long to figure it out; it was a straight shot up I-20 and Robby had become more tolerant of the expressway system. However, Kim did bring up the fact that he didn't want to go through Louisiana because the police had such a bad reputation when it came to their treatment of black men. "Look, man, we ain't goin' through no Louisiana. We're gonna steer off course and go up to Arkansas, then back down to Mississippi and into Alabama. The man is really hard on us and I don't want no trouble. And I don't want ya'll in any trouble because I'm with you."

Robby looked away, eyes half shut, deep in thought. Being raised in Atlanta and having parents that came from the deep South, he was no stranger to the racial problems that still permeated throughout the area, no matter that it was 100 years after the Civil War. His graduating class in high school was the first to integrate in 1966, and he well remembered how bullies would not allow the black students to use the restroom, forcing them to hold their pee all day until they got home. He thought about the black boys he grew up with in the projects of Atlanta, many of whom became his best friends; he remembered back to a few times when black men had saved his life in Nam... specially one time when a black man who was an incredible shot pulled him out of a river. He looked across the vast Hilton property and thought that, no doubt in days gone by, it was worked by slaves. He reached into his pocket, pulled out a bag of Levi Garrett, took a pinch, and allowed it to settle in his mouth, savoring the taste.

"Kim, I can't blame you for being scared, and if you want to spend the extra time and money, you go right ahead. But know this, nobody ever got anywhere knuckling down to the man; and know this too, you have Moose and me by your side and if anybody, I mean anybody, fucks with you, they fuck with all of us and I don't care who they are. It's your call, bro."

"Uh...uh...in that case, let's go straight through then. The fearsome foursome might now be the fearsome threesome, but we're still fearsome!"

"OK then, what's the logistics?"

"We're looking at about 600 miles, which comes out to about 12 hours. That means if we leave in less than an hour, we'll be in Birmingham by 10:00PM...that's 2200 hours, Moose," Kim said with a huge smile, touching the side of his glasses.

Just then, Roger and his mom came up the driveway from their walk around the property. The men went inside to get their gear and say good bye to Lula Mae and Hatti Ruth. They thanked Mrs. Hilton for her hospitality and headed out to the bus. As they loaded their gear, Roger gave them his address and phone number so they could stay in touch and so Moose could send him his money order when he sold the van.

Robby stood in front of Roger, firmly shaking his hand and said, "Well I guess this is so long. Hold it in the road. If you're ever in Atlanta, look me up. I'm in the phone book under the name Robert H. McLeod."

"What's the "H" stand for."

"Homer."

"What? Homer? Well just damn. I was going to name my first son after you...but never mind, now."

Both let out a subdued laugh that displayed more emotion than it did a sense of mirth. Kim and Moose took their turns saying good-bye to Roger, not really sure how to express how they felt about this man and the strong bond that had grown between them, even though they hadn't even known each other that long. But it wasn't necessary to say anything .

Starting down the long driveway that would take them back to the expressway, Kim looked back and saw Hatti Ruth standing there, waving away. He thought this was the first time he hadn't flirted with a young lady. Since meeting Karen, he'd only had eyes for her. Sweet, smart Karen had not been out of his mind from the moment they'd met.

Chapter 15

· · · · · · · · · · · · · · ·

On the Way to Kim's House...

As Kim predicted, they entered the expressway at exactly 10:00AM, and with a little luck and a few good decisions, he would be seeing his family tonight around 10:00PM.

After hours on the road, Moose looked at his Timex watch and noticed it was 5:00PM and said, "Isn't it about happy hour?"

"Well yeah, but you're driving."

"Ah, shit, man, what's one beer?"

"OK, but just one. We don't need any drunk driving tickets to slow us down."

"Hey Kim, gimme a Budweiser, since Robby wants to be a killjoy. OH yeah...the king of beers! Thanks."

As you might expect, Moose had another beer, but promised to stop at two...well maybe three. They entered a town called Hickory, Mississippi. The sign said, "Welcome to Hickory, the small town with the big heart – Population 600."

The town had only one traffic light, which turned red. By the time Moose had pressed his foot on the brake pedal, he came up a little late and found himself at a complete stop under the light instead of in front of it. He muttered under his breath about spilling some beer, put it in reverse and backed up...right into the only police car within 25 miles.

"We're fucked," said Kim with thoughts of long jail time if they find out what was in his duffel bag.

"Everybody just stay cool, maybe it won't be so bad," said Mr. Optimistic, Robby McLeod.

———

Robby had always been in the big city and was surprised to see the officer looked just like all southern sheriffs are portrayed: big belly, sunglasses, hat on with a slight tilt, with a .38 pistol that looked like it hadn't been shot since Pat was a calf and she'd been giving milk for years.

And then it got even better...Moose handed him an expired New Jersey license and a military ID. The sheriff said two words, "follow me."

They parked the Microbus on the street in front of a small building separate from the others on Main Street and found out soon enough that it served as the court room and the jailhouse. With only a "come on" from the sheriff, he marched them into the building, opened the door to the communal cell, and without a word motioned them inside and closed it with a clang.

They all sat on the metal bench that ran the length of the cell and didn't say a word, each deep in thought, hoping for the best and preparing for the worst.

As dark approached, the sheriff came up to the bars and looked at the three road warriors who were now in all kinds of trouble. He looked at Kim, and then at Robby and Moose, then back at Kim and said, "We do things a little different down here, boys. First of all, we don't have no integrated jails. So you come with me, boy. I have a special place for you."

As the key rotated, the lock made a loud thump, and Moose jumped up, yelling in his biggest booming voice, "YOU AIN'T TAKING HIM NO DAMN WHERE. The only way to take him is to kill us both and that AIN'T HAPPENING!!!"

The sheriff paused and they could see him rolling the matter over in his mind. Finally, he spoke in an annoyingly arrogant southern drawl, "That's Ok, boys, I'll deal with ya'll in the morning. I'm also the judge in this town and ya'll can wait all night and wonder what's gonna happen around 10 o'clock when you come before me in court. Since you acted this way, I'm suspending your phone call until 8:00AM. That is, if I get here on time."

The sheriff wandered back out of the room and the three men slumped into their places back on the bench. It was an ok jail as far as jails went, but not a great jail. The smell of urine was so pungent you could almost taste it on your tongue. The floor was sticky from many weeks, if not months, of neglect. There was one set of bunk beds, and in the corner was a commode with no commode seat that had a faucet behind it so you could get a drink of water, but who would want to.

Thinking back to the Hilton ranch they had just left and the jungle he'd "visited" for a while, Robby said, "Holy shit. Viet Nam was better than this."

He sat back, in deep thought, trying to come up with a plan of escape, like he did so many times in the past as a Marine in battle. A few moments later, he sat up straight, raised his arms heavenward, and calmly said, "I have a plan. I'm gonna use that business card I got from Senator Ronald B. Richland when I saved his nephew's life and we'll see if he really meant what he said about helping out. It's our only hope as I see it. Anyway, we all get a phone call. Each of you be thinking of who you're gonna call. By the way, there are only two beds, and you two can have them. I'll sit on the floor and sleep as I can...don't sleep much anyway, especially tonight."

8:00AM came and went...no sheriff. Then he appeared at 8:47, bringing a tray of white bread with peanut butter that had been applied in a most half assed fashion; and to top off the meal, he served grape drink in tin cups. "Here's your breakfast... eat, and then I'll let you out one at a time for your phone call."

Robby arranged it so he was the last one to use the phone, knowing most government workers don't start until 9:00 and he wasn't taking any chances with not being able to connect.

"Well, did you talk to Senator Richland?" asked Kim nervously.

"No. But I talked to his secretary who said she would give

him the message as soon as he arrived."

"Oh great! Oh fuckin swell! Our future lies in the hands of a white man, a government worker, who has never met us. We are in such deep shit, we'll never get out. It would've been better to been shot in Tijuana," moaned Kim, who was beginning to panic, pacing back and forth in the cell.

"Stay cool, sailor boy. I seen Robby pull off more than one miracle. I'm thinking he's good for another miracle or two. I'm sorry, you guys. It was my drinking that started all this shit. If I had been sober, we'd never been put in this shit hole. If we get outta this, I will NEVER drink and drive again." said Moose, quite sober now. Kim and Robby nodded, not sure if his repentance was sincere, or regret because he was caught.

Robby cleared his throat, "Well, that is cool that you learned a lesson from this, but it will not help the situation now. As I see it, our only salvation lies with a man in Washington we have never met."

10:00AM came and went. At 10:30 there was still no word, no sheriff, no day in court.

At 10:47, the sheriff unlocked the door, and Robby noticed an unusual expression on his face. It was a look of agitation, tinged with anger that he was trying his mightiest to control.

The sheriff cleared his throat and said, "I just got off the phone with THE Senator Ronald B. Richland, the last real Democrat in the South. You boys are free to go. Why he wants anything to do with you boys, I'll never know. But thanks to him, you can leave. He told me that ya'll are some kinda war heroes and could use a break. You boys are behaving more like a bunch of damn hippies than soldiers, but I gave the senator my word to cut you loose. Sooo....Git!!!

"Thank you sir, we promise to go straight and not get in any more trouble," said Robert McLeod, who was trembling at the knees.

In total disbelief they all walked to the van that was still parked at the curb from the night before.

Robby walked to the driver's side, and as he opened the door, he looked in the back and saw that everything was just how they left it: the empty beer cans, crushed cigarettes, even the duffle bag was right where they left it.

Before he entered the Microbus on the driver's side, he stopped and turned around because he felt the presence of someone behind him...you guessed it...the sheriff.

The sheriff looked at Robby with a gentler though still stern look and said, "I was a Marine once. I was all over a bunch of islands in the Central Pacific...wound up on Tarawa...November of '43...saw 3,000 of our boys die to secure that god-forsaken place. I understand what ya'll have been through, but it don't give no cause to break the law."

"Yes sir!"

Robby turned and slid into the driver's seat and Sheriff Blankenship closed the door, took off his mirrored sunglasses, and looked through the window directly into Robby's eyes, and said, "This never happened. We never met. I don't know any of you. But don't ever come through this town again and do anything illegal."

"Yes sir." They all said in one accord. Then one last time, as they drove off still in disbelief, Robby made his request, "Hey Kim, plot our course and give me an ETA."

Chapter 16

. . . .

Homecoming for Kim

Kim consulted his map and reported back, "We take two lefts and go East on I-20. I'm thinking our ETA to be around 6:00PM tonight. Before we get on the expressway, let's stop at a pay phone so I can call my mama and tell her we're on our way."

"Sure man, no problem. Let's just get out of this town first... don't want no part of Hickory, Mississippi, you know?" Robby said, still reeling from the whole experience.

"Oh hell. I don't want no part of Mississippi; we can wait till we get to the Alabama line. If I get locked up again, at least it will be in my home state."

As always, Kim was right on target. They rolled into Birmingham at 5:42PM. Moose awakened from a nap, and said, "This reminds me a lot of Pittsburgh with so many steel mills going on."

The air was dirty and thick with soot from the coal-burning furnaces in the mills. To make matters worse, all you could get on the radio was country music and country music annoyed Robby, since he was raised on rock-n-roll. "Their singing sounds like a dying calf in a hail storm." he would say. The only thing Robby liked about it was that it was a big city in the South, and that made him feel more at home. And besides, he was now less than three hours from home.

Kim started giving him directives on how to get to his house, taking them off the expressway at an exit near one of the old mills. Two rights and a left and they were on Kim's street. After passing the mill, Robby couldn't help but notice the condition of the street and how the houses had deteriorated considerably. The streets turned into a tar and gravel mix, causing the tires to make a loud noise. They were being jarred and bounced around in the van from all the potholes, many of them full of water. The houses didn't fare much better...rows of shanty houses that were in need of paint, and in some cases, could use a window pane or two. The mill-village houses reminded Robby of shoe boxes all in a row that were narrow and long with the door at the far right or far left of the house. He couldn't help but think it was such a contrast from Roger's house.

When they turned onto Kim's street, they were met with a big surprise. The entire street was lined with people clapping, waving handkerchiefs back and forth, holding homemade signs that read "Welcome Home Kim." House number 502 was his and they pulled up to a driveway full of cars and a yard full of partying well-wishers. Someone had a bar-b-que grill going that looked like a 55 gallon drum in a previous life. Scattered throughout the yard were coolers full of beer. And there she was...Kim's mama, wearing her best Sunday dress with a flower in her hair that a neighbor had picked for her.

Kim introduced his mama to Robby and Moose and gave her the white goat skin rug and Aztec blanket he had bought for her in Tijuana. Within the hour they'd made the rounds until everyone on the block had met Kim's traveling companions, and finally, thankfully, they were eating real Southern pork bar-b-que with baked beans and coleslaw, and plenty of beer.

Above all the party noise and loud thumping music, Kim said, "Hey guys, how about you stay and party with us? This will go on all night."

Robby thought really hard about this, torn in both directions, and finally said, "You know Kim, I'm partied out for a while. I'm three hours from home and I'd really like to just to keep chipping away at it until I get home myself tonight. But I know where you live now and we'll get together soon. Give me your mailing address."

Robby and Kim shook hands one more time and then Moose extended his hand and said, "I would be proud to share the battlefield with you, sir," and then reached out to give him a one-armed hug that took Kim right off his feet.

One more round of good byes and one more pork sandwich to go and they headed toward the van. As he touched the door handle, Robby looked back to see Kim and his mom sitting on the dilapidated porch in ladder back chairs that had turned grey with age. They just kept grinning at each other as they sipped on a can of beer and smoked Kool cigarettes.

He thought back to the other day when he'd observed a son and his mom sitting on a porch in the lap of luxury. He thought how the bond between a mother and her son knew no boundaries. It was not hampered by too much money, or by too little. It endured all things, hoped all things, and healed all things. Kim was just as rich as Roger...he just doesn't have a mom with lots of money.

Chapter 17

. . . .

Back in Atlanta, the final parting

Robby knew it was around 9:00PM when they left Birmingham, which would make it around midnight when they arrived in Atlanta. Well, the clock would actually read 1:00AM, because he would be entering a new time zone when he crossed the Georgia line. Keeping up with all these time zones would soon be a thing of the past because he had no intention of traveling or leaving his hometown again.

As they headed eastbound on I-20 once more, Robby turned on the radio and put the station on WSB, 750-AM. For two reasons he did this; first of all, this station was very strong and you could barely get it on the outskirts of Birmingham, and the closer you came to Atlanta, the stronger and clearer the signal. So he made a game out of it, using the AM station the same way one would use a homing device. The second reason he had the radio on AM-750 was because that was all he had. The Blaupunkt was an AM radio, only. FM radios were barely heard of.

Robby was quite familiar with this stretch of highway, having once had a girlfriend in Birmingham and he had spent many a weekend traveling this very same road. He kept the gas pedal to the floor board, making that old bus do whatever it would do...70 downhill...50 uphill.

As he drove near the Six Flags amusement park, they crested a very steep hill that overlooked downtown. Robby reached over and shook Moose's arm, "Hey Moose, wake up. This is my favorite view of Atlanta!"

From atop the hill, the entire skyline of the city sparkled against the backdrop of a dark sky. "Look man, you can see the capitol, the Equitable building and over to the left is Buckhead. That's where I'm gonna live someday...in Buckhead. That part of the city never sleeps and is full of fun all the time...kinda like Tijuana ...but safer."

"That's cool, little bro. How far to your place, and did you call anyone to tell 'em you're on your way home?"

"Not really. I called my cousin and told him the date of my discharge, but didn't tell him my exact time of arrival. I did tell him to have my house ready. He's been looking after it in my absence, so when we get there, we should have at least water and electricity going...maybe even the heat. We should be there within the hour."

"What??? You own a house? You never told me that."

"Well, you never asked. It's just a small two bedroom house with one bathroom and a floor furnace in the hallway. They built thousands of them around here after World War II. I bought it about a year after I got out of high school, while still in college. I got it at a good price and I'm holding on to it. I'm sure it'll be worth some money someday since it is in this nice area called Grant Park. It cost $8,500.00. It ain't much, but it's all mine. If my cousin came through and all the utilities are turned on, we can spend the night there."

"Oh hell, we can spend the night there even if it has no power. Christ knows we've slept in worse places....ha ha ha."

They took the exit near the State Capitol building and drove three miles east on Memorial Drive, made a few right turns, and...home at last. As he pulled into the single lane driveway barely big enough for one car, Robby felt as though it had been a lifetime since he had seen this place, and right now, it looked pretty good. By most standards it was a humble home on a small city lot that happened to be on a dead end street. The good news was it was a dead end street. The bad news, it was on a dead end street, and they were forever getting traffic from lost people who used his driveway for a turnaround. But none of that mattered now. He was finally home and glad to be there.

When Robby arrived home, there was no mother or father to greet him, no parade, no large group of friends...not even a dog or a cat. It was just him and the house...nothing else. Moose asked him why didn't anyone meet him and he just said that he had no one. He lost his parents when he was eight, was raised by his grandfather who had died a month before he'd enlisted in the USMC, and most of his friends had either moved on or were killed in Nam.

"So is that why you volunteered for so many crazy missions? Because you had nobody to come home to?"

"Uumm...never even thought about it," said Robby, a bit surprised that Moose was so intuitive.

He unlocked the door, and reached for the porch light switch...we got power. Yay!!! The porch light, although not extremely bright, lit up the entire front yard, putting a hazy glow on a 1957 Volkswagen Bug sitting in the side yard.

"That's my old car. It's the one I used when I went to school and lived in Buford. I just couldn't bring myself to sell it when I went in the service. It's a good car, never had a minute's trouble. Tomorrow, I'll see if I can get it running. It hasn't been cranked since I left and I hate that because the worst thing you can do to a VW is not run it."

Moose nodded and said, "Well, the Nazi Bastard has sure been run...we run the shit out of it, and it still has to go to Jersey."

"Yeah, it has been run a-plenty, but there are still plenty of miles left in it. It'll get you home with no trouble."

Robby went through the house and turned on the rest of the lights. Everything was just the way he left it. There was even a dish cloth draped across the kitchen sink.

The house had the smell of a slightly mildewed old dog because it had been closed up for a while, except when his cousin came by to check mail and look around, and occasionally slept there when his wife went beyond her normal bitch mode into ultra-bitch mode, making coexistence impossible. He opened all the windows making the house fresh and cool, but still a little musty smelling.

"Shit. All the sheets and the mattresses smell old and musty. I'll need to get started on some big time cleaning in the morning. This stuff is so smelly, I think I'll just sleep on the floor tonight in my sleeping bag...tomorrow is another day, you know?"

"Yeah. Like I said, we've slept in worse places."

Moose and Robby sat at the yellow Formica top table in the kitchen and drank the rest of the beer and tequila that was in the van, along with sandwiches and coleslaw that had been sent along with them from Birmingham. They talked about all the times they had until the drinks were gone and the conversation expired. This would be the last time in their life they would fall asleep in a sleeping bag because they had nowhere else to sleep.

The distant sound of a train woke Robby up and he immediately knew he was home...never thought he would've missed that damn train and its noise. To his surprise, Moose was already up and was outside, putting his gear in the Microbus, getting ready to leave.

"Hey, man. Not even a good bye kiss?"

"I was just getting everything ready to go while you were still stacking Z's."

Robby grinned and nodded at Moose and gave the bus a walk-around, checking the tires, the oil level, and making sure all the lights were working. He reached in his pocket and said to Moose, "Here are all our addresses, so when you sell the van, you can send us money orders. All the paperwork is in the glove compartment. The extra key is in the ash tray. Kim left the maps for you, and you can keep all those 8-track tapes, all except for the Steppenwolf and Chuck Berry. The guys wanted you to have all the other supplies left in the van, the rope, tents, cooler, compass, maps, magazines, sleeping bags and all the spilled beer, dirt grime, and dirty socks...all yours."

Robby tried to think of something to say to a man who had saved his life numerous times, a man who would give you his last dollar if you needed it, to a man who had the biggest heart, the bravest spirit, and the meanest punch of any man on the planet. What do you say to a man when you have laughed together, cried together, told each other lies, and had each other's backs? What do you say when this may be the last time you'll ever see him? Robby swallowed, looked deep in the eyes of Moose Forrester and said, "We really kicked some ass didn't we, sir?"

"Oh hell yeah, little bro. It was a good thing about what happened in Dong Ha, after all. Had you not been there to save that Lieutenant's ass, we would still be in jail in Mississippi. You saved everybody's ass that day!"

"I guess...I guess so. Well, so long and call me if you need me. Semper fi."

"Semper fi."

Robby watched the Microbus crank one last time. The engine turned over three times, a puff of smoke and then began running as good as ever. He watched Moose leave the driveway and head back to Memorial Drive. He waited to see if he would miss third gear... like he had done a few times before.

* * *

"And that's Robby's Volkswagen story-just the way he told it to me not long ago while we was sittin and drinkin coffee in my new house. But, I'm here to tell you, that ain't even half the story. This story I just told you ended in the spring of 1969. Robby has another Volkswagen story that started up all a new 44 years later, when he turned 65. Yes sir. That's right; a whole new story with a whole nother Volkswagen began in the spring of 2013."

~ Jimmy Johnson

Chapter 18

· · · · · · · · · · · · · ·

Springtime, 2013...Forty Four Years Later

As he awoke, he looked at the alarm clock beside the bed and thought to himself, "Why am I looking at the damn clock? I've been retired for six years now and I still get up at 5:30 every day. What difference does it make what time it is, and why can't I sleep any later than 5:30?"

Perhaps it's routine, maybe habit; perhaps all the years spent getting up early to get to the jobsite and help the kids get up and off to school. Oh hell, it could be just another sign of getting older...maybe all of the above. But every morning, Robby McLeod woke up at the same time and had the same routine for as long as he could remember... same routine, different setting.

A few years ago, when the economy was on a down swing and real estate was cheap, he bought a high-rise condo complex in Buckhead, North Atlanta and renovated the entire top floor for his personal use. One half of the top floor was remodeled and converted to his living quarters and the other half as a studio reserved for his passion, the practice of tai chi. The studio was 4,000 square feet of hardwood floor with mirrors on three walls so he could always see what was going on with his students. The other wall was solid glass from floor to ceiling and through it you could see the sun set over downtown. The room had the appearance of both comfort and class. In days gone by, Robby was accustomed to neither, but times have changed. He used this beautiful room three days a week for teaching this ancient art to the elite in this very fashionable part of town. He also had a full sized gym, which he seldom used.

Every morning was the same: as soon as he got up, he shaved, brushed his hair and looked in the mirror. Robby noticed that his silver hair fell half way down his back between his shoulder blades. Hummm...the last real hair cut was in 1969, as a Marine. Since his sister, Patti Ann, showed him how to braid his hair, it's remained that way for over 25 years. As he braided his hair, he thought of when it was reddish brown, then dark brown, and how now it's silver with some reddish blonde streaks.

Today, the weather was cool and dry so he headed up to the roof for his workout. He grabbed the handrail and taking two stairs at a time, climbed the narrow, steep set of metal steps and opened the heavy steel door at the top of the stairway, plunging onto the roof into a pre-dawn sky lit by stars and complemented by a full moon. It was early April, and the cool crisp morning air brushed against his face. It was much better than any drug designed to wake you up and get you going. Just breathing in the air this time of year was enough to give you energy for the rest of the day. As Robby stepped out onto the roof, he breathed in deeply, detecting the different aromas that accompany the city of his birth, the scent of flowers and pine trees mingled with bacon cooking in the diner on the ground floor of his condo as well as the ever-present hint of diesel exhaust coming from the MARTA buses. He thought back to his childhood, when he walked these same streets, and noted that the smells are the same as they always were...enough reminiscing, time to get to the workout.

Robby spent the first half hour stretching and practicing the postures of qigong, an exercise and healing technique developed in China more than 4000 years ago. Standing in the opening tai chi posture, he imagined himself as an ancient Chinese soldier going into battle, and when he got the full picture in his mind he began the 108 moves. It seems an impossible and beautiful dance to someone unfamiliar with the complicated and long, drawn out sequence of memorized moves, but to him, it's the only time he felt at home and at peace with himself.

By the time he'd finished, the sun had risen over Buckhead and the city beneath him had come alive. The sweet smell of bacon and flowers was replaced by the acrid smell of exhaust fumes as rush hour began and the streets ran amok with public transportation and commuters trying to get to work. Calm silence had made way for honking horns and the sounds of people hurrying to work in the high rise offices that tower over the city.

One more ritual that he did daily: he went to the edge of the roof and leaned over the safety wall to look at Peachtree Street. Today, he noticed the Dogwood trees that had just begun to blossom. Atlanta may be the Deep South, but there are definite seasons. In this "City of Trees," spring brings the blooms of the Redbuds and Dogwoods and summer brings a green canopy that half covers the city. Autumn swoops in with the vivid yellows, oranges and reds of turning leaves, while winter trees lend a stark and lonely vision to the landscape saved only by the array of brilliant lights in the form of Christmas decorations and the seldom-seen dusting of snow. It doesn't matter the season, there are always interesting things going on down on Peachtree Street – parades, pretty women in short skirts in the summer, dog walkers, the occasional panhandler, and even a famous 10K run... always something. Every day he ends this ritual by looking heavenward, then at the tree tops, then at the street....one last deep breath and ready for the day.

Today was a special day for Robby. He'd been looking for a Volkswagen van, a 1962 Microbus, and he found one for sale that was advertised as being totally restored about 80 miles north of Atlanta. He had looked at several in the past, but was never impressed enough to buy one. He wasn't going to give up until he found the right Microbus. To many men that came of age in the 50s and 60s, seeing a '57 Chevy or a '66 Mustang brought back a thousand memories, and it was something like that, but much more.

He had been back inside just a few minutes when there was a tap on the door. "Oh shit!" he said aloud, then thought to himself "That must be Deri. I asked her to meet me at 7:00 and I've lost all track of time." His heart beat a little faster at the prospect of seeing her, and the idea that they'd be spending most of the day together was just about the best thing that could happen. Since his wife died a few years ago, Deri is the only woman that excites him and makes him laugh.

They had been just friends for over 25 years although there had always been a very strong attraction between them. They often had lunch, had done quite a bit of business together and had even counseled each other about various aspects of their lives in the time they'd known each other. But, Robby was happily married for 22 of those years and after the grieving for his wife had lessened, Deri was in an exclusive relationship and so it went, until about 2 months ago. They still hadn't pursued a more intimate relationship even though they had both thought about it quite a bit lately. But, what if it changed the great relationship they had now? Rob and Deri had this very conversation, to which Robby said, "Let's just go with the flow and see what happens."

Her full name was Deri Thomas. "It's like Sherry, with a D," she'd been heard to say with a wink and a smile. After retiring from real estate at 50, she had opened a chain of yoga and Pilates studios throughout the city. Her passion was staying fit and spreading the word about her exercise programs. That was one of the common denominators between Robby and her... the desire to stay fit. They both enjoyed running the Silver Comet Trail or hiking along many of the nature trails that you could find within a half-hour drive. They'd always been competitive in a fun and friendly way, neither of them taking their sometimes silly antics too seriously.

He did a quick step to the door, pulling it open. "It's 6:59. You had a minute to spare. By the way, how do you look so freaking good this early in the morning?" said Robby while trying to control his excitement. She entertained him with her best model pose, wrinkled up her cute little nose and said, "You'd look this good, too, if you'd spent the ridiculous amount of money at the hair salon yesterday like I did!"

For a brief moment Robby just stood there looking like an eighth-grader the first time he saw a nude photograph. She was not a young woman, but she was very attractive and in Robby's eyes, no one was better looking than Deri. Standing in the doorway, the morning sun from the window shined directly on her, making the hallway look so very dark in comparison. The lights that were supposed to illuminate the area were just not adequate. She lit up the hallway the same way she lit up a room. She literally took his breath away.

He looked at her from head to toe. Her hair was blonde with very light reddish lowlights, recently trimmed in a way that emphasized the shape of her thin face with slightly high cheek bones. Her dark blue eyes seemed to sparkle and dance. She was wearing a pink cashmere sweater that tied in the front about waist height, and underneath, a light violet silk tank top. His eyes fell upon her firm breasts and he couldn't help but notice that her nipples were still erect from the chilly spring morning.

So as not to appear staring, he said, "Nice looking tops. They, uh, go great with those black pants."

"Why thank you, kind sir," she replied as she walked through the door. "It's too cool for a light top but not cold enough for a sweater. By noon, it'll be time to shed some clothing."

"Hummmm...can't wait till noon," Robby thought to himself.

"I see your toenails match your sweater...that must be why you wore those open toed high heels, not so that you'd be taller than me," he teased her.

With raised eyebrows, she immediately retorted, "Well, they aren't THAT high, and besides, I AM taller than you."

Quickly, Robby snaps back, "I know, I know, you're 5'9" and I'm just a short fool. The thing is, when we go out on the town and you're wearing your three inch heels, you top out at six feet, and I look like your little boy in the seventh grade."

"Oh, you're silly." Deri leaned against the wall, winked at him and said, "So, handsome, you think you found the right party wagon?"

Chapter 19

· · · · · · · · · · · · · · ·

On the Highway...Singing and Talking

"Let me change, and we'll be on our way in 15 minutes. Thank you for going with me. If I buy the VW bus, I'll need you to drive my BMW back home. If I don't buy it, there's plenty to do in Buford. There are some shopping malls close by that I think you might like."

"I really don't mind driving your new 640i and I'm quite certain it'll be a better ride than that old bus you've been wanting forever. I'll make some tea while you dress; and please, don't wear that damn Hawaiian shirt." She gave him a smile, and in her sweetest voice said, "And, please try to look more like Kevin Costner than the Skipper on Gilligan's Island."

As Deri made tea, her mind turned to the relationship between her and Robby. They shared the same work ethic, they both stayed physically fit, and shared a sensibility and sense of humor that got them through tough times. Beyond that, they appeared to be total opposites: she always dressed in the highest of fashion while Robby was blue jeans and t-shirts. She was cutting edge and kept up with all the new technical advances and was the first to buy the next generation device. Robby was still wondering why they discontinued 8-track tapes and Deri was barely able to talk him into buying a flip phone with a camera. She could be extravagant and loved to spend her money on high quality merchandise, while Robby made the most out of every dollar and ate at the Quick Fill service station. Deri was professional, gracious, tactful, and diplomatic; Robby would tell you to go fuck yourself if you annoyed him too much.

While Robby was changing, Deri found her way outside on the balcony. Standing there, sipping hot tea with a cinnamon stick, she looked down at Peachtree Street, watching a runner jogging down the sidewalk dodging the commuters. She looked north and south, and then east where the rising sun was reflecting a multicolor sunrise onto the mirrored glass of a high rise hotel. She thought for a moment about the first time she and Robby met and how far the both of them have come since then. As she sat down, she heard the sliding glass door and Robby appeared wearing khaki pants with Dockers shoes and a light blue shirt with button down collar and the sleeves rolled up one fourth of the way.

"Oh my, don't you look dapper!" Robby nodded as if to acknowledge her compliment and with a slight grin, said, "Well, I should. You bought me everything I have on. Anyway, it's 7:20. We need to haul ass. I promised Mr. Holcomb we'd be there by 9:00 to look at the Microbus."

Deri knew when he said it's time to go, he means it is time to go right now so she placed her cup down on the glass top bistro table and walked out with Robby.

They walked down the hallway toward the elevator, their shoulders so close that they were almost touching. They bumped into each other accidently, start to grin at the same time and the race is on to the elevator. Deri's long strides got her there first, and he could have caught up but he really wanted to watch the sway of her hips as she got just in front of him. He didn't mind "losing" to Deri.

Standing at the elevator, they looked at one another in silence. Just as Robby was about to speak, he heard a ding, the door opened and another ding. With his left hand, he gently guided her into the elevator. As he touched her, he thought her to be the epitome of hard and soft. Because she was athletic, the muscles in her back were hard and lean, and yet, her skin was soft and smooth. Robby looked at her, and didn't think about the fact she was up at 5:00 this morning to do her nails and hair. Nor did he think of how she went carefully through her closet to get the right outfit that would please him the most...something sensuous but not too revealing, something sexy but professional. He didn't think that her trip to the salon had anything to do with the trip to Buford. All he could think about was how beautiful she was.

As the elevator started to descend, Robby thought about what it would be like to place a warm, moist kiss on Deri's lips...a long, slow kiss. She was saying something to him but he couldn't hear the words...his eyes are taking her all in and he was fantasizing about his lips tracing that graceful neck to her shoulder and down further to...all of this paradise was abruptly interrupted by the ding of the elevator, the door opening just a little too soon.

They resumed their race across the parking deck, with one trying to walk faster than the other, heads straight, arms pumping, grinning like a pair of kids. As they approached the car, Deri slowed down to give Robby a chance to catch up and open the door for her. He'd always opened the door for her, for as long as she'd known him. As she slid in, she casually looked around at his new BMW 640i...it was not nice to gawk.

"Nice car, I love the triple black."

"I like it so far. It gets better gas mileage than some of the others."

"That is so you, Robby. You buy an $80,000 luxury car and you're concerned about the gas mileage."

"UH...it's not what you earn; it's what you save that matters. Anyway, I really thank you for being willing to go with me and drive the BMW back."

"No problem. I'm sure I'll enjoy driving the 640i back home more than you will that old VW. And besides, there's nothing like the smell of a new car with fresh, new leather."

Robby thought of a line in the movie *Christine*, but decided not to say it, because it would not be a very nice thing to say to a lady. Instead, he said, "Next stop is Buford, Georgia. Buckle up, boys and girls and enjoy the ride."

He had not driven thirty feet before he became annoyed. "WELL JUST DAMN! I can't believe there are already seven cars at the security gate trying to get out. OH COME ON PEOPLE. It's 7:30 on a Saturday morning. Doesn't anyone stay at home and watch Bugs Bunny anymore?"

"Be patient, Rob. It's springtime on a Saturday in Atlanta; everybody will be out today. And besides, these people you are fussing at are PAYING you to be in this parking deck."

"Yeah, you're right. Thanks for reeling me in. I guess it would look kinda bad if I cussed out the people who are giving me money to be here. Oh lookie lookie, I see Peachtree Street."

They turned right, drove two blocks, turned again, and were on I-85 headed north to Buford.

"How 'bout some traveling music to soothe our souls?" Robby said as he got out a Steppenwolf CD and put it in the sound system, cranking up the volume. He thought the first song was perfect for the ride because it's about getting out on the highway. Deri was thinking of the MP3 player in her purse that contained a thousand songs, but said nothing about higher technology.

They both started singing to the song as loud as they could. Robby knew the song because it was popular when he was 21 and just out of Viet Nam. Deri was about 16 when the song came out and "born to be wild" seemed like just the anthem for coming of age.

After the sing-a-long, Deri started thinking back about the tea she left on the balcony and that she should have washed the cup or at least put it in the kitchen, and then her thoughts returned to the balcony. Actually, Robby had three balconies. When he bought the high rise, he removed all the interior walls of the three condos on the top floor that faced the east side. The master bedroom had its own balcony, as well as a Jacuzzi, with a shower large enough for two with a molded built in seat, two separate rooms with large oval commodes and a urinal that's hung on the wall. "Yes, a urinal," he'd say. "This is the bat cave, thank you very much, not *Better Homes and Gardens*."

The other balcony was connected to the great room. That one room was once an entire condo. Now it was one room with a large screen on the wall, a card table for eight, sparsely placed furniture, and an old recliner that he sleeps in more than the bed. When Robby was a child, he lived in the projects downtown, or in a mobile home, and was always cramped for space. He fixed that.

The third balcony complemented the kitchen/dining area. The kitchen was surprisingly small, but very efficient. He had installed a breakfast nook and a large wet bar that surrounded the kitchen and would rival any bar in any restaurant in Buckhead. This was where friends and family gathered to talk and laugh and seldom go anywhere else in the condo. When you left the bar, you walked through a saloon door that took you to a dining room with a custom table that seated twelve. It was in this kitchen where Deri made the tea and it was this balcony where she had stood and pondered.

Deri turned down the volume and asked, "Robby, do you remember when we first met?"

"Oh yeah, it was January 10th, 1974. You were a receptionist at a real estate office and I came by once a month to wash the windows. You approved my invoices. I was twenty-six, you were twenty-one."

"How do you remember these things?"

"I remember everything we ever did, everything we ever said; that's just the way it is."

"Back then, did you want me? You know, a woman can tell if a man really wants her, so don't lie to me. Did you want to have sex with me when we first met?"

Robby glanced over at her, "Well, who wouldn't? I never made any advances because I was married and had a family, and I'm not into sport fucking. I've always believed sex is an expression of love between two people, and not just some itch that needs to be scratched."

"All you would have to have done was ask. When we first met, you were so good looking and built like a Roman god. The first thing I noticed about you were your hands and slender fingers, and I fantasized about having those hands on me. I really wanted you back then."

"Great! So you wait thirty-nine years until I'm too goddamn old to do anything, while we're driving 90 miles an hour to tell me this! Deri, your timing is incredible."

"Oh stop. You are not too old. I know these things. You're in better shape than most men who are thirty years younger. And I think you're still sexy, just in a different way."

"Yeah, like in a grandpa McCoy kinda way."

"Now, I'm being serious. When I was on your balcony this morning, I was thinking about when we first met and how much has changed since then. You've gone from a karate instructor who was washing windows to make ends meet and I've gone from a receptionist who was raised on a farm in Texas to what we are today. I just wonder where did the time go? Where DOES the time go? I'm concerned about how fast the time goes by, and...uh..I just....uh...I just...Well, I just would like for us to spend more time with each other before another twenty-five years fly by. Maybe we could arrange a day trip every week or two or something."

"Well just put me in a dress and call me Nancy. I've been thinking the same thing! Time has flown by because we've stayed so busy building our own little empires. I mean...like...shit... most people my age are sitting in a retirement community clubhouse, with a bunch of fat women watching Oprah and I Love Lucy reruns, and their biggest accomplishment all day is that they didn't pee in their pants. Most friends my age are either dead or too sick from a major disease to do anything or go anywhere. And look at us! We're the picture of health. There's nothing physically or medically wrong with either of us. And what do we do? We work our asses off. We stay so busy, we're lucky to see each other for two hours in a month. We have to check our calendar and mark it six weeks ahead just to do lunch. I want to grab this time while there's time left and spend it with you."

For a brief second, Robby took his eyes off the road, looked directly into her eyes." One more thing, since my wife died and my kids are grown and gone, the only time I am totally happy and feel young again is when I'm with you."

"Oh Robby, that's bullshit."

"No," he smiled at her, "Bullshit is missing your exit because of being in deep conversation. We need to turn around and get on I-985."

"Once we get to Buford and you buy that Volkswagen, we can meet tonight and talk more about all this."

"That's fine. But, I'm not going to buy it; I'm just looking at it."

"That's bullshit, too."

Chapter 20

. . . .

Nothing Really Changes

The closer they got to Buford, the quieter Robby became. He wasn't the same laughing and joking around person that he was on the highway.

"Are you getting a little apprehensive about seeing the VW?" asked Deri.

"Yes, but mainly I've been thinking about all those memories I have connected with a '62 bus. We're almost there. We go to Main Street, cross the tracks, turn left on Mill Street, go by the cemetery then to Buford Dam Road. Lake Lanier Heights is off Buford Dam Road and his house is the first one past the county line."

"Oh my. Did you use your GPS for those directions?"

"Hell no! One of those things will take you eight different ways to Sunday and get you all turned around. Do you know what GPS stands for? It doesn't stand for Global Positioning System. It means Goddamn Piece of Shit. I called Mr. Holcomb and he gave me directions which I wrote on a paper plate. Anyway, I used to live in Buford and I know right where it is. When I left home at 18, I didn't believe in renting, so I bought a small mobile home. Back then we called them house trailers. The closest place to Atlanta that allowed house trailers was Buford. So I moved here and went to school in Atlanta. That became a bit inconvenient, so the following year I sold the trailer and bought a little house downtown. That was almost 50 years ago and it seems like just a very few years have gone by...maybe five or six. What causes that? Old age, maybe?"

As they drove by the historic cemetery on Mill Street, Robby slowed down and said, "The old cemetery hasn't changed a bit. It's good to know some things are still the same. You see those little pink flowers that are blooming around the perimeter of the grave yard? They were there in the same place in 1967. They always bloom the last week in March."

"I know...Thrift...the flowers are called Thrift."

Robby turned to her and grinned. "Oh hell, I bet that is one hard word for you to say. How long did you have to practice?"

"Look here, Mr. McLeod, I grew up just as poor as you. We wore Goodwill dresses and shoes from Shoetown. And just so you will know....oh look, there's the street sign that says Lake Lanier Heights Road. I thought it would be bigger."

Robby drove past the driveway before he saw the county line sign. He backed up and looked down the driveway. The property was steep mountain terrain that plummeted straight into Lake Lanier at the bottom. The 250 foot long driveway was narrow and went straight down to the house, and looked more like a pathway that could have used a load of gravel, or two, or three. Currently, the driveway had a few potholes and some mud from all the April showers. There was no garage or carport. The gravel driveway stopped at the side of the house. The house looked as though someone burrowed a hole in the side of the mountain and placed a house there. Whoever built it was smart because they built the house on two levels which created less digging and a more stable house.

The house had seen better days. It was wood frame with clapboard siding that needed paint ten years ago. The roof had been patched so many times it looked like a quilt of many colors. To the left of the house, his eyes fell on what he thought to be the van. It was a vehicle all wrapped up in a brown tarp like you buy at the hardware store. All he could see was the front bumper exposed and it looked to be in good shape. Robby decided to back down the treacherous driveway. He was thinking if Deri drove it home, it would be much easier for her to pull out of this narrow, slippery passageway in drive, rather than reverse.

Robby practically ran around the car to open the door for her. As he opened the door, he looked at his watch. It was 9:01. He heard a dog barking in a shrill, little voice. He looked like so many breeds of dog, you wouldn't know what to call him.... a real Heinz 57 variety. A man with a shaved head and a white mustache came out the door and down the steps.

"Hey. I'm Dan Holcomb. You must be here about the Microbus."

"Yes sir. My name is Robert McLeod; this is my friend, Deri Thomas."

Mr. Holcomb first shook hands with Robby, then took a long look from head to toe at Deri, and very gently clasped her hand. As he let go he turned his head toward the VW and said, "This here bus reminds me of my dad's he bought new in 1962 because it had the 40 horsepower engine. I was fourteen then. We took it on a trip across the Rockies and my dad raced a '59 bus up a steep grade. He was going 15 miles per hour and the '59 was going 12. He was so excited about beating that 36 horse bus. I was so embarrassed, I hid under the seat. To get that excited about four horsepower...it just ain't right. We went hunting and fishing in it and I took my first girlfriend to the movies in it."

"No kiddin'," Robby smiled and shook his head.

"Yep, everybody raised in the '60s has a Volkswagen story."

"Yes sir. I have my own Volkswagen story...one you wouldn't believe. By the way, is that it under the tarp?"

"Yeah it is, let's have a look at it."

He had taken a nylon cord and looped one end to the grommets in the tarp and the other end he tied to rocks on the ground. He had also taken the cord and wrapped it around and around the bus and tarp, making it look like a large man-made cocoon. He picked up a rock and started to untie the cord but the knot was too tight. Robby figured that he was untying the cord instead of cutting it so he could save it. Robby waited a minute, thought "Oh hell" and said, "Mr. Holcomb, let me just cut this off and if I don't buy the bus, I'll buy you a whole case of this jet string."

Robby took out his Explorer pocket knife and pressed between the rock and the cord and the tip of the knife broke off, making the Explorer look like a homemade screwdriver. After a heavy sigh, he started cutting each cord with extreme prejudice, as if he were in a knife fight. Slice, slice, slice, pull, pull and in seconds the tarp was on the ground.

With the tarp gone, there stood in front of Robby a 1962 Volkswagen Microbus that looked just like it did the day it was made.

Dan Holcomb watched Robby's eyes as they took in the vintage Volkswagen bus. It was hard to tell what he was thinking; there was a faraway gaze that looked at once sad and in the next moment his eyes became bright and the edges of his lips would look like they were about to come up into a smile, and then those clear, green eyes would cloud over with pain.

Mr. Holcomb didn't know what kind of memories he was witnessing as he watched the man take in the old VW bus and he wondered if he should just go on and ask him...

His thoughts were interrupted by Deri, "Robby are you OK? Your hands are trembling and your face is pale. You're not having a stroke, are you?"

"No...no...I'm fine...just had a couple of memories bounce back on me." He continued to look at the Microbus, never taking his eyes off it, even though he was talking to Dari.

The VW bus was two-tone; the top was the color of vanilla ice cream, the bottom was that peculiar color of Volkswagen yellow. The front displayed the famous "V" and it glistened in the morning sun. The white came down the center of the V and right in the middle of that was the newly chromed iconic VW logo. Not a dent or scratch in the body. The tires were new with original VW hubcaps, also newly chromed. Robby opened the little back door and looked at the engine and wasn't surprised to see that it also looked new and freshly painted; the old dog house design engine with 40 horsepower. He checked the oil, and yes sir, clean as grandma's kitchen floor. This was exactly what he wanted.

While looking at the dipstick, Robby said, "All you needed to do was check one thing in a VW. Check the oil, and maybe the belt from time to time and that was it. There was no radiator, no water, no windshield washer fluid, no power steering fluid, no pollution devices, no computers…just a dipstick and a belt."

Before Dan could catch up to him, he had opened the driver's door and stuck his head inside. The same care and craftsmanship that was on the outside had carried over into the inside. The rubber floor mat was new and smelled of Armor All. The seats had been newly upholstered and were the color of coffee with lots of cream. The headliner was perfectly clean with no rips or tears. The shifter between the front seats still had the original shifting knob. It was ivory and looked like a mushroom.

Then Robby's face turned red, eyes became as big as saucers and his slight smile turned into a frown that would scare the Devil himself.

"Why would anyone take out the Blauplunk Radio and replace it with a Kenwood sound system? That's like wallpapering the Sistine Chapel."

Deri, who had stayed in the background said, "Maybe there was a reason for it."

"It was me," Dan Holcomb squeaked out, sounding like a teenage girl confessing to stealing mom's birth control pills. Straightening up some and lowering his voice a couple of notches he said "I had to. I took it to a Braves game last summer and someone broke into it and stole the radio. I hear they are in big demand with collectors. I didn't have the money for anything but the Kenwood."

"No problem, I can fix that. Deri, you're right. There is a reason for everything."

Robby looked at the dilapidated house and then back at the pristine van and asks, "How did you come to own this van?"

"Well sir, in 1969 I was twenty one and worked for a garage in a place called Surf City, North Carolina. We got a wrecker call about a VW bus that done fell in the ocean. Someone drove it off the pier. I was late getting there because the drawbridge was open. It was a crazy looking drawbridge, turning sideways instead of hinging upward. Anyway, by the time I got there, it had set in the ocean so long everybody thought it weren't good for nothing but scrap metal. My boss let me have it for $20.00. I been fixing it up piece by piece throughout the years. It wasn't originally yellow. I took it apart, cleaned all the salt out of it, got all the dents out and sanded it myself; my cousin painted it. I would get a break on parts because I was a Volkswagen mechanic for 30 years. I guess I worked in about every VW dealership in North Carolina. But I'm retired now. It's just me and my dog, Rebel."

"You mind if we take it for a ride?"

"Sure, that's fine. I trust y'all. Drive it all you want. It may need some gas, and don't go on Shadburn Ferry Road. They're paving it and the bus'll get tar on it for sure."

Robby jumped into the driver's seat and turned the switch. The motor turned over about three times and something caught the corner of his eye. It was Deri, arms folded, leaning back on her right leg, eyes wide in surprise. Not only did Robby forget to open the door for her, which he ALWAYS did, he damn near left her in the yard. With a sheepish look, he motioned with his head for her to get in.

Just as Deri sat down and started looking for a seat belt, there was a puff of smoke at the rear window and a tic tic tic tic tic tic. Running, it sounded like a wind up watch...very German, very Volkswagen. The van went up the steep, muddy driveway like it was a 4x4. They turned right and headed to town.

"Oh wow!!! This thing shifts perfect and will stop on a dime and give you nine cents change."

She looked at his face. Robby looked like a little boy the first time he rode on the sidewalk in a brand new Radio Flyer.

All of a sudden in all of his excitement, Robby pulled over to the side of the road, leaned over and planted a hard, lingering kiss onto Deri's very luscious lips...a long deep kiss, the kind of kiss where you come up for air and go back again...so full of the passion that had been submerged for many years. The surprise of it made both of their eyes widen and they reluctantly pulled apart not sure exactly how it had happened, but quite pleased that it did.

Robby was the first to recover and said, "Well, oh, my, that was nice. By the way, the skin above your lips looks a little chafed. Sorry about that."

Deri cleared her throat so she could speak without squeaking, "It's because of those horrible cheap razors you buy. My god, Robby, you could afford to hire someone to come by twice a day and shave you with the best products on the market, but instead you buy the cheapest razor you can find and use them too long and your stubble is downright dangerous, Mr. Sandpaper Face. And, I just had a facial yesterday."

Immediately, Deri felt bad about scolding him after receiving a kiss that nearly knocked her out of her seat and rattled her brain with the pleasure of it. The last thing she wanted to do was discourage a second kiss! "It's ok," she said with a smile and a tilt of her head, "I think I can find it in my heart to forgive you this once."

"OK, OK I get it. I tell you what I'll do, just for you. I'll stop buying those pink plastic razors at Big Lots and start buying the Walmart brand instead," he said with his most sincere face, belied only by the devilish twinkle in his eye.

Robby pulled back onto the road and grinned like a little boy with a new-found toy as he shifted into the next gear.

After a moment, Deri said, "Robby, I know you're busy, but I am going to need food soon. I've been up since 5:00 with nothing but a half a cup of tea."

"OK, how about we go to the Dairy Queen in town?"

"You're kidding me, right? You know I can't eat anything at a Dairy Queen! Is there a smoothie store or a salad bar or something even remotely healthy somewhere close?"

"I'm pretty sure not. We're in Buford, not Buckhead. I tell you what we'll do. Let's split a grilled chicken sandwich, and tonight I'll take you to that French restaurant you like so much, The Bistro Niko. And, I'll even tell you my Volkswagen story over dinner."

As they headed back to Dan Holcomb's after lunch, Deri looked over at Robby and noticed a tear running down his cheek.

Deri didn't think that she'd ever seen Robby shed a tear except when his wife died and, rather alarmed, she blurted out, "Robby, honey, are you all right?"

Robby turned to look at her. His eyes were fire truck red with tears running down both cheeks and an expression of frustration and sadness she had never seen before.

"Robby, baby, talk to me. What in the hell is wrong?" she said with a tinge of panic in her voice, and Deri never panicked.

"Nothing has changed. It's all the same. Same horror, same sadness, same nightmare, same Microbus taking me home. Everything is still the same."

"Robby, I'm not sure it's such a good idea to buy this car."

"It's not a car. It's a Microbus. And I'm buying this Nazi Bastard no matter what."

Deri was not one to use endearments like honey, or baby or sweetie. It was the first time she had said those words to Robby, and of all times, they fell on deaf ears. Robby quickly pulled himself together, coming back into the present and gathering his focus. They were going back to Dan Holcomb's house to do what they do best...wheel and deal.

Chapter 21

· · · · · · · · · · · · · ·

Spread the Love

As they backed down the driveway, they noticed Dan was sitting on the porch steps, scratching Rebel's back. This time, the dog did not bark. Apparently, getting a back rub was more important than protecting house and home.

The fact that he was still sitting on the steps with a kind of sad look on his face, and had made no effort to get up and greet them told Rob and Deri that he really didn't want to sell the van. They looked at one another, nodded, blinked and slowly walked to the bottom step of the porch.

The first to speak was Deri, "It really is a nice car in a quaint sort of way."

Robby tried not to show any emotion and said to himself, "Goddamn, I can't believe she just said that."

Then, after the slightest glare at Deri, he looked directly at Mr. Holcomb, "It is really a fine piece of workmanship. What are you asking for it?"

"Well sir, I'll take $30,000."

"Well yeah....I'm sure you would. But we're not even close. I'm thinking $10,000."

"Naw, I can't go 10. They got 'em on eBay for $30,000.00 and mine is in better shape, and has all genuine Volkswagen parts. Everything is original, except the radio. I'm sure over the years I've put $30,000.00 in it and would like to get it back."

"Just because they are ASKING 30K doesn't mean they are GETTING 30K. Most collectors are paying between 10 and 12 thousand."

Now it was Deri's turn. In her sweetest voice she says, "Mr. Dan, you know, this is not a 1967 Shelby Mustang or a 1960 Corvette. It's a 1962 Microbus. It's the muscle cars of the '60s that bring the big bucks. There is a very slim market for this kind of vehicle and people are not willing to spend a lot of money for them. I know how you feel about wanting to get the 30, but the numbers are just not there. $12,000.00 really is top dollar."

Then she placed one foot on the second step, leaned over, exposing her breasts a little, innocently widening her eyes as she took her right hand and gently patted his hand and said, "Wouldn't you really like to see your van go to a nice home where it will get the best of care?"

Dan simply melted before her eyes. She looked at Robby, expecting him to close the deal and nods.

Robby asked, "Just out of curiosity, why do you want to sell it, anyway?"

With a slight clearing of his throat, Mr. Holcomb reluctantly drew his eyes away from Deri and looked over at Robby. "Well, you see, it's like this here. Last November, I lost my house in a divorce. It was just a five room farmhouse in Salemburg, North Carolina, but it was all mine. Now it's all hers. My uncle used to own this lake house and when he died, my two cousins inherited it. They just used it as a party house. Those two knuckleheads never appreciated it, never took care of it, and never fixed anything. I got the chance to buy it, so I did, even though it needed a lot of repairs. I figure if I can get $30,000.00 that'll be enough for me to fix up the house way I fixed up the bus."

Robby turned to the right and looked toward the street. He turned to the left and looked in the woods. Then he walked away from everybody and walked down to the lake and stood on the old dock and stared at the water. He stood there motionless for what seemed like an eternity. Deri and Dan were both wondering: "What is he doing? What is he thinking? Why is it taking so long?" Finally, he came back up the hill, walked beside Deri and nodded at her. She knew that meant to get the zipper pouch. Mr. Holcomb had not moved an inch from his position on the steps, so Robby asked Mr. Holcomb if he would please walk with him to the van...he had a couple of questions. He opened the side door of the van as Deri walked up and handed him the pouch.

Without a word, Robby unzipped the pouch and laid 15 bundles of one hundred dollar bills on the floor of the van. In his lowest, calmest voice, "Mr. Holcomb, in each of these bundles, there are ten one hundred dollar bills. That means there is a thousand dollars in each bundle. There are fifteen bundles, which equal $15,000. Look in my money pouch and see, it's empty. I have no more money. I'm all in at fifteen thousand. But here's what I'll do: I'm a developer and a builder who constructs high rise office buildings and multi-family dwellings. I have a storage basement full of carpet, flooring, sheetrock, wiring, pipe, commodes, sinks, counters, and God only knows what else. All that came out of $300,000.00 condos and you can take all you need to fix up this house. You'll have to call me or Deri before you come, because we have a security gate, as well as a not-too-bright security guard, named Gordon. So, let me ask you this, would you rather have this $15,000, all in hundred dollar bills, and the materials to fix up your place, or would you rather keep the bus?"

Without a word, Dan handed him the extra key.

Mr. Holcomb shook hands with Robby. Robby looked him right in the eye, and for the first time, he noticed they had identical eyes. They were green with brown specks. They squeezed each other's hand in a strong, firm fashion, much stronger and warmer than normal, and nodded to each other. Sometimes you say more when you say nothing at all.

Robby and Deri collected the paperwork for the bus, left their business cards and headed back to the driveway and

Robby's now two vehicles. As Robby put the spare key in his pocket, he took out the key to the BMW and dropped it in Deri's hand.

Deri gave him one on those looks of disbelief and said "Well, Mr. Businessman, how much money did you lose on this deal? What in the hell were you thinking? MY GOD, Robby, I totally had him! When I leaned over and talked to him and he looked in my eyes and then down at my breasts, I owned him! He would have taken 12K for that car as fast as a kitten takes a bowl of cream. Instead, you give him $15,000.00 and a key to your warehouse. Why?"

"Because he's family."

"Family? What do you mean?"

"He said he lived in a farm house in Salemburg. Salemburg is a small town with a population of about 600 where everyone is related. For one hundred fifty years nobody moved in or out of the county. Therefore, all are distant cousins. Everybody in Sampson County is somehow related. His name is Holcomb. My mother's maiden name is Holcomb. There are only three names in the county: Holcomb, Underwood, or McLeod. If you have a name other than those three, it means you're not from around there. My parents are from Salemburg and moved to Atlanta after World War II looking for work, and I was born here in the ATL. If we're not related by blood, we are a kindred spirit and he needed a break. I spread a little love, and gave him a break, that's all."

"Well," Deri says with a sigh, "I guess the world does need a little more love."

"Oh geeeez. Do I hear a song coming? Love, sweet love?"

Robby turned to get in the van, and paused for a moment, looking at Deri, "By the way, Deri, I'm going to take the surface streets home. I need some time to get accustomed to driving this Nazi Bastard. And, besides, wide open, it'll go 59 miles per hour...65 downhill. That's not the safest speed on I-85. You'll have no trouble getting back to Atlanta with all your navigating gizmos. No need to follow me...just take off and I'll see you tonight at the Bistro."

Chapter 22

· · · · · · · · · · · · ·

A Lucky Day

Robby turned right on Buford Dam Road. He knew if he turned right, it would dead end into Atlanta Highway. Turn left on Atlanta Highway, make no turns, and it becomes Peachtree Street and goes right by his building...in about two hours. One right, one left, too easy.

He chose Buford Dam Road because you drove over the dam and it hugged Lake Lanier for many miles, providing a scenic, relaxing, laid back atmosphere that personified his Microbus. He opened the windows and left the radio off. There was just something about the sound of the wind and the hum of the little engine in the rear. He began daydreaming about Deri and didn't stop at a red light in time. Instead, he stopped directly under the light and backed up far enough to be out of the intersection and see the light. In a moment, it turned green and just before he let out the clutch, the motor went dead.

"Oh just fucking swell!!! Why couldn't you have quit on me before I bought you? Deri is going to laugh her cute little ass off when she finds out she has to come get me and take you to the shop after only one hour. Ah....come on and CRANK you Nazi Bas....."

Just then a City of Buford garbage truck sped through the intersection running the red light with its horn blasting as loud as possible. It went by the van so fast that the wind turbulence made it rock slightly back and forth. This monster of a truck jumped the curb and crashed into an old abandoned Sinclair service station. There was a rusty old sign on the side of the building, but you could still see the etching of a dinosaur. The truck came to rest under the sign.

Robby opened his flip phone and called 911, then jumped out of the Microbus and ran over to the garbage truck. He saw the driver was an older black man with his head on the steering wheel, blood dripping from his forehead. He opened the door and carefully assessed the situation. The driver appeared to be in his mid-60s, a little overweight, with grey hair around his ears. Rob noticed a very small scar on his neck not much bigger than the size of a pencil eraser. He was wearing a dark blue uniform with the name 'Jimmy' on the name patch. In one swift motion, Robby took out his knife, cut off the bottom of his own shirt tail, folded it three times and placed it on the man's forehead.

"Hey Jimmy, you OK? I checked you out and it looks like all that happened is that you bumped your head on the steering wheel."

"Oh Lawdy Lawdy Lawdy. My brakes give out comin' down dat hill and all I could do was blow the horn and pray. Oh Lawdy, I'm glad you wasn't hurt. When I was coming down dat hill, just a prayin', I saw you back up and stop. And then, when your light turned green, you be still and I went right by you. If you'd a moved when the light changed, I'd a killed you for sure...oh Lawdy."

"We're both fine. You just be right still and everything will be everything, bro. I hear sirens. They'll take care of you. I'm gonna cut out."

"Hey Mister, are you one of those psychic people?"

"No, I'm not psychic."

"Well then, how did you know my name?"

"It's written on your shirt."

"But how did you know I was in Viet Nam? You called me bro."

"Lucky guess."

"I know, you one of those old hippies. I can tell by your long hair and your hippie van."

"NO. I'm not old, I'm NOT a hippie. And this is NOT a hippie van. It is a classic Volkswagen Microbus."

Robby was beginning to get impatient with so many questions coming from a man he tried to help, from a man who has the bottom of his favorite shirt pressed to his bleeding head. He didn't want to answer the question as to how he knew Jimmy had been in Viet Nam even though it was easy. It was the scar on his neck. Robby and friends called it a 5 millimeter hickey. Sometimes when firing their M-16, the casings would discharge and hit them on the neck, burning the neck and leaving a burn scar that looked like a hickey.

"You'll be ok, I've got to go," he said, heading back to the Microbus.

As he touched the bus door handle, Robby became dizzy and an overpowering feeling came over him. His legs trembled so bad, he could hardly stand up. The realization that he had cheated death one more time hit him hard. Slowly he climbed into the van, still shaking all over, and noticed a strong odor that smelled like dirty clothes, sour beer, with some marijuana mixed in. He turned to look at the back seat and all he saw was a torn headliner, ragged seats, and a filthy floor. He closed his eyes, shook his head and pressed hard on his temple with the palm of his hand and took two very deep breathes.

As quickly as it came, it left. As he took several more deep breathes, he was now calm, regaining his confident attitude, even a feeling of well-being. The van once again smelled like Armor All and new vinyl, and looked all new again. He realized that it was all just a flashback. When he first came back from the war, he had them often and anything would set them off: a baby crying, a siren, fireworks, even the 11 Alive News chopper had caused flashbacks in the early days. Thankfully, it seemed only a traumatic experience would set one off now.

Oh yeah, he'd forgotten, the van had stalled and wouldn't start. He held the key in the ignition for a moment and then turned the key, bumped the starter and...tic tic tic tic, that unmistakable sound. Right now, it sounded pretty damn good. His imagination was still playing tricks on him though, because as soon as the van started, he could've sworn he heard a whisper, "I gottcha back, bro." This too, faded away, and with one more breath he was determined to dismiss the whole episode from his mind.

Putting the whole episode behind him, Robby decided just to kick back and enjoy the ride back to Atlanta. As he cruised down the road, enveloped by the peacefulness of the lake to his right and the dense forest to his left, he thought there's nothing better than North Georgia in the springtime. Not to mention he finally owned a little bus that he'd been craving for many years and had high prospects with a woman he adored. At 65, everything seemed to have finally come together and maybe, just maybe, he had found paradise.

While in this euphoric state, a vision from the past hit Robby so hard it jarred his very soul:

He is back in Viet Nam, in a river, trying to climb up the bank, but he keeps slipping and falling down back into the water. It didn't help matters that there were six Vietnamese shooting at him. In a blink, a young black man ran down the hill, under heavy fire, and took a one-knee-down position about ten feet from the bank of the river. POW POW POW POW POW POW...six shots blasted the air and the six men trying to kill Robby fell dead into the river on the other side...all head shots. As he gave Robby a hand up from the slippery bank he shouted, "Lawdy, Lawdy Lawdy, I think I been shot in the neck!" Robby looked quickly at his neck and says, "Naw, you just got your first 5 mm hickey.

Welcome to the Republic of Viet Nam."

Oh...my...God, Robby thought to himself. Could Jimmy be the same man that saved his life in Nam? Was this a chance meeting, a one in a million shot? Was it the VW Microbus that brought them together and once again his life was spared? Oh hell no, just a coincidence. Everything's cool...take a deep breath...stay on course.

After a few moments of quiet, he made a decision. He must, once and for all, get rid of these demons inside him. He bought the van for a reason, to help him face those demons from the past that continued to haunt him.

Robby decided now would be a good time to stop, get some coffee, and find a place to think things through. He found a picnic table far removed from the others and sat on top of it drinking his coffee, looking at the lake. It was 11:30 and still plenty cool...a typical April morning. He heard a distant drone of a boat's engine and a steady splashing sound. About 800 yards out, there was a ski boat with a skier attached yelling WOOOOOO!!! How do they do that, and why? It was still 45 degrees, then add the wind chill due to the boat speed and then add the water on the skier's body. That would bring down the skin surface temperature down to about 10 degrees, or less. Why? Oh well, Robby thought to himself that he had done crazier things in younger days for the sake of having fun.

While sitting on the table, listening to the waves splash on the shoreline, his thoughts again returned to Deri. He had known her longer than anyone outside his family and they were the best of friends. There had always been a special fondness and physical attraction there, but they had never been together in an intimate way. Although they had entertained the thought, the timing was never right – they had never been single at the same time, until now. But this time Robby made a vow to himself that he would allow nothing to get in the way of a romantic encounter. He'd made another decision. He wanted to make love to Deri tonight and he wanted it to be a very special. After all, she did say, "All you had to do was ask." So what if he was 25 years late, who's counting? He jumped off the table, walked quickly to the Microbus, ready to head back to Atlanta, knowing there was the woman of his dreams waiting at the end of the line.

Chapter 23

· · · · · · · · · · · · ·

There's a Moon out Tonight

After his long layover at the lake, with all his thinking and planning done, he realized the Nazi Bastard needed gas. He also decided never again to call it the Nazi Bastard, even in fun. He deliberately stopped at a very large, busy filling station, because he knew it would have the freshest gasoline. He went inside the convenience store and bought nothing because of the ridiculous prices. $1.79 for a can of Coke? I don't think so. Robby was sure Walmart sold a whole two liter bottle for 99 cents. He got a sip of water from the water fountain attached to the wall...water was free.

When he went out to the bus, he found a couple of guys checking it out and Robby showed the Microbus off a bit, giving them "the grand tour." An older lady with grey hair walked quickly with the slightest limp toward Robby and the bus and exclaimed, "Oh my, oh my! This is just like the van my boyfriend had when we met. I was a student at Southern Cal and he played in a band in one of the clubs close by. We had such fun in that van...traveling, picnicking, and all that. We drove it to a few concerts, and since we had very little money, the van became our motel room. Well now, I guess I said too much...he he he."

Robby smiled since he understood all about how an old car could prompt a memory, and said, "Uh...did you and your boyfriend get married?"

"Oh heavens no...I married an accountant. My boyfriend with the van was wild. He's probably dead or in jail, now. Oh...

so sorry... I have taken up your time with my old memories. Oh look! Here comes my grandchildren and husband...gotta go... nice to meet you!"

It took him 45 minutes to get away from the gas station... seems everyone wanted to share their Volkswagen story. Robby knew this was something that he was going to have to get used to. After all, the bus had great appeal, and it sparked a lot of memories in many people. On the downside, he was a very private person and didn't like attention drawn to him. He had plenty of kindness toward people, but very little patience. He supposed it was time to work on having patience with others and just maybe, the van could help him do that.

He pulled into the parking deck and looked at his watch; it was 3:30. Holy sheep shit, so much to do between now and 7:00 o'clock. He opened the door to his condo and looked at his watch again...3:45. He thought to himself, "Damn, I have exactly three hours to be at the restaurant and before that, I've to get all cleaned up, find some nice clothes, buy a bottle of wine, and clean the bat cave. Oh god...clean the bat cave...assholes and elbows, let's get moving."

* * *

It was a good thing the restaurant was in walking distance of the condo because there was no time left to sit in traffic. He exited the elevator on the main floor, briskly walked out on the sidewalk, turned left and in ten minutes, there he was. Whew! He made it. It was exactly 6:45.

He always arrived early for two reasons; first of all, that was his nature, that's the way he is. He's always early or on time, it was a point of pride and discipline. Deri is either damn late or just a little late. The second reason sounds a bit silly for a sixty five year old man, but he liked to arrive first so he could watch her walk in the door and cross the room. There's something about the way she entered a room that was downright appealing. Sitting outside, under the canopy, Robby waited at a small table right against the wrought iron fence that bordered the sidewalk on Peachtree Street...the perfect spot to watch her as she walked in.

As he waited, he wondered if this fence is to keep people out, or to keep them in until they've paid. His mind continued to wander as he people-watched. He saw two gay men walk by, holding hands. One was blonde with spiked hair, whereas the other guy was large, robust, with a crew cut and a Celtic tribal tattoo around his large biceps for all to see, since he was wearing a sleeveless t-shirt. He thinks of a bumper sticker he saw once: "I'm not black and I'm not gay, but I live in Atlanta, anyway." A short, rather heavy black woman walked by wearing a skirt that was an entire four inches below her ass, with high heels that would pass for stilts. She was followed by a young man in a cowboy hat with a mouth full of chewing tobacco. He thought back for a moment to when he was a Marine and chewed Levi Garrett chewing tobacco.

Just then, Deri appeared at the door that led into the sidewalk café. He is not disappointed by her stunning appearance. She was wearing a long black skirt that was split up the front to mid-thigh, with a silver blouse and black jacket that matched the skirt. She saw Robby and walked to the table, her hips swaying from side to side in perfect time with her arms.

"So, I see the old bus made it home. I was hoping you would call when you arrived," she said as she gracefully slid into her seat.

"Uh...sorry...I've been rather busy since I got home. I already ordered your drinks: a glass of bottled water with lemon, your favorite chardonnay and an extra glass of ice."

"You're sweet." Deri settled in and looked around the room. She turned back to him and smiled, "OK, Robby, I've been thinking about it and waiting all afternoon. You promised to tell me your Volkswagen story, so now give."

Robby thought for a moment and began his story, "Well, it started when four of us guys were all discharged from the military around the same time, and we all met by chance in a bar in San Diego. There was Roger Hilton, from the Army; Kim Hernandez, from the Navy; a Marine buddy of mine called Moose Forrester, and me. The four of us were getting acquainted and kept drinking most of the afternoon. We decided, in our drunken stupor, that the smartest thing to do would be to pool our money, buy an old car and travel across the country, dropping each other off at our homes along the way. The last one home would sell the car, split the money four ways and send each of us a money order. If it worked according to plan, we could travel, see the country, and drive home, all for free. So we bought a '62 Microbus for $500, and we drank, smoked and partied our way across the United States. We got in and out of serious trouble a couple of times, had some...uh...short term relationships, and probably hit every bar from coast to coast, where we engaged in more fights than in Viet Nam. The sailor and the soldier lived in Texas and Alabama, I lived in Atlanta, and Moose lived in Jersey. I was the next to the last to get home, and then Moose drove home after leaving me at my doorstep. That's the last I heard from any of them."

"I thought you said Moose was going to send you the money back when he sold the bus."

"I never heard from him again, or anyone else for that matter. It's not like Moose was the most dependable man on the planet. He was the sorta guy who could lift a ton, but didn't know how to spell it. Moose would kill or die for you, loyal to a fault, but he was rather loosely wrapped."

"Oh, didn't that bother you? I've seen you go after people who owed you money and it's not a pretty sight. Didn't you try to find him?"

"No. For one thing, maybe he never sold it. Maybe he had to keep it because he couldn't afford anything else. Besides, there's something about us you could never understand, totally. Unless you've been there, you just don't get it. We were bros. We were a brotherhood; we had each other's backs. We pulled each other out of the mud with bullet holes in us. We marched together in the sweltering heat with the smell of our buddy's brains on our shirt. We...we...uh...never mind. You get the picture. Moose was 6' 4", weighed 235 pounds. Once he threw me on his shoulder and ran 100 yards, under fire, to a Huey, because I had been deeply cut and my guts were hanging out. After what Moose and I had been through together, who gives a shit about $125.00?"

"Oh."

"Perhaps we need to order now, and forget about what went on in '69. For the rest of the night, let's stay in the moment, for the moment. It's a beautiful evening, there's a full moon out tonight, and we're in your favorite restaurant. After we've eaten, there's something I must ask."

"Something you must ask? Oh Robby, you know I don't like surprises, ask me now."

Robby cleared his throat, looked at the floor, cleared his throat again, and looked up directly into Deri's deep blue eyes and said, "I know I am about twenty five years late, but I've purchased a bottle of chardonnay; I even cleaned the bat cave. And...I've been thinking about nothing but you and I want to be with you all night long. Soooo....what I want to ask you is, after dinner, will you please come with me to my place and we share some wine and laughter and hold each other as the sun rises on the balcony?"

This was the last thing Deri expected. She was more than just fond of him, and more than once had wondered what it would be like to spend the night together; and here it is...THE question. Deri smiled slightly, never taking her eyes off his and said, "You know, I'm just not very hungry anymore. Perhaps we could go to your place for a while?"

It was unusually quiet during that two minute ride in the

elevator. Robby didn't know why Deri was so quiet, but he knew why he was quiet. He was nervous as hell. Actually, hell is not nervous. Hell is hot. He was as nervous as any boy would be on his first sexual encounter. Nervousness mixed with excitement. Deri noticed his fingers trembled as he pressed the number 12 button and she smiled, giggling a little inside at the thought of one of the most powerful men in the city being so nervous and excited.

"I have wine and tequila. Would you like some of either?"

"No, but I need to take off this jacket. I was expecting to be outside tonight, not in the bat cave."

"Let me help."

Robby unbuttoned the only button on the jacket, slipped it off her shoulders and allowed it to fall to the floor. As it fell, he pulled her to him and first kissed her lightly on the lips then began to kiss her with a passion that he thought was long gone. Their breath came faster and faster and keeping his lips on hers, he held her against the wall. He gently placed his lips on her neck and slowly unbuttoned her blouse, leaving a trail of kisses across her neck and down towards her breasts. The last two buttons would not move. He slid his lips back up her neck and whispered in her ear, "How much did you pay for this pretty blouse?"

"Um, $125.00, on sale, maybe, I think..." she murmured, unable to concentrate on anything but Robby's body so close to hers.

"I'll buy you another one; no, I'll buy you two," he whispered into her ear as he ripped the blouse apart, the two stubborn buttons sailing through the air.

A magical moment more special than he could have imagined had just began for Robby.

Chapter 24

· · · · · · · · · · · · ·

Time to Let It All Come Out

As always, Robby woke up at 5:30. As he opened his eyes and looked around, he was momentarily confused when he realized he was in a place other than his bed or favorite recliner. He looked upward and saw stars and as he started to pull the comforter off, there was a naked woman lying on her side with her arm across his chest. He looked to the left, and there was his patio furniture.

Ahh... yes. Now he remembered. After a couple more love making sessions, and a couple glasses of wine and shots of tequila, he remembered they decided what a great idea it would be to make love on the balcony under the stars. So, Robby removed the comforter from the bed and laid it on the concrete floor. She didn't like the hard floor and was afraid of spiders, so they made love standing up with Deri's hands braced against the wall of the balcony, looking toward the mirrored hotel. Apparently, shortly after that, they fell asleep on the balcony, all rolled up in the comforter. Some would call it passing out, but they didn't pass out, they fell sound asleep. You see... wealthy, mature adults don't pass out...they fall asleep.

He gently rolled out from under her arm and made his way to the master bathroom, awakening a little more with each step. He noticed clothes scattered in a haphazard fashion throughout the condo. Deri's shoes and jacket were in the great room...her torn blouse, in the hallway. Her skirt was on the floor mid-way in the bed room. Her black bra was at the foot of the bed, matching panties that were more lace than panties he found straddled on the ceiling fan. It was apparently a team effort because his clothes were in the same areas as hers, except he never did find his underwear...couldn't quite remember if he was wearing any.

As he was brushing his hair, he smelled the intoxicating aroma of coffee. Just then Deri entered the bathroom wearing nothing but one of his t-shirts. She looked in the mirror and noticed that there was no red mark above her lip. She glanced at the counter and saw a brand new triple-bladed fusion razor and special gel from a shaving boutique and was surprised at how touched she was that he had not forgotten her chafed lip. She quietly slipped up behind him; put her arms around his waist, and with a little more than a whisper, "I have coffee ready and some tea. The sun is coming up and there is nothing more in the world I want to do but sit with you on the balcony and watch the sun come up."

As they half lie next to each other, settling into each other's arms on the patio chaise lounge, covered with the once discarded comforter, they stare into the lightening sky and think back to what had been the perfect night.

After she'd taken a few sips of her tea, while stirring with the cinnamon stick, Deri said, "Robby, tell me your Volkswagen story, but this time, I want to hear the real one. Not the one you told me last night to blow me off. Please Robby, tell me the story, the whole story."

Robby looked in his coffee cup, took a small sip, rolled it around in his mouth , and said, "Well, it all started in the spring of 1969 in San Diego. Well, truthfully, I really don't know where to start."

"Well dear, you can start anywhere you want. Why not start with why you bought that silly car in the first place."

Robby was a little miffed because she had just called his Microbus a silly little car, but for now, was most willing to put up with it. After all, he had recently called it much worse; so...on with the story...

"Well for a couple of reasons. For one thing, it was at a time in our country's history when we didn't know if somebody was going to welcome us into their heart, or treat us like we were drug addicted alcoholics who loved killing for no reason. Due to the different reactions you would get, I didn't like to be in public in my uniform and wanted to be by myself and just be left alone. I thought it to be a good idea to travel alone, or with some chosen friends who were like-minded. Then, there was the money... cheaper this way. And, believe it or not, when I was a little boy, my favorite TV show was Route 66. There was just something extraordinary about traveling the country, single, with friends."

"I can see that. Well, what were some of the highlights of the trip?"

"Mmmmm...not much at all...quite boring, in fact...long hours in a van that would barely hit 60 MPH."

"Robby McLeod, I know when you're lying. Now come on; I know you...no need to hide from me. So, how was the trip?"

He told all. Well, all except for tying the bandito to a cactus in the desert...that would've been a bit unseemly to explain to a lady. He thought best not to mention how Moose gagged one night at a roadside grill. It's doubtful she would see the humor in that. He spoke of the grandeur of the Grand Canyon, the beautiful water, the clear nights where you could see forever. He told her of the many nice people they met along the way, including a sheriff who turned out to be an OK guy after all. He mentioned the fight between Kim and two bullies and how Roger came to the rescue. He spoke of the grandeur of the Hilton Ranch, and all the happiness at Roger's house; then to Kim's house, where luxury would be the last descriptive word, and yet, the love and joy were the same. With a deep, somewhat trembling voice, he recalled arriving at his cold, dark, empty house, only to watch Moose leave in the morning.

For the first time in his life, he spoke to someone who was not in the old Microbus in '69 of the horrors and nightmares he had as a result of being in warfare. With trembling and tears, he told her of the death and destruction he witnessed, as well as many a close call he had with death: coming back to base with bullet holes in his shirt, his buddies shot and falling to the ground right beside him, snipers missing him by an inch, driving a gasoline truck under fire that in the end had over three hundred rounds in the cab, almost drowning, being pulled out of a river under fire...hard, painful times, indeed.

"...So, anyway, like I said, we dropped Roger off at his home. We spent the night there in Canton Texas, and after a brief stay in New Mexico, where Kim met a sweet young lady and a couple of really serious idiots, we headed to Birmingham and left Kim at his house amidst a block party of Biblical proportions. And then, to my house in East Atlanta ...and that's how it ended. Moose drove off in our Microbus and I never saw any of them again," said Robby, clearing his throat as he held back the tears.

Fighting back the tears and holding it all inside suddenly no longer worked in the presence of his new found love. He completely let go of all his submerged emotions and cried like a little baby.

Although Deri never had children...never wanted any...she was loving and maternal. She held Robby close to her chest, kissed him on the forehead, and rocked him back and forth in her arms as if he were a child who had just scraped his knee running on the sidewalk.

In her gentlest, kindest voice, "It's OK, honey. You just let it all go....let it all go away with those tears. You are going to be just fine...just fine."

Chapter 25

. . . .

Deri's Idea

By now, it was almost noon and they had been sitting together on the balcony all morning.

Robby took a deep breath, wiped his eyes on the comforter, and said, "Let's go inside. It's getting hotter than a June bride on a feather bed. Let's go in and enjoy some A/C and maybe a light lunch."

"Not so fast, Mr. McLeod. You haven't told me everything. You haven't told me the real reason you bought that van. By the way, I did some checking. A Microbus just like that one sold at an auction in Vegas for $50,000.00 about six months ago."

"I know."

"But you didn't buy it for an investment, and you didn't screw yourself like I thought you did when you gave Mr. Holcomb all that money and access to building materials; but just the same, why, Robby why?"

"Well, it's rather simple. I was lucky in one respect. Most guys who came out of Nam were jetted home in a matter of days from their last battle. They never had time to decompress, to think things out. When World War II was over, our soldiers mostly came home on ships that took a couple of weeks to get home and during that time they talked to their buddies who were the only ones who understood. It was time well spent readjusting to the real world in civilian life. The Microbus was like my ship across the sea. It gave me time to adjust to the world ahead of me, time to talk things out with men who understood and cared. By the time I arrived in Atlanta, I had made a kind of peace with myself as to all the terrible things I did, as well as all the slaughter and carnage I witnessed all around me. But the one demon I cannot shake can be summed up in one word: WHY? Why am I still alive and why did men better than I am blow up right beside me and the only thing left of them was a hand? Why did we really go into that goddamn war anyway? It was rumored among the ranks that the U.S. thought there were large pockets of oil off the coast of Viet Nam and we were not there to stem the tide of communism; we were there to gain control of Nam and get cheap oil. So, were we fighting for oil, instead of freedom? Why? A Marine officer told me once we were there as guinea pigs, testing out the new M-16 rifles. Why? Why? Why did all this happen, and why was I allowed to see it and survive it? Why did I deserve to live? I was thinking since the old VW bus helped me get through the horrors of war, the new bus would help me find out the why of everything. It has plagued me all my life and maybe the answer lies deep within me when connected with the Microbus. So...I figured why the hell not? So I bought it, and quite honestly I don't know where to start or what to do next."

"Oh Robby, you're breaking my heart. Is that the reason for all the sleepless nights? The reason you stay up late and finally fall asleep in your recliner watching boring TV?"

"....well....I guess...so... never thought...that is the reason for the sleepless nights and the nightmares...guilt...I'm thinking lots of guilt."

"Well, then, I know just what you need to do. To coin one of your phrases, 'it's too easy.'" Here's what you must do: just as the trip across the country with your buddies helped you in 1969, this time you take a trip in your new Microbus and find these same buddies...Moose, Kim, and Roger. I bet when you see them again and talk to them, or when spending time alone in the van while traveling, it will come to you. I'm just sure it will. Besides, the time away will do you some good. I'll use my people search program on my computer and locate these guys for you...name, address, directions...everything."

"It may take weeks; I can't stay away from my business computer that long."

"OK Mr. 19th century. You can buy a phone that will enable you to send and receive emails and do everything else your computer does right from your car, anywhere in the country. I'll go with you, help you buy it and show you how to set it up and use all its features."

"No kidding. A jive-ass phone can do all that?"

"Oh Robby, you slay me. It's a good thing I love you so much."

"YOU love ME? I love you, too!" He rubbed her bare leg, raised his eyebrows up and down and in his best Groucho Marx said, "Let me take you to the drive in and I'll prove how much I love you."

"Oh god. You're awful. I have a better idea; take me to the phone store and let's get busy on planning your trip of a lifetime."

"I know my first stop already. I'm going back to Buford and talk to a garbage truck driver named Jimmy."

Chapter 26

. . . .

Headed down the highway...again

April 12 , 2013

Today was a special day for Robby. First his birthday...65 today, and second, his first trip in the Microbus. Not exactly a cross-the-entire-country jaunt like in 1969, but a day trip to Buford to find Jimmy and talk to him.

In his shirt pocket was his new phone that Deri taught him all about yesterday at his kitchen table...rolling her eyes when he complained, "I feel like I'm back in school trying to learn a new thesis or something. Why does a phone have to do so many things? You know, when I was 21, all I had was a phone that plugged in the wall that sat on a little table in the hallway, and we did just fine!" With a large dose of patience, Deri continued her smart phone class until he began to see how handy this could be on the road. Although, he would never admit it.

After driving the bus around for two days and totally ignoring his BMW, he felt more confident about navigating the Atlanta expressway system, a trial for both body and soul, but he was up for the challenge. So there he went, back out on the highway, 44 years later with a different bus, but the same feeling of excitement that came with the anticipation of a new adventure. He had barely hit 4th gear on I-85 when the phone rang. He knew it was Deri because his new phone had a personalized ring. He smiled as *You Shook Me All Night Long*, by AC/DC played ...how does it do that?

With a swipe of his thumb, he answered, "Well hello there... miss me already?"

"Yes I do, a little. But that's not why I called. That security guard, Gordon, the one you call 'as dumb as dog shit in a watermelon patch,' was caught in Mrs. Brawner's condo peeing in her potted palm."

"Potted palm? You mean a houseplant? Just when you think you've heard it all...oh Christ! OK, here's what we do: If you haven't already done so, fire his stupid ass and tell him if he wants his last pay check he can take us to court and he can explain to the judge the thrill that goes with pissing in somebody's houseplant. Take the money that would have gone to him and apply it to the cleaning service. I want them to thoroughly clean the entire condo and find the biggest, best looking palm in the city as a replacement. Run all this by Mrs. Brawner. I need you to do whatever is necessary to make her happy and make this go away...holy cat shit...pissing in the plant. All right, thanks for calling."

The only reason he ever hired Gordon was because he felt sorry for him, being an unemployed veteran. Robby thought to himself that the reason some people are unemployed is because they are unemployable. He dismissed the whole matter and began to focus his attention on the hum of the engine in the rear.

Still amazed at how Buford hadn't changed a bit in almost 50 years, he parked right in front of City Hall. The lady at the counter had a name plate that said Anne Jones. As he approached the counter, she put down her bacon biscuit, took a quick sip of lukewarm coffee from a Styrofoam cup, and with her biggest smile and heavy southern accent said, "Hey, can I hep yew?"

"Yes Ms. Jones, I'm looking for one of your garbage truck drivers named Jimmy."

"Why, I know just who you mean and I'm so sorry to tell you this, but he doesn't work here anymore. His name is Jimmy Johnson...you know, like the football coach."

"I really need to talk to him; do you know how to get in touch with him?"

"He had this accident just two days ago, and it rattled him so bad he said he just couldn't drive anymore. He said something about getting a job washing cars at the Chevrolet place. Maybe you could try there. We're not allowed to give out names and addresses, but if you don't see him there, he hangs out a lot at the diner you passed as you came into town."

"Thanks, you've been very helpful."

"Oh, yew welcome.," drawled Anne, as she brushed the biscuit crumbs from her blouse, hoping this handsome man didn't notice.

Robby decided to try the diner first since it takes only ten minutes to apply for a job in a small town dealership, but you can spend hours in a diner.

Sitting at the counter, beside the coffee pot and cash register was Jimmy, still wearing the uniform of the City of Buford, complete with city logo and name tag.

With a look of a bombshell exploding near him, in total shock and amazement he blurts out, "Lawdy, Lawdy. Lookie here! Hey ya'll," he said to the other two men sitting at the counter, "this is the man I talked about who was so nice to me when I had my accident. Mister, please have a seat and I'll buy you some coffee."

"Thanks, I'll take you up on that. Actually, I was looking for you. I had some questions to ask, if you don't mind."

"Naw man, ask me anything you want. If I don't knows the answer, I'll make something up...he he he."

"OK then, are you a good shot with a rifle?"

Jimmy got a surprised look on his face when he answered, "Well...yes suh. I don't know why you'd ask such a question but I'm a good shot. When I was a child we lived on a farm in Hog Mountain and had to hunt the woods for food. My daddy would give me nine bullets and I better come home with nine squirrels. Missing was not an option. He'd whoop my ass if I missed; and if you know you gonna carry a ass whooping, you learn real fast to shoot straight."

"Mmmm, I thought so...when you were in Viet Nam, were you ever in Quan Tin?"

"Mister, are you sure you ain't one of them psychic peoples? First you called me bro and figured I was in Nam and now you know where I was while I was there?"

"OK Jimmy, I'll tell you how I know. It's the scar on your neck. Those kind of scars come from the empty casing ejected from an M-16. There was a black man who once saved my life... the most incredible shot I ever saw, he helped me out of the river and I told him..."

"...you told him he had a 5mm hickey, then you said, uh... welcome..."

"...yeah I said, welcome to the Republic of Viet Nam," finished Robby with a slight smile curling the corner of his mouth.

"OH LAWDY LAWDY LAWDY!!! It's you!!! That short Marine! You know what? That was my first day and I was as scared as a shot cat running to the doctor, and when I saw how calm you were, it made me calm some. Thinkin' back 'bout that experience kept me calm in many a tumble."

The two of them did something that would've never happened 50 years ago, in Buford or anywhere else in the South. They stood up in the middle of the diner and hugged and patted each other on the back. Two grown men who, on first glance could not have been more different: Robby a white, college educated and well-to-do man raised in the city, and Jimmy, a black man from the country who didn't finish high school and had seldom seen anything past minimum wage. Yet, in spite of the differences, Robby felt more of a kinship with this man than he did with any of his high rolling friends in Atlanta. They were long lost brothers who were finally re-united.

Jimmy said, "Sir, let's sit down and have another cup. Uh... what's your name...I don't even know your name, and if you told me, I done forgot."

"My name is Robert McLeod. Everyone calls me Robby... some just say Rob, and leave it at that."

"Well, now Mister Rob, nice to meet you again and I thank the Lord we got together after all this time."

"Ummm...I don't think the Lord had as much to do with it as the Microbus. Were it not for the bus, we would have never met; but just the same, good to meet you too. Another question, are you looking for a job?"

"OH YES SIR! I AM!"

"Let's go over to that empty booth, where we can talk a little more private. Well, I got something for you if you're interested. I need a security guard at my building in Atlanta. It is exactly 38 miles from where we're sitting right now...traffic's a bitch, but if you leave here at 0600, you'll be there by 0700. You can work from 7:00 to 3:00 and miss most of the heavy traffic both ways. I have a lady, named Deri, who handles the hiring and all the paperwork that goes with it. She'll also clue you in on the job description...you know, what to do, when to do it, and why...that kind of bullshit. If you have a pistol and are licensed to carry, that's a plus, but not a requirement. How are you fixed for money right now? Do you have enough to last you two weeks? We hold back a week on the payroll."

Looking down into his coffee cup, too embarrassed to look Rob in the face, he says, "Well, sir, I guess I could use my electric bill money for gasoline until I get paid...don't want no hand-outs."

"Hand-out my ass! You saved my life, man." Robby took three one hundred dollar bills from a worn and tattered wallet and slid them across the table, and said, "View this as your Christmas bonus. Oh yeah, speaking of money, I'll start you off at $35,000 a year. That's about $670 a week. I'll tell Deri that, too; she handles the payroll. Here's Deri's business card; call her before you come in and she'll set up a time for y'all to meet and do all the necessary paper work. I know this is short notice, but if you can start tomorrow, that would be great."

Jimmy is speechless. He'd never dreamed of making that much money. He made $325.00 a week working for the city... plus all the free garbage he wanted. For sure, this was a godsend.

"Oh yes sir, thank you, Mister Rob. I'll be there tomorrow at 0700 sharp. I promise I won't let you down."

"I know you won't."

By now, the two of them had gone through an entire pot of coffee and were working on a second pot when Robby happened to look at his wrist watch. "Oh crap, I need to go right now if I'm going to miss the traffic. Hope to see you tomorrow. If not tomorrow, I'll see you around sooner or later; I live there."

"Yes sir."

Jimmy watched the Microbus turn onto Main Street and continued to watch through the window until it was no longer in view. A voice from the booth behind him asked, "Hey Jimmy, who's the old hippie in the van?"

Jimmy sat up straighter, feeling more confident than he had in a very long time. He turned around and said, "Well sir, he AIN'T old, he AIN'T no hippie, and that AIN'T no van; it's a classic Volkswagen Microbus."

Chapter 27

. . . .

A Few Surprises

Robby had been on the road about 20 minutes when Deri called again, saying, "You don't waste time getting a new security man, do you, dear? Mr. Johnson has already called and set up an appointment with me. He wanted to meet me at 6:30, obviously having no idea that I don't do anything until 10:00. So, we made the appointment for 11:15 and he was really concerned because he said he had promised you he would start at 7:00. I told him not to worry, I would cover for him and everything would be fine. That is OK, isn't it?"

"Sure, that's all right. This guy is much smarter than Gordon, far more loyal, and knows where to pee."

That cleared, Deri, barely able to control her excitement, continued, "I have some news for you; in fact a couple of surprises. I have located Roger and Kim...can't seem to find Moose, but I'll continue to search. Roger, of all things, lives north of Atlanta in Alpharetta, and his office is in the Coca Cola building right downtown. All this time your condo was not even 10 minutes from his office. I talked to him briefly and he has quite a story to tell you. I set up an appointment for you to see him tomorrow at 11:30. He seemed so nice and he's really looking forward to seeing you."

"Well just damn...how about Kim?"

Deri went on, practically giddy with her success, "Kim lives in Muscle Shoals, Alabama and he told me he thinks of you all the time and has prayed for you on numerous occasions. He laughed and said you needed someone to pray for you. He so very much wants to see you. He was hoping that you could come see him next Saturday."

"Back in '69 that was the only time Kim and I would fuss and fight...you know...when he brought up all that stuff about God, and all...Well Deri, you did good. No word about Moose?"

"No Robby. It would help when you have a best friend, to at least get his real name. Moose is just a nickname and there's no record of a Moose Forrester in the United States. And not to bring up a touchy subject, but when you have a best friend, it's a really good idea to make an effort to contact him a little more often than once every 40 years."

"I know...I know, Deri. I did try once in the summer of '69 and couldn't find him. Then, life got in the way. Next thing you know, I was married, had children, ran two businesses, went back to school...busy, busy, busy. Then you wake up one morning and the baby girl you remember sitting in a high chair in a little two bedroom house is now a 40 year old woman with her own family...a family you see at Christmas and Father's Day. Like I've said, where the hell does the time go?"

"I understand, Rob. Come to my house tonight around 6:30. I have everything you need to make the trip to see your friends: maps, phone numbers, emails, directions...everything."

Deri lived north of Atlanta on the shores of Lake Allatoona so Robby left in plenty of time to allow for traffic and for the not-so-fast Microbus. Punctual as always, Robby entered her driveway at exactly 6:29.

All he was going to do was get the information packet from her, visit for a bit and then head back home once the traffic thinned out. As he reached out to ring the doorbell, which sounded more like the chimes at the Crystal Cathedral, he was surprised to see Deri already opening the door.

There stood the best looking woman he'd ever known wearing nothing but a short cotton skirt and a purple tank top.

Robby's eyes became as big saucers as she grabbed his sleeveless t-shirt with one hand and pulled him through the living room, past the kitchen and then in and out of the dining room, leading him to one of the sofas in the family room at the rear of the house. In a low, sultry voice she said one word, "sit."

He sat on the sofa, his mind spinning with anticipation, wondering just what she was up to. Without a word she grabbed his ponytail and gave it a slight tug causing him to look up at her as she climbed onto the couch, straddling him, and gave him a long passionate kiss. Her fingers ran down his chest and grabbed the bottom of his t-shirt, pulling it off and throwing it to the floor. Slowly she stroked the hair on his chest, sensuously nibbling on his nipples. She slid her hands down to his jogging shorts and they found their way on to the floor beside his shirt. Deri kneels on the floor in front of him and begins to stroke his hard, throbbing penis, places her mouth on him, sliding half way down the shaft as she uses her hand to stroke the bottom half. Robby reaches out to grab her hair and gently pulls up and down. After a moment, Deri breaks free, pulls the tank top over her head, kicks off the skirt and climbs up, straddling his body as she slowly lowers herself on him, gradually quickening her pace, sliding up and down on him as they both moan with surging pleasure until climaxing and falling into each other's arms on the sofa.

As they lay there catching their breath, Robby gazed out of the huge picture window that overlooked the lake, and can't remember feeling this way before; intensely satisfied, relaxed from top to bottom, and absolutely loved by an incredible woman. Still in a haze of euphoria, all he could say was, "Wow, I never saw that coming. This was too wonderful for words."

"Well, Robby," she said, cuddling deeper into his arms, "I've been thinking about you all day and every time I think of you, I start to breathe really hard and I start wanting you in the worse way. Since we spent the night together last Saturday, you have not been out of my mind for a minute."

After basking in the afterglow of their perfect love dance, Deri pulled back to look into Robby's eyes. "Let's get dressed and I'll get all the information that I printed out for you and then we can eat. I cooked your favorite meal, spicy Thai pork."

Eyes raised in mock surprise and seriousness, he said "Oh really? I was actually looking forward to a hot dog at the Quick Fill, but I guess I could force myself to stay for supper."

With a heavy sigh, Deri said, "Men!"

Chapter 28

· · · · · · · · · · · · · ·

Hello Roger

Robby didn't make it back to Buckhead that night, but stayed with Deri, where they sat on the deck, held hands and watched the stars come out. As they gazed skyward, Deri said, "Why don't you just spend the night."

They talked and cuddled, laughed and cuddled, then, fell asleep as they cuddled more. For the both of them, it was paradise to have someone to hold...to feel a warm, unclothed body in their arms held so tightly, hanging on and never wanting to let go.

When Robby woke up, he slowly pried his way loose from Deri, moving carefully so as not to awaken her and looked at the clock beside the bed...5:30AM...well, well, big surprise. With his shorts and shirt in hand, he turned around to get one last look at Deri, sound asleep with half her body out from under the covers. He stared in amazement for a moment, watching her as she lay across the king-sized brass bed, her strong, muscular shoulder, a supple breast, and an athletic leg peeking out from the mauve satin sheets. He couldn't leave without going back to the bed and kissing her cheek, whispering "Bye bye...love you...see you later." He groped his way through the house, unfamiliar in the dark, trying to re-trace his steps because he knew he came in with shoes...well, kinda like shoes...his $2.00 flip flops. Oh yeah... the family room...there they are...upside down and spread five feet apart. Now that he's in full uniform, Robby headed back to his condo to put on his other uniform...Hawaiian shirt, Dockers shoes and cargo shorts. On second thought, since he was going to meet Roger, he thought maybe he should wear something more befitting the occasion.

As he took the elevator up from the parking garage, he thought to himself, Deri is not only good looking, good cooking, and great loving, but that woman can make a really good map, too. He had no trouble finding The Coca Cola building and Roger's office up on the 20th floor.

Just as he had no trouble finding Roger's office, he had no trouble getting in to see Roger as he was waiting for him in the reception lobby. Robby took one look, broke out in a big smile and said, "Hey Roger, what happened to your hair?"

Grinning like a pair of fools, Robby and Roger stepped towards each other, reaching out to warmly grasp hands. "UH... it left. By the time I was 40, all I had was a hula skirt, so I shaved it all. Now it's all white and very short. And look at you!!! You haven't changed a bit except, for that long hair. Last time I saw you, it was a military buzz and was...uh...not silver. Somewhere between red and brown, if I remember correctly."

"Well, you know, time changes things...but not all things."

"Man, it is so good to see you; come in my office. Do you still like coffee?"

"Oh yeah, that's where I get all my vitamins and minerals, is from coffee; I'd love a cup."

Roger opened his office door and motioned for Robby to enter. He took a quick look around the office and noticed it was a corner office with a wall of solid glass where you could see for miles past the concrete, congestion, and noise of the city... out past the suburbs to where there was nothing but trees. He noticed far in the distance an outline of Stone Mountain to the east and just a few blocks away, the Capitol Building brandishing a gold dome, gold mined right there in Georgia.

As he sat, a 5x7 photograph caught his attention on the credenza behind Roger's desk. With a surprised look on his face,

Robby said, "I don't remember that picture ever being taken. What's the story on it?"

"My mom took that picture of us just before y'all left for Alabama. She had bought this new Kodak camera, an Instamatic 104. You know the one with the flash cube? Mom always tried to be cutting edge, but photography was not her forte. When we were saying our good-byes as the three of you were getting ready to leave, she took the shot...it's been in that frame and within my sight since then."

"My, my. We look like children...hugging and laughing...you and Kim with a cigarette in your hand...gee whiz...Kim looks like a little boy dressed up like a sailor. At the time, I was thinking we were all grown up and had our act together. Little did we know all that life was going to offer us, both the good and the bad."

Roger picked up his phone, pushed a button and said, "Felicia, please come here for a moment."

From the office next door walked a beautiful lady, about 30, with long curly red hair, very attractive in every way, dressed professionally yet somehow quite sexy. She had an air of class you don't see often. He handed the picture to Felicia and said, "Would you please take this and make two...no, three copies of this picture. Use our finest photocopy paper and place them in a protective envelope. Please do it now, so Mr. McLeod can have them when he leaves."

"Certainly," she said, almost singing the word in a happy melody, rather than just making a statement.

As she turned and walked by Robby, she looked at him and gave him a wink and a smile.

"Wow Roger, that's one good looking secretary you have there."

"Yes...quite pretty...she's my daughter."

"Well that explains why she acted as though she knew me; you must've told her about my coming for a visit."

"Yeah, she knew you were coming and I have talked about you

in the past. She said she feels like she already knows you, wants to talk to you, but later. Now is our time to get re-acquainted. Let's take our coffee in the conference room where we can sit at the table, have a place to put our cups and our elbows and catch up on the past 40 years."

As they walked toward the conference room, Robby noticed several pictures on the wall in his office: several 8x10's of horses, one with Felicia holding the bridle, adorned in riding gear, a large family portrait of him, his wife, and daughter that looked to be taken about 10 years ago. He saw no art, no certificates, no diplomas...just horses, family, and the fearsome foursome with the Microbus in the background.

As he sat in the conference room, Robby glanced quickly around the room and to no surprise he found everything to be first class...right down to the napkins. Although feeling somewhat small sitting at a table for 20 people, he felt right at home in Roger's presence, even though they had been apart for decades, and had only known each other for less than two weeks, they had created a bond that would last a lifetime. He reached to the center of the table, grabbed the chrome-plated coffee decanter, and gave himself a warm up. He first looked down at the bubbles in the coffee he had just generated by pouring too fast, looked at the view through the window, then directed his attention to Roger and asks, "So, tell me about yourself. How did you end up in Atlanta and how did you end up on the 20th floor in the Coca-Cola building?"

"Oh hell, I don't know where to start."

"Start at the beginning. What did you do right after we left your house in Texas?"

Roger laughed, "Oh, that's easy. I went back on the porch and lit another cigarette."

"Very funny...yeah , funny as a screen door in a submarine. Really, man, did you go back to school, or what?"

"I did the 'or what.' As it turned out I didn't go right back to school as I had planned. I bought a 1968 Oldsmobile 98. You know... the kind of car with a trunk big enough to serve a four course meal to the Vanderbilts. Believe it or not, I drove back to San Diego, where I became acquainted with a man who had invented these little battery operated burglar alarms. You would attach them to a door or window and the slightest movement would cause them to make this god-awful sound that would irritate the piss out of you until you turned it off. It may have even scared an intruder or two...Who knows? I loaded the trunk and floorboard with those alarms and set out selling them all up and down the west coast. I paid $2.00 a piece for them and sold them to housewives for $10.00. I wholesaled them to hardware stores, independent grocery stores, drug stores, and the like for $5.00. On a good day, I would sell between 75 and 100 alarms... making a profit of around $500.00 to $600.00 a day. Not bad for a box kicker, right?"

"Oh yeah, that's good money. What made you go back to San Diego?"

"It's like this. I just couldn't find myself. I really couldn't decide what to do with my life. I had thought of marketing bottled water, but realized I needed a big pile of money for that, so I abandoned that idea for a while. I didn't want to go back to school because the idea of sitting still all day and listening to dull professors while in a classroom full of 18 year old boys didn't appeal to me. So I stayed on the road until I decided what to do with my life. And you ask why I went back to San Diego? This sounds a little corny, but it was there that my life really began. It began in that bar where we formed the fearsome foursome. Before that, I was either a boy who did everything his mother said, to a student who did everything his professor said, to a soldier who did everything the Sergeant said. It was in that bar in San Diego I first became a real man who was doing things for himself instead of someone else. I went back to that same bar to recapture that feeling. As fate would have it, I met this man with the alarms in that same bar; sitting at the same damn table we sat at."

"Tell me what happened next that got you to this position, and what made you wind up in Atlanta?"

"I stayed on the road for three years straight without a break, selling those alarms, socking all the money away...even sleeping in my car at times; which was a trick I learned from our time in the VW van. I called home once a week to check on mom. One time when I called, I was in Cheyenne, Wyoming...a wintery, rainy night, in a phone booth that was wet, cold, and smelled like every cowboy in the state had pissed in it. She wanted me to come home for a visit and she sounded so serious I headed home as fast as that 98 Olds would take me. By now, I was sick of the road life and was yearning to be home again and eating some of Lula Mae's cooking.

"Three days after I arrived home, my mom died...lung cancer. She was 44; all that time she never once said a word to me because she didn't want to burden me with bad news. To the end, her concern was for me, not for herself. The last day, I stayed by her bed and we talked all day and into the night. One thing she said several times was, 'I wish I'd never started smoking those goddamn Pall Malls.' And another thing she kept saying was, 'Follow your dreams. Don't be afraid to take chances. Remember...even a turtle would never get anywhere if he didn't first stick out his neck. If you think you can change the world by selling bottled water, then, damn it, do it, and don't let anyone stop you or talk you out of it.'"

Roger wiped tears from his eyes with one of the linen napkins and said, "I'm not sure if she kept repeating those words over and over because she wanted to be sure I got it, or maybe it was the influence that all the pain pills had on her, I'll never know. But I do know this: that was the last day I smoked a cigarette and it was the first day of my life as a bottled water entrepreneur."

Roger cleared his throat, poured the last of the coffee, took a sip, looked back at his office and said to Robby, "Oh yeah, how did I get here, in the Coca-Cola building. That was the easy part. Perhaps you remember a conversation we had before going to the Grand Canyon and you mentioned the best water in the country was in the North Georgia Mountains because it was filtered by granite from deep in the earth. Do you remember saying that?"

"Yes, I remember. And I still believe that. It's still one of the few places that isn't polluted to the point you have to wipe your feet when you get out of the lake."

Roger continued, "Well I did further research and found out the water you talked about is in the top three percent in the world when it comes to purity...in the world...three percent! So, I packed up the Olds one more time and moved to Georgia. Since it was the granite filtering that made the water so pure, I started at the source...Stone Mountain, Georgia. You were right; it's one big ass rock. Back then, it was just another small-town-America kind of place that thousands of people would avoid in preference for the big city. There was a drug store, the First National Bank, US Post Office, a hardware store, two cafes, a train depot, and three police cars...that's all."

"I went to one of the drug stores that had a counter with a soda fountain and a row of tables along one wall, which looked to me like the gathering place...you know...like a neighborhood bar without the alcohol. I introduced myself and asked if anyone knew of some land for sale that had plenty of water. The owner of the place laughed and said, 'Just pick a spot and dig down about four feet and you got water around here!' Then they proceeded to tell me all about the moonshine stills they had around these parts and how popular their whiskey was because of the clear water. That is, it was popular until the government began to meddle in their business. Now, I'm thinking, if this area supplied illegal whiskey for all of Atlanta, it certainly could supply bottled water for the same."

"I had a good feeling about this place, so I walked around town, looking for a building I could use for my headquarters. One block off Main Street I saw a rather unkempt, run down building for sale. Looking from the outside, it looked perfect for a warehousing and distribution center; there was even a loading dock in the rear and an overhead door in the front. The owner, Mr. Hall, happened to be there and he showed me the place; it didn't take long since it was a small place...about 2,400 square feet. That old metal building had held many businesses throughout the years, but the last business was a car repair shop, which means it was a nasty mess. Through all the debris and filth left on the floor, I noticed a galvanized pipe protruding out of the concrete floor; it was about three feet high and looked really old."

"I asked the owner about the pipe, and he said, "'Oh, that old thing; I never capped it off. Well, it's like this. Back in the '20s, there was a much smaller building here, a wood frame structure that was a barber shop, in fact, it was my barber shop. That there pipe come up inside the shop into a sink where we washed up. The other end of that pipe's about 200 feet down; it's a bored well and they had to drill through solid granite for a week before they hit the water. I quit barbering and tore down the old barber shop, poured a concrete slab where the parking lot and shop use to be so I could build a nice new building and rent it out. The ole boy that poured the concrete didn't know what to do with that water pipe, so he just left it there and built around it. But don't worry, young man, we're on city water now and you don't need that old well anymore. If you want to buy it, I can cap off that pipe.'"

"Cap it off? No sir, there is no need to cap that old thing off. I'll take it as is. How much are you asking?"

"Well, you know, this is 1973 and things are really expensive nowadays...I'll take $35,000 for it just the way it sets."

"Ok. I'll take it on one condition; I need you to get a good lawyer to draw up the papers and I would like for you to pay the legal fees. I can give you a cashier's check as soon as you get the appointment with the lawyer."

"Consider it done. I have a lawyer friend of mine, Mr. Venable, who'll treat us right."

Roger got up to go to the small break room next to the conference room and refilled the decanter. He walked to Robby's side of the table to freshen up his coffee with the skill and dignity of the finest waiter in any four star restaurant. Next he walked to his side of the table, poured a cup for himself and tossed two oat and chocolate chip power bars on the dark cherry table.

As he sat back down in the plush swivel chair he said in a rather nostalgic voice, "And that's how it all started. I cleaned the place up, put a filter on the pipe and began bottling water. I started off loading my Olds with cases and five gallon jugs of water and selling it in office parks and small vendors. In a short time, it had grown so that I purchased a larger warehouse and bought the top of a mountain in Blue Ridge that even had more water. I named the company 'Mountain Water Company.' I got my first break when all the Colonial and Big Star grocery stores in Atlanta carried it and put my water right beside Coke and Pepsi products. It was no time other stores wanted my water and I landed a contract with K-Mart. The K-Mart contract put me over the top and I went nationwide. That's when the Coca-Cola Company started giving me lots of attention. It seems they were a little concerned that my pure, clear water was going to make a dent in their artificially colored, sugar-water sales, so they bought me out with the agreement that I would stay on board and be in charge of the water division. They changed the name of the water to a classier name, but it still comes out of the same hole in North Georgia."

With a smile, he spins around and looks out the conference room window. While holding his coffee in his right hand, he gestured with his left toward the window and said, "That's why I picked this office...from here you can see Stone Mountain, and that's where it all began. From time to time I look out this window, see the mountain, and think of two people: my mom and you. It was my mom who encouraged me to follow my dream; it was you who said it might work if I pumped enough time and money into it and recommended the Georgia Mountains for the best water. So that's about it for me. I live in Alpharetta with my wife and a few horses."

"Speaking of horses, whatever happened to the place in Texas?"

"Oh yeah, I guess you didn't know. My parents divorced when I was young and that was my mom's place. When she died, I inherited it, but I just couldn't bring myself to live there. I sold the house, property, horses, furniture...everything. When all expenses were met and all bills and taxes were paid, I walked away from the table with barely $900,000. I took 600,000 of the money and divided it among the hired help on the ranch who had been so loyal for so many years. Lula Mae and Hattie will never need for anything the rest of their life, neither will Jose-Zapata, who tended our horses for many years. I took the balance of the money and placed in an interest bearing account and I use the interest it brings for charity. I never touched any of my inheritance, because I wanted to make it all on my own. Now, that's enough about me. It's your turn. I've seen your name in the newspaper from time to time, and heard your name mentioned among the good-ole-boy network in Atlanta. So, don't give me that 'I'm just a poor little city boy, raised in the ghetto' act. I know better." With a devilish smile, he said, "Please, sir, tell me, did you ever perfect the art of drinking tequila? Been in any good fights lately?"

Chapter 29

· · · · · · · · · · · · · ·

Robby Shares His Story

In a flash, Robby called to memory his wilder days and laughed, "Oh hell... I drink on very rare occasions these days; and, although I still work out with the martial arts, I haven't looked for a fight in quite a while. There's really not much to tell. I took one day at a time working toward my goal, and when I reached my goal, I'd set another one."

"So that's it? That's all you're going to say? Uh...I don't think so. Ok, then, what was your first goal?"

"To finish school and get my degree, to be the first in my family with a college education."

"Did you graduate?"

"Yes. In fact I got two degrees...one in physics and one in business administration."

"Umm. I never got my degree. OK, so that was your initial goal; what was your ultimate goal?"

"That night we spent in the Grand Canyon, I made it my ultimate goal to live in the tallest building in Atlanta, so I could go on the roof and look at the stars with no distractions. Regardless of my ups and downs, I never lost sight of that one goal."

"Did you reach that goal...are you on top of the world, now?"

"Yes, as a matter of fact I am! It came to me a little later in life than I wanted, but yes I am happy how things turned out. I live in a high-rise condo in Buckhead where I own the entire building. I also own a few strip malls and other high rise multifamily dwellings. I have four children who are all grown and gone and doing well. My wife passed away a few years ago and I haven't remarried."

"Sorry to hear about your wife."

"Thanks."

"So, tell me, how did it all get started for you? I mean...uh... like...I told you my story, so what's yours?"

"Well, it was my intention to earn a lot of money in the karate business. I had it all figured out how many students I needed to become a millionaire. It would've been a chain of schools all over Atlanta. But it just did not come true no matter how hard I worked at it. Looking back, the numbers were just not there...I mean to say that back in 1969 and 1970, Atlanta was still a big town and not the huge sprawling metropolis it is now. Back then, karate was not a household word and there were still many people who had anti-Asian sentiments. Some even called karate 'Jap Crap.' So, the timing was off, there weren't enough people to fill up a school, and there was so much overhead, it was hard to make the big bucks I wanted. For several years I worked hard with marketing, advertising, personal demonstrations, and finally had two schools going and both making enough to support my family, although it was difficult and a constant strain to make all the books balance. I took on all kinds of odd jobs to help keep the schools afloat: window washer, repaired lawn mowers...I even installed swimming pools for a while just so we could pay our household bills and keep the schools out of the red ink. I so loved the martial arts and I still do; and I truly wanted to share this knowledge while bringing in big money. I mean, really, who doesn't want to get rich doing something they love?"

"Then one day I realized there is a big difference between a karate school and a karate business. I had a karate school that maintained strict discipline with a strong regard for ancient tradition. I did not have a karate business and I stubbornly refused to make the compromises necessary to turn it into a business. I failed as a karate entrepreneur and stabbed myself with many pains in the process."

"Then, a few years later, somewhere around '74 or '75, here I am sitting in my little two bedroom cottage in East Atlanta with a wife and baby...looking for the brass ring that I missed on the first try. I never gave up, but kept trying; hell, I even did radio commercials for a while...always hoping this would be the break I needed. All the while my wife and I were making improvements on our house. I was blessed with a wife who was quite pretty and just as handy with a hammer and saw as I was; she simply had a knack for fixing things, and I loved restoring that old house and admired those who fixed up an old place rather than tear it down. Throughout the late '70s, the neighborhood started going downhill, but we hung on and by 1980, the East Atlanta/ Grant Park area was the place to live. One Saturday afternoon, while we were working in the yard, a man in a suit parked in our driveway, took some pictures, and walked up to me and offered me $100,000.00 for our house.

That was the break I needed. As you know, for 20 years there was an enormous boom in construction. Throughout my neighborhood and all around Atlanta, there were hundreds and hundreds of houses...little frame houses...built right after World War II, for soldiers coming home. By now, the soldiers had moved on and left behind these houses that by now were in the hands of slum lords or at the very least, in bad need of repairs and modernizing. With the money from the sale of my house, I bought two houses and my wife and I renovated them, sold them, and doubled our money. We kept doing this...doing all the work ourselves and kept growing until we started hiring people. Once, we bought an entire block of houses that had been a mill village, made them into modern bungalows and held the mortgage on them. There was a lady, named Deri, who recently passed her exam and got her real estate broker's license; we made a good team...I would rebuild these old houses and she would market and sell them as desirable homes. I guess you could say we made each other rich. In the meantime, I attended every seminar and code class I could, increasing my knowledge of the construction industry. I began to see a trend of demolishing old, nasty apartment complexes downtown and replacing them with high rise condos. So...as they say, the rest is history. I focused on multi-family dwellings, once I learned you could make about five times the money with half the trouble compared to restoring houses.

All the while, I never abandoned my martial arts. It's what kept me centered and focused; it's what saved my life in Nam. I discovered Tai Chi in 1975, practiced it every day and have done so for the past 40 years. I teach karate and boxing at the Boy's Club and Tai Chi at the Senior Center and do private lessons at my personal studio. Here I am late in life, enjoying the best of both worlds...I teach the martial arts and I realized my dreams and goals I set that night at the Grand Canyon back in '69. It's been a road full of unexpected twists and turns, many speed bumps, many uphill climbs...but we made it, and the ride ain't over yet."

Roger found he had been leaning forward as he listened to Robby's story. He leaned back, "Quite interesting...like you used to say, 'Semper Fi, do or die.' You mentioned a lady named Deri, who did all your real estate transactions. Is this the same Deri that called me?"

"Yes sir, it is. She still handles my investments."

"It's a good thing to have known someone so long you can trust. By the way, she mentioned that you bought a van like the one we traveled in and you plan on re-tracing our steps. Is that true?"

"Well, you could say that, to some degree. This Microbus isn't quite like the one we crossed the country in, and I paid a hell of a lot more than $500.00 for it. But I do plan on going to visit Kim Hernandez and then travel cross-country and see my son who now lives in Oregon. I'm hoping that the trip will get rid of some demons that have been pinned up inside me since the war."

"I see. We all have our demons that haunt us from the past. It's a good thing you could find the same kind of the van and be able to take a month off to travel. Did you by any chance drive the van here?"

"Yes, I did. Let's go take a look at it."

As they stood up, Felicia entered with the pictures of the foursome in front of the original Microbus and handed them to Robby.

"Wow! Thanks! You even went to the trouble to frame them. How did you do that so fast?"

"It wasn't that fast; ya'll have been talking for over two hours. That gave me plenty of time to go to Atlanta Art Supply and get nice frames for you and your friends."

Roger added, "I thought you would like to give one to Kim and Moose when you see them."

"That's very nice of you. I'll give one to Kim...we haven't located Moose yet, but Deri is still working on it and if anybody can find him, she can. She's like a pit bull that never gives up."

Felicia detected the visit was not quite over, so she respectfully brought up work, "You know, dad, you have a board meeting at 2:30...it's 1:40 now"

"OK. I'm going to go look at Robby's bus and then back to the conference room."

As they were on the elevator, headed to the underground parking, Roger smiled a slight smile and said, "Somehow, I remember you as being taller."

"Oh fuck you, Roger." And they both burst into laughter as if they had never been apart. Before they could heap on any more good natured insults, the elevator door opened, they turned left and there it was, on the second row of cars, a VW standing out like a diamond in a coal pile. Roger stopped in amazement, slowly walked around. He rubbed his eyes, looked again, rubbed his eyes, looked again. First he saw this beautifully restored yellow Microbus and then suddenly, there was a flashback to the old tomato soup red VW with dents, scratches, and no hub caps.

"Oh...my...God!!! Seeing this has brought back a thousand memories. There's some things I haven't thought about for years. Like that night in the desert on the outskirts of Tijuana. That night, you stayed cool and saved our lives. I was so scared, I couldn't move and here you calmly took care of business like it was nothing."

"Well, compared to what Moose and I had been through, it WAS nothing."

Roger looked across the parking deck, eyes half closed, not seeing the dozens of cars, but the Mexican desert and, his voice filled with emotion, says, "I guess you know, if you hadn't reacted the way you did that night in the desert, none of this would've happened...all the high rise condos, the shopping malls, the pure, clean water in bottles throughout the nation...none of it would have happened. We would've been buzzard bait. It was your brave action during that split second that allowed all this to happen."

"Oh sure it woulda happened...Atlanta would have given birth to another big-time developer and there woulda been born some other dedicated fool who wanted to change the world one water bottle at a time."

They hugged as if they were long-lost cousins at a family reunion, and Roger stayed until he heard that long ago sound of a 40 HP engine turn over and start running. With a small puff of smoke the pristine bus left the parking lot. Roger stood there until Robby was completely out of sight, while Robby took one last look in his rear view mirror.

Both knew that it would not be the last time their paths would cross.

Chapter 30

· · · · · · · · · · · · · ·

The Day Trip

While driving back to his condo, his mind was rolling around the rich experience he just had with Roger for the past few hours and thinking about what Roger said to him in the parking deck.

He swiped his phone and said, "Call Deri." Oh great god and goose bumps, it called Deri. He suddenly felt a part of the 21st century...in control of a diminutive device that was assembled by employees in third world countries who earn 50 cents a day... somewhat like a Captain Kirk of a very small *Enterprise.* If he continued in this pattern, soon he might reach the status and skill level of any middle school mall rat, who can't walk 20 feet in any venue without a phone stuffed in their ear, or bumping into people or cars while texting.

While the phone found signal and began to ring, Robby savored the moment: he found the Microbus that had been only a flight of his imagination for many years; he had fallen madly in love with a long-time friend; he just had a momentous visit with a friend from the past, and the ultimate climax...he is in charge of a smart phone. Life is good.

"Hello, this is Deri."

"Yeah, I know it's Deri, I just told my phone to call Deri."

"Oh god, are you still playing with that phone? Does this mean I should no longer call you Mister 19th Century?"

"Yeah, it's great. I even checked emails this morning at a stop light. That is until some bastard started blowing his horn at me. Anyway...uh...why I called...Since I have two days before

I leave for Alabama to see Kim, how would you like to take a quick trip up to the mountains. The scenery is just gorgeous this time of year, the weather is perfect; we could spend the night and come back Friday morning. So...you wanna head out on the highway?"

"Sure, that would be great. I would love to go. Can we leave in the morning? It'll take the rest of today to shut down everything and get ready. I assume we're taking your van, correct?"

"Well...yeah, that's why I bought it...to travel."

"OK...just wondering since the only air conditioning is putting all the windows down, I'll need to bring extra moisturizer, you know, with all the heat and wind blowing in my face. Say, Robby, are you ever going to drive your BMW again?"

"Of course I will. I'll drive it to funerals," he said with as much seriousness in his voice as he could muster.

The next morning, Robby picked Deri up and they traveled the back roads and old highways from the days before I-85, stopping at every old general store and antique shop on Highway 411. Deri brought her MP3 player and they sang all the old music as loud and carefree as if they were teenagers who had borrowed dad's car. They stopped at Tallulah Gorge and spent two hours hiking. As they crested a hill that over looked the canyon, Robby stopped to catch his breath, take in the scenery, and broke out in his adorable grin, "You know, this reminds me of the time we hiked the Grand Canyon...only smaller, easier, and not so much mule poop and flies. And you are much prettier than the guys I hiked with back then."

Robby saw her wrinkle up her nose and give out a little giggle. Oh god, he would say anything to hear that giggle. You know the kind of giggle that makes you smile all inside.

That evening they found a small bed and breakfast with a porch that stretched across the back, complete with amazing mountain views. After having a down home supper served by the B&B, they ordered glasses of wine, settled into two of the rockers on the porch and watched the sun go down in a brilliant orange and pink sunset.

That night, snuggled under the covers of the four poster bed and on the edge of sleep, Robby whispered, "I could fall asleep like this every night."

All too soon, it was morning and the fun was over...it was time to eat breakfast and head back home.

Deri couldn't believe no one at the Mountain City Diner even knew how to cook a poached egg, so she finally convinced herself just this once she would fall into the trap of good ole country cooking: eggs fried in bacon grease, grits with a large scoop of butter, pork sausage, and white bread that had been toasted slightly, and surprise, surprise... covered in butter, with a little packet of grape jelly on the side of the saucer.

Deri looked at her plate, then looked across the street through the window to see the steep cliff where the side of the mountain had been blasted away to make way for the highway back in the '20s. She looked down at her plate again, stirring the food around with her fork, shoving the eggs to one side of the plate and then to the other. She squirmed in her seat, shifting to the right and then to the left before squarely facing Robby. With uncharacteristic hesitancy she said, "I think we need to talk about us."

"Us? Ok, I'm Robby, you're Deri. That's us. What else is there to talk about?"

"Robert McLeod, don't be a smart ass, I'm serious. I really value our relationship and there is no one I would rather spend time with. I know quite well how much you enjoyed being married. But...you see...uh...I'm not so sure I ever want to get married again. First of all, I would have to change my name, and then change all my credit cards over to my new name. And you know how many cards I have. Not to mention my property and car and insurance and who knows what else...it's simply mind boggling the things with your name on it. As you know, I was married once for a short while and it didn't work out so well. I really enjoy being with you, more than just about anything, but I like going my own way and doing my own thing without having to answer to anybody. I hope you understand."

Robby, who always enjoyed having a constant companion, and so hoped to marry Deri someday, saw all those fantasies disappear faster than the pancakes from his plate. With the hope and dream dashed, he smiled slightly, and with all his strength, tried not to sound the least disappointed, and said, "I do understand, and I respect your thoughts on the matter."

That evening, when he arrived at the bat cave, he packed everything he needed for the trip in the Microbus, and slept in the recliner in his clothes so there was nothing to do in the morning but drink coffee and leave by 6:00.

Chapter 31

· · · · · · · · · · · · · ·

Kim...Really?

His first stop was an unplanned brief layover in Birmingham. As he entered the old steel mill town, he noticed one thing different...no steel mills. All he could see was abandoned mills, yet another testimony to days gone by. He could vividly remember how he drove to Kim's house that night, even though it had been 44 years, almost to the day, it felt more like a month ago. What causes that? On an impulse, he left the expressway and traveled to Kim's house, wondering what it would be like now. Maybe his mother would still live there, or perhaps a young couple, just starting their life together? But that wasn't the case at all. The street where Kim had lived was hardly a street any more...mostly potholes, broken pavement, and mud. All the houses where Kim's neighbors had lived were boarded up, some with all the windows broken and the roofs caved in. He pulled into Kim's driveway, which was so overgrown with weeds, you could no longer even tell if you were in the driveway, or if you had simply pulled into the yard. The porch where he and his mother had sat was gone...only the stone steps remained, giving silent testament to the fact that once there was a porch that held a hundred memories. There were no longer any windows or doors at this original home of a very good sailor, his mother, and his many brothers and sisters.

"Well shit," Robby said to himself, "Last I remember, this street was full of laughter and joy at the sight of one of their own coming home."

He took one last look around, remembering the smell of the bar-b-que, the tubs of iced-down beer, and all the hand shaking and hugging going on to loud music from the porch. He said aloud, "Oh well, it is what it is...next stop Muscle Shoals, Alabama. I hope Kim has fared better than this street has...and his mother, too."

As usual, he took the old highway to his destination rather than I-65 out of Birmingham. It wasn't long before all he saw was open farm land: cotton fields, corn, mustard greens, a sunflower farm which looked so different from the surrounding fields.

Driving north of Highway 43, he saw a sign telling him Muscle Shoals was 10 miles away. As he passed the sign, he pulled off the road to visit a country store that had gas pumps and advertised clean rest rooms. Robby could use a little of everything that place had to offer: gasoline, a snack, and a clean place to pee. As he got out of the van and began to stretch, a man who seemed to be in his early 70s came around the corner and said, "Fill it up?"

"Sure thing, sir!" said Robby, a bit surprised to see someone who still gave service at a service station. He had not seen anything but self-service stations in years. Then he thought to himself, "I guess it's true what they say, 'When you enter Alabama, you set your watch back one hour, and you set the calendar back 25 years.'"

The man who was pumping gas couldn't be quiet about the Microbus. He broke out in a big grin and said to Robby, "I had a bus like this back in '67...took it to West Virginia in the winter time...damn near froze to death! It had very little sign of heat. I mean it was as cold as a frog stuck on a frozen pond. Of all places, my girlfriend lived in Beaver Lick, West Virginia...yep, Beaver Lick. I made many a trip back and forth to West Virginia in a bus just like this one, except mine was blue. Is this a '64?"

"No sir, a '62."

"Oh, well they all looked about the same. I still miss mine...

sold it to get married. This June me and the missus will be married 43 years. "

"Yes sir, nice talking to you."

"You too. The gas comes to $35.16; you can pay inside. We ain't got no pay at the pump here."

Robby had gotten more accustomed to people with their Volkswagen stories. "Maybe I oughtta write a book about people's VW stories…naaaa…who would ever buy such a thing?" he thought to himself as he shifted into fourth gear.

His daydreaming about writing a book was interrupted by a woman's voice coming from inside his phone, which said in her sexiest voice. "Your destination is 100 yards on the right." At first he thought Deri may have keyed in the wrong address, because there was a white, single story building about the size of a small barn. Until he saw the sign that read *"Loving Arms Ministry – Kim Hernandez, Pastor"*

He was so taken aback, still staring at the sign, he missed the driveway and drove right by the small, country church. He quickly screeched to a stop, backed up and entered the gravel driveway. He jumped out of the bus with phone in hand and walked as if he were in a race to the church sign. He aimed his phone and squeezed off 12 pictures of the little white plywood sign that had obviously been hand painted a few years ago. He said to himself, "Deri ain't gonna believe this! That crazy little shit, so full of mischief and mayhem…now a preacher? Really? Oh say it isn't so! When I knew him, he practically started every sentence with 'god damn.' This could be a little awkward."

He walked around the church, making a complete circle… looking and smiling the whole time. At the rear of the church, he noticed something you don't see every day. There was an old out house that was still standing as a testament to the way things were not long ago in rural Alabama. He looked down the hill, into the valley, and then up the next hill, and at the top of that hill he saw a white double-wide trailer with blue trim, that had a porch that covered the entire front of the house. There was a gravel driveway that connected the double-wide to the parking lot of the church. As was the custom, often the church provided their pastor with a home, and this looked like one of those deals. It was only 100 yards away, and he could see a black person sitting on the porch.

While getting closer to the house, he was able to see it was a woman, not Kim. Only when he drove right up to the house did he realize it was an elderly African-American lady with hair as white as the cotton in the surrounding fields. As he turned off the engine and pulled back on the parking brake, he heard a rather weak and scratchy voice call out, "Robby McLeod...is that you? Are you that old friend of Kim's?"

"Oh my goodness! Are you Kim's mother?"

"Oh yes sir, I am!"

Robby immediately noticed that other than hair color, she had not changed a bit. She was wearing a yellow dress with a white collar and buttons to match with a sapphire pin attached that looked like a blue bird. Could this be her Sunday dress...the best she had...and she wore it because Robby was coming today? He felt honored that she would go to the trouble for him. She did have one other thing that caused her to look a little different: she had a small, clear hose underneath her nose that was attached to an oxygen tank beside her rocking chair on the porch.

"Mr. McLeod, you're looking good. The years have been good to you. How old are you now?"

"I just turned 65."

"Well, I gotcha beat. I turned 89 last   January."

"Ma'am you're looking mighty fine, too. But please don't call me Mr. McLeod, call me Robby; and forgive my forgetfulness, but I can't remember your name."

"Well, sir my name is Cassey."

"Miss Cassey, it is so good to see you after all these years. Is Kim around? I'm sure looking forward to seeing him again...so much to talk about."

"He'll be back shortly. Today is the day he cooks lunch for the homeless mission in Russellville. He runs three outreach ministries for the poor and homeless: one in Russellville, one in Haleyville, and a large one in Birmingham that has a second-hand store and free meals every day.

You know, I'm really proud of my boy...he's done good. Back in the day, he worked with many of the famous leaders to help make things better for us colored folks here in Alabama. He marched with Hosea Williams, Andrew Young, and I don't know how many others. Once Hosea stayed at our house, and let me tell you, he was just full of fun! He made me laugh a hundred times! And then he asked me if I would like to go in town and have some fun that night. Now ain't that something! I don't think he meant nothing by it, but I didn't go anyway. I told him I won't go to town with a married man. And he smiled at me a big ole smile and said to me, "Dat's right...I know dat's right."

Oh...something else...schools. My boy Kim has done a whole lot to improve schools in Alabama. He put on a drive that raised money to get computers in these little schools that couldn't afford such a thing."

"MY, my, my, Miss Cassey that is quite a story. I'm so curious. How did it come about that he got religion and became a Minister?"

"Well, sir, I'll tell you how it all happened. He went to New York to visit my ex-husband and his brother...said he had some business with them and his uncle. I told him they was no good and stay away from them, but he insisted on going, and he promised me after that, he wouldn't have nothing to do with them no more. That night, after he had done his business with his uncle in Harlem, he was on his way to the subway and he was robbed of all his money and these hoodlums stabbed him in the back and beat him and kicked him until the police caught sight of it and put an end to that mess. He almost died in the hospital, and he did lose one kidney, but he come out alive. While in the hospital, he became a changed man. He found the Lord, and he was sure the Lord had a hand in him being alive. One night he had a dream...he called it a vision...but anyway, he seen himself in front of the throne of God himself, and Kim said, 'Thank you Lord for sparing me.' And the Lord said, "I spared you because it is not yet time for you to die, there are many good things you are destined to do. I spared you once in the desert through the hands of Robby McLeod, and today I spared you through the hands of the police. This time, make it count....make it count."

"It seemed when he got back from that trip, one day it all came to him, and since then he has been busy serving the Lord and helping everybody he can."

"Miss Cassey, I hope you don't mind my saying, but that was about the last thing I expected from Kim. However, I'm so very proud of him, and can't wait to see him."

"Well, son, you don't have to wait no more...here he comes."

A dark red mini-van with a magnetic sign on each side was coming toward the house a little too fast, leaving a cloud of dust behind, with the horn beeping over and over, almost like playing a tune. Robby and Miss Cassey stood up as the van came to a sliding stop less than two feet from the steps. Kim leapt from the van that had barely stopped, yelling, "ROBBY!!!" and ran with outstretched arms toward Robby, who is doing the same from the other end. Finally the two brothers meet once again. Robby was the first to speak, "I'll just be damned...oh excuse my language...but, my goodness....look at you!!! You look great! You look the same way today that you looked in 1969. Even your glasses are the same, and that goofy grin. Say, man, who's that pretty lady getting out of your car? Is that your daughter?

"No Robby, this is my wife Karen."

"Karen? Wait, is this the same Karen you met in New Mexico? The same Karen you never stopped talking about? I can see why you thought she was so special." Robby stepped towards her with his hand outstretched. "Karen, I'm Robby, and it's a thrill to meet the lady who stole Kim's heart!"

Karen flipped her long, raven hair from her shoulder and let it softly land on the center of her back, and as she did so, Robby noticed a few strands of silver-grey that give her hair more accents and testified to her maturity.

She reached out to shake his hand, smiling as she said, "I'm glad to meet you, Robby. Kim has said so much about you, I'm certain life wouldn't be complete had I not seen you in person. I heard what you said about my looking like Kim's daughter and I'm beyond flattered! You know, I'm 62 years old now. I was just 19 when we met."

Kim chimed in, "Well, I'm a young, handsome, 70 now...yes, the big seven-zero. It seems like just last week we were coming home in that old Microbus, which, by the way, looked nothing like this one. That yellow bus looks brand new!"

Like a proud father, Robby said, "Yeah, it is like a new one; it's a fine piece of workmanship. It's nothing like the old one, and neither was the price I paid for it. Maybe in a while, we can go for a ride...just like old times, but not quite as many miles. Changing the subject, your mom told me what happened to you in New York City. I'm really sorry you lost all your money that you received from that special sale you put together for your uncle."

"Oh that. I didn't lose that...well at least not that much. My uncle convinced me that walking around with $40,000.00 in cash wasn't the smartest thing to do in Harlem, so he wrote a check and we deposited it in the bank. I kept out $1,000.00 in cash for a plane ticket back home. All those crooks got was less than a thousand."

"It looks like lady luck was shining on you. Uh...how did it happen that you married Karen? I take it that you went back to New Mexico?"

"Yes, I did. When I got out of the hospital, it took me a while to heal from my wounds and it took longer to get my head on straight. During that time, Karen and I wrote letters back and forth for a good six months and it was her constant contact and great advice that pulled me up out of the mire and put me on the right path. I bought a brand new Chevy Impala, white with red roll and pleat interior, air conditioning, radio, and white side walls. I drove out to New Mexico in much better surroundings than I did the time I traveled with you guys."

"So, we married and came back to Alabama. It was during a time of such change in this country and Karen and I were right in the midst of all this history. We worked hard with civil rights, made much progress improving the education throughout Alabama, especially in the poor rural schools. We set up soup kitchens, and used clothing stores in three locations, and built the church you passed on the way to the house. That's what I did with all that dope money...plus a lot of donations, and thousands of unseen hours performed by hundreds of volunteers who were determined to help make a difference."

Kim reached around Karen's shoulder and gave her a firm, loving squeeze and said, "This little lady is the best thing that ever happened to me. She's the reason I quit smoking and drinking; she feeds me good food that she raises in our garden, but best of all...she makes me laugh. I don't even want to ponder how I woulda turned out had I not met her. She has been like the rudder on my ship of life...always steering in the right direction. I think often of you and realize if we hadn't made that trip and you hadn't wanted to stop at a motel with a bar attached, I would never been so blessed with such a woman."

Robby didn't know what to say; he didn't even know what to think. He had an idea that Kim would have turned out just fine regardless of how he traveled home or where they stopped to spend the night, or if he had never met Karen, he would prevail, overcome, and come out in the end victorious. Kim was a fighter...as was Robby...'we never give up' he thought to himself. Then on the other hand, he thought about how good life has been for Kim and he is happy to have had a small part in making it happen the way it did. He swallowed hard, cleared his throat because he was getting a little teary-eyed, and said, "Well, I'm glad it all worked out for you, and it was my honor to have a part in it." With a smile emitting from the corner of his mouth, he added, "Besides, us Marines gotta look after our sailor boys; if we didn't, we wouldn't be able to hitch a ride when we go to battle. And I'm thinking," he said with a wink, "it was you and Moose that were interested in the attached bar, not me; but, hell, that was a long time ago."

Robby's face lit up and he said, "Oh, I just remembered something, I have a surprise for you. Walk with me over to the van." On the front seat of the passenger side were two 5x7 pictures. He took one, turned around, and holding it with both hands, he extended the picture to Kim as he bowed...the ancient way of showing deep respect to someone you have given a gift. In a low voice, he said, "This came from Roger...the Fearsome Foursome...never knew this picture existed until a couple of days ago. Roger made three copies: one for me, one for you, and one for Moose...that is, when we find that son of a bitch. Oh man, there I go again. Sir, I apologize for my language."

"Oh thank you, Robby. I'll treasure this picture forever. I have just the place for it in my pastor's office. No need to apologize for your language. You can't say nothing I ain't heard before...you can't even say nothing I ain't SAID before; and besides, I am not your judge and jury, I'm just a buddy from the past."

Then, just as quickly as the smile appeared, it left Kim's face, and the corners of his mouth turned down slightly, as he said, "Hey, let's go for a ride. Just give me a minute to put this picture in my office, say my goodbyes and we'll be back on the highway. I want to show you the Tennessee River and the Dam. It is just a short drive from here."

Chapter 32

. . . .

Kim's Turn to Talk

Kim couldn't hide how impressed he was with Robby's new-found vehicle. With eyes as big as the glasses he wore he exclaimed, "Geee Whiiiz...this is a bad ride, man...a BAD ride!!! It looks brand new; it even smells brand new. Even though it doesn't look the same, it feels the same, and sounds the same; all except for all that rock-n-roll music coming from the 8-track player. This brings back a thousand memories...things I haven't thought about in 40 years."

Robby nodded and smiled, "Yeah, I know what you mean. We all have our Volkswagen story, don't we? Even though we shared the same highway in the same Microbus at the same time, we all had different experiences. Some experiences I never mentioned...like the one in the desert outside of Tijuana."

"I never talk about it," said Kim, sounding a little cold and distant.

Robby noticed that Kim had become very quiet and not his normal jumping up and down happy as a farm boy at the fair kind of guy, but he let it go and decided not to pry, and at the same time hoped he had not struck a sore nerve mentioning the TJ experience. Instead, he settled in and turned his attention to the hum of the engine and took in all the scenery which was so different from his home place...miles and miles of flat land with nothing but several varieties of produce coming out of the ground...no high rises, no apartments, no restaurants...nothing but a farm house with a barn every mile or so.

After a few miles of silence Kim spoke up, "Robby, there's something I must tell you. I asked you to take a ride with me, not only to see the river, but I wanted to tell you this while we were alone."

"Tell me what?"

"Sadly, the reason why you have not been able to find Moose is because he passed away."

"OH NOOO! When did he die? What happened?"

"He passed within four months after we all got home in '69, sometime in August. Robby...he killed himself."

"OH SHIT, I thought there was something like that going on. All this time, he never got back to me, and that wasn't like Moose. I had my doubts about him being alive when Deri, my assistant, couldn't find him. She even looked into the death records of New Jersey, but turned up nothing. So, that made me feel he may be still alive somewhere. I tell you, that is sad; and I am shocked, but not surprised."

"What do you mean that you are not surprised?"

"It's a long story, Kim, how much longer until we get to the Tennessee River?"

"What do I look like...your navigator?" Kim couldn't keep the sly smile from his face. "Sorry man...couldn't resist...about one half hour."

"That should give us enough time. This is a secret I've kept all these years...one that I no longer need to keep, I guess. Anyway, here goes:

"There were three of us jarheads that were going to be discharged about the same time...within about four days of each other. We were in a safe zone where there was no VC for miles and we were waiting to get measured for our new uniforms and once we got them, we were to catch a ride back to the USA. There were three of us walking across a grassy plain with a slight breeze...a dusty, hot breeze, but nevertheless, a breeze. It was Moose, me, and one of our buds named Johnny Spears. Me and

Johnny came in the same day and were to be leaving Danang the same day. He had a baby he had not yet seen, and was too excited about getting home and seeing her and his wife. We called him Swords. Every time we called him that, he would laugh and say, 'It's Spears, not Swords, you stupid bastards. Spears beat Swords.'"

"I heard the distant pop of an AK and heard Johnny moan...a goddamn sniper shot him in the neck...blood gushing out the right side just like you turned on a faucet. Immediately, Moose and I went into combat mode, even though it was a safe zone. I had several clips which I had duct-taped the ends together so I could change them out faster and gave them all to Moose. As I was kneeling on the ground with Johnny, doing what I could for him, Moose had flushed out the sniper. What he did was he stood up and dared the bastard to shoot him. Just then, a round of ammo hit the ground about three inches from his heel and that was all Moose needed to see where the sniper was. He was hidden in a tree at the edge of the grassy plain. Moose ran toward the tree, cussing and shooting at that tree for all he could, changing out the clips and flipping them over as he ran; he must have put about 200 rounds in that tree, if not more. He was so angry, so pumped...out of his mind with anger. As best I could tell, one round grazed the sniper enough for him to drop his weapon and partially fall from the tree. I saw the AK hit the ground and the sniper came crashing down, but was caught up in some low hanging branches. By now, there was nothing else I could do for Johnny, so I ran to help Moose. I thought I had entered a foot race because running close to me was a guy with a camera, who I found out later was from *Newsweek*. The cameraman arrived first to see the sniper was nothing but a boy from one of the villages who had picked up a rifle and was playing with it. He couldn't have been more than 12 years old. He finds himself with a shoulder wound, and caught hanging by one foot about six feet off the ground. Three things happened at once so fast, it's hard to describe: I was looking for something to administer first aid; whereas Moose, so full of anger, pulls out his bolo knife and cuts the boy's throat, while screaming, "Here, that's for killing Swords...." Meanwhile the photographer is taking pictures by the dozen and yelling, 'I'm gonna be famous and you're going to the stockade!' That was right before that photo man felt a hard thump to the back of his head, fell to the ground, and dropped his camera. That's because I hit him in the back of the head with the butt of my M-16 and then filled his camera full of holes. For good measure I took all the film out and exposed it to the sun; then I smiled and said, 'Nobody's getting famous off this; nobody's getting in trouble over this. This is war, you stupid little bastard. If this incident ever comes up anywhere, any time, I will hunt you down and fix it so you will regret the day your momma met your daddy. You got that?'"

"He rubbed the back of his head and nodded yes and reached out to get his destroyed camera, which I kicked out of his hand. I told him to get outta my sight, and he ran away."

"That bothered Moose more than I saw anything ever bother him. He served three hitches in a row, 39 months, but this really got to him. He cried, ranted and raved and screamed WHY? WHY? Why did Johnny Spears have to die on his last day in a safe zone? Why did he wind up killing a child who killed Johnny? Looking back, through the eyes of a more mature adult, I think it was because in Moose's mind, for him the war was over...the killing, the carnage was all behind him now, and like a lightning bolt, he was dragged right back in the fight and he wanted no more of it...you know...like it was never going to go away."

"Although we never mentioned it again, I could tell that it tortured his soul."

By now, they had reached the river and Kim directed him to a parking lot at the base of the Tennessee River Dam.

Chapter 33

· · · · · · · · · · · · ·

What Happened?

Robby took a panorama look at the sight and was speechless. The river and the dam were much bigger than he imagined. Robby guessed it was about a mile across the river as you could barely see the pine trees on the other side. Along the river bank he could see a cross section of the local culture: an elderly black man sitting perfectly still on a plastic bucket using a pole he had made from an Oak branch with a line and red cork attached; a young white man with a three tiered tackle box that, when opened, displayed every fishing lure you could buy at Walmart, using a new Abu-Garcia rod and spinning reel...constantly casting his latest lure in all directions; from downstream came a bald, overweight man who had a Yellow Lab who was constantly jumping in and out of the water, playing along the shoreline, barking in excitement while really pissing off the serious fishermen. Scattered upon the river was an equal cross section of culture of fishermen in boats, from the small $200.00 Jon Boat to a $250,000.00 Cabin Cruiser.

Robby's eyes caught sight of some new park benches that had been recently placed along the nature trail that ran parallel to the river, where one was occupied by some young love birds who were holding hands, but the others were vacant. Spotting a bench that was farther away from the love birds and more private, Robby said, "Let's get out and walk for a while."

As the trail turned away from the river and started an upward climb, Robby saw the remote bench he had seen from the van. As they topped the hill, he noticed that Kim was really breathing hard and could use a short break, so Robby motioned his hand toward the bench at the top of the hill and said, "Let's stop at that bench for a minute and cool our heels, man."

With a nod and grin, Kim said, "Oh yes sir! I'm not in as good of shape as I used to be. I see you're still fit, but I been eating too much fried chicken and watching too much TV."

As they take their place on the bench, they notice the higher elevation gave them a spectacular view of the river and dam. While still gazing at the enormity of all that water with the surrounding nature, staring at a large pontoon boat, and not looking at Kim, he reached deep inside and barely uttered a sentence that was just above a whisper, "Do you know how he died? Do you have any details?"

"Yes sir, I do. I owe you an apology. I assumed you knew...I'm truly sorry for your loss, and I'm sorry you found out this way."

"It's OK, Kim. You didn't know. Besides, back then we didn't have emails, Facebook, and social media to keep up with everybody...not sure if that was a good thing, or bad...just the way it was, I guess... no apology necessary." Robby turned his gaze from the pontoon boat and looked directly at Kim, "So, what happened?"

Kim felt like someone at confession, a little nervous, wanting to get the words out, but somewhat fearful at the same time. He looked across the broad expanse of the river, and along the river's edge he saw, of all things, two little boys playing soldier... using sticks for rifles. He closed his eyes, took a deep breath, and began.

"About a year after I was attacked, those guys that beat and stabbed me went to court, and I had to go back to NYC to appear in court and testify what all they had done to me. While I was there, I got to thinking about Moose and wondering how he was doing...maybe I could go by and visit since I was this close by, you know. So, I called long distance information and asked the lady for every number of every Forrester in Bloomfield, New Jersey."

Surprised, Robby said, "Bloomfield? How did you know he lived in Bloomfield?"

"The night we were in that bar in New Mexico, where I met Karen, he said the place reminded him of a bar back in Bloomfield. So, I took a chance and figured that bar was in his hometown. So anyway, I started calling every Forrester in Bloomfield and finally talked to his mother. On my way back home, I went to her house to pay my respects, and she told me the whole story."

"I sat in this living room with one of those large grandfather clocks ticking away, and on both sides of the clock were pictures of Moose...from early childhood on: one on a pony, one in a football uniform, another in his Marine Dress. Funny thing, he looked so young in that picture. I perceived him as an older man when I knew him. Anyway, she told me that when he got home all he could talk about was all the fun he had traveling the country with you, Roger, and me. He was not so happy a person, though. His mama told me of his nightmares...screaming 'NO!' in the night, and waking up the whole house cussing and screaming. In the four months he was at home he was hired and fired from three different jobs, was arrested for drunk driving, and got a girl pregnant. His father had enough and thought a change would do him good. His momma had a sister who lived in this little town in North Carolina and her husband offered him a job. It was there that he killed himself. He's buried in a Veterans Cemetery in Jacksonville, North Carolina. That's why your secretary couldn't find him in the death records in New Jersey; he's buried in North Carolina. I visited his grave on my way home. His name is Clarence Obadiah Forrester II."

"NO WAY...Clarence? No wonder he was called Moose. Clarence Obadiah is just not the name for a warrior...more like the name of a janitor or a bicycle repair man...or something like that. Please forgive my asking, but do you know how he killed himself? What happened?"

"I do. I made a detour on my way back to Alabama and visited his aunt and uncle. They lived in the very small beach town on one of the tiny islands off the coast of North Carolina. It was so small it had only one fishing pier. At the entrance to the pier, there was a bait shop and a very small diner that sold hamburgers, hot dogs and fries. Moose's uncle owned both those places. He taught Moose how to flip a hamburger and drop French fries and how to sell bait next door. He put Moose on the night shift, working 11:00 to 7:00. Since there weren't many people fishing at night, he took care of both places. One night a Korean family came in around 5:00 in the morning and wanted to buy some live bait so they could start fishing before sunrise. Word has it that the little Korean boy kept staring at Moose until he became very agitated and yelled at the little boy, saying, "QUIT STARING AT ME, YOU LITTLE GOOK, YOU KNOW WHAT I DID, DON'T YOU? YOU KNOW WHAT I DID!!! YOUSE JUST GET OUTTA HERE...GET TO FUCK OUT!!!"

"The Koreans that caused him to freak out were a family who lived there and ran a Handy Pantry store down the street. They knew about Moose and his problems from talking to his uncle and decided to leave and discuss the matter when Moose was gone and his uncle was at the bait shop."

"Moose found a saw in the broom closet, walked to the end of the pier and sawed the three posts that supported the safety rail in place. He tossed the saw in the ocean, went back and got in our VW van and drove it off the end of the pier to his death."

"I went to the pier where he died, walked to the end where I saw a railing that looked new compared to the rest of the weather-beaten railings. Believe it or not, it was in that spot that the Lord told me what to do to make my life count for something. As I was looking across the ocean, feeling the pounding waves gently shake the platform, I saw the church, and all the homeless centers and hundreds of people marching arm in arm, with Karen at my side. So I left that pier with a resolve to marry Karen, become a pastor, and do good unto others."

"It's bugging me to death...I can't remember for the life of me, what the name of that little town was. It was kinda like a California name...just can't place it. I remember this, though...I was delayed getting out of town by this crazy draw bridge; it turned sideways instead of lifting up."

Robby felt a cold chill come over him...feeling like one great big icicle. His hands were shaking, cold and clammy. His eyes were watery with a heart pounding so hard he could feel it. He looked over at Kim, doing all he could to control his emotions, he said, "Surf City...the place is called Surf City."

Kim lost it, for a moment he forgot he was a pastor, and blurted out, "How the fuck did you know?"

By now Robby had stood up and looked down at Kim, and with a slight smile, said, "Lucky guess." He looked again at the river, remembering that Mr. Holcomb had said, "It wasn't always yellow."

"Kim, we gotta go. We gotta go right now!"

As fast as their old legs could carry them, Robby raced back to the Microbus with Kim about three steps behind, calling out, "What's going on, Robby?"

"You'll see."

Robby opened the engine compartment door and looked at the underside. He knew from his VW repair days that when a car was repainted, they would often put just one coat of paint on the underside of the hood, whereas several coats would go on the outside. He opened his Explorer knife, and with the broken tip, used it like a scraper and removed the layer of yellow paint; and there it is. Without a word, he motions to Kim to look where the paint had been removed.

"OH...MY...GOD. Tomato Soup Red...oh Jesus...could it be?"

Without saying a word, Robby walked briskly to the passenger side, opened the door and felt under the dash to discover his fingertips run across two 1/8 inch holes where an

8-track tape player used to be.

With tear-filled eyes, in a voice that quivered, Robby said, "This van is not **A** Nazi Bastard." And together, in unison they say, "It's **THE** Nazi Bastard!!!"

They stand there staring at each other, then at the van and back at each other, then back at the van again. Suddenly, they both break out in exuberant laughter, not really knowing what to do or what to say, or even why they were laughing. After a few moments, they just stood there and did nothing, said nothing. There are times in your life where an experience transcends all thought, all action, all words. This was one of those times. Without a word, Robby ceremoniously removed the photo that was intended for Moose from the picture frame, and kisses the picture. He carefully places it behind the sun visor on the driver's side. Finally Robby broke the silence, forced a slight smile and said, "Well, what's for dinner?"

Chapter 34

. . . .

1969 Again...Almost

It was 1969 all over again. That evening when Robby and Kim returned, the parking lot was full of the smiling faces of people who loved Kim and by extension loved Robby, although they had never met him. There were not dozens...there were hundreds who came from all over Alabama to witness the reunion of half of the fearsome foursome.

Robby saw people of all races, all shapes and sizes, all levels of wealth...from the very rich to the very poor, with one thing in mind. They all wanted to meet the man who influenced their pastor, their leader, their mentor... the one who had influenced them. To Kim's surprise, Karen had put this all together, starting the moment she heard Robby was coming.

"Say Kim, this is like old times! Every time I pull in your driveway, there's a big party going on. Although, this time the ice tubs are full of Pepsi, tea and Fanta Orange instead of Budweiser and Colt 45," Robby said, breaking out in a big smile for the first time all afternoon.

"Yeah, times they do change." Then Kim walked to the tables where a banquet had been spread that reflected the love and hard work of all who came. In a loud, booming voice Kim shouted, "OK EVERYONE...please gather and join hands for a word of prayer before we eat. Quickly, everyone came together and Kim began... "OUR DEAR FATHER IN THE HEAVENS, please accept our thanks for this wonderful time we have to get together with our like-minded brothers and sisters. And thank you, Lord for placing Robby on this earth for the good of many. Wrap your loving arms around him, Lord, as you guide and protect all of us. Bless this food and forgive us for the times we fall short of your glory. In Christ's name...Amen!" Everyone at once said 'Amen,' including Robby, who had joined hands with a retired school teacher from Selma.

Robby shook hands and hugged so many people, he felt like a rock star...or at the very least, a small town politician. All said the same thing, "...so nice to meet you; Kim has mentioned you so many times, I feel like I know you...welcome..."

The party was winding down and people were going home about the same time a real party just got started good back in '69...10:00PM. Robby didn't mind though; he understood that most would be getting up in the morning for church. Never mind that many were older than his antique Microbus and this was no doubt quite late for them...and he hated to admit it...for him, too.

Kim said, "How about you spend the night, bro. Our house is only a two bedroom, but we have a small efficiency apartment I built inside the church for someone who might need a place to stay...looks like that's you, tonight, ha ha."

For the first time since his arrival, he saw the old Kim... dancing as he talked and laughed, going through the crowd, telling corny jokes, being everyone's comic and good friend.

"Sure man, I'll stay the night, but I'll need to leave early in the morning. I think I'll go to North Carolina and visit Moose's grave before I head home, and then I may drive this old van to Oregon to see my son...Oh, by the way, why did you say in that prayer that I was placed here for a reason? For the good of who?"

"Sir, I know how you feel about God and religion, and can hardly blame you. I just said what was in my heart. I didn't think about it ahead of time. It came out of my mouth the way it was supposed to come out...don't know...I really don't know. It just came out that way. Maybe someday it will be revealed to you."

The next morning, Robby was awake, dressed, and outside

the church apartment by 5:45. It was the time of day when the stars are giving up their extravagant display to an intense sun that was barely peeking over the horizon. While standing in the morning dew on fresh mown grass, he faced the sun and began the tai chi routine he had done every day for many years. His exercise program was interrupted by the smell of bacon as it traveled across the valley and up the hill right into his nostrils... so much for concentration. He realized there was no need to return to his routine, because he saw Kim walking toward him, no doubt to invite him to breakfast.

"I knew you would already be awake. I was going to call you on your cell phone to tell you breakfast is ready, but I don't have your number."

"Uh...I don't know it either... never call it."

"I'll show you after breakfast how to get your number out of the phone. In the meantime you call me when you get a chance and your number will be stored in my phone."

"Geee...what happened to writing a phone number on the back of a match book?"

"Well, I guess that went away with smoking, and 8-track tapes, ha ha ha!"

"Y'all have any biscuits made?"

"You mean like cat heads? Oh for sure! Mama taught Karen how to do all kinds of good Southern cooking. Bless her heart; when we met, all she knew was hot dogs and mac and cheese. But now, she holds her own with the best of them. Come on, bro, let's eat."

After a superb breakfast, Robby walked the driveway back to his van, ready to leave having packed everything last night. As he touched his door handle, he turned to take one last look. Cassey and Kim were sitting on the porch in large white rocking chairs, much the same way they did 40 years ago in those weather beaten ladder back chairs. He noticed a book in Kim's lap, thinking he was studying for today's sermon. He got in his

Microbus that now had even more meaning than before. The kind of meaning that caused you never to sell it at any price... maybe be buried in it. As he pulled out the clutch, he stuck his entire arm out the window and gave the people on the porch a big full-body wave good bye. By now, Karen had joined them, standing by the screen door, waving with one hand, a dish towel in the other hand.

He reflected on how rich Kim is; and once again he got the feeling it is not the last time they will get together. But for now, he has plans.

Chapter 35

· · · · · · · · · · · · ·

Again?

Robby reminded himself that he had to call Deri and tell her he won't be returning on schedule because he was going to the Veteran's Cemetery and maybe on to Surf City, North Carolina. He thought about calling her right then but decided to call later because this time of day she'd be dead asleep. Heading north into Tennessee and then going east into North Carolina is the way he wanted to go because he would be able to see more mountains than on any other route.

By afternoon, Robby left the flat land, into hilly country and then into beautiful mountainous terrain. Something he didn't think all the way through: there are some very steep mountains in East Tennessee, and, the Microbus did not excel at climbing long steep hills. What was he thinking?

He wasn't sure where he was but he was sure he was climbing the steepest, longest hill he had ever seen. Just as he thought he couldn't go any slower, a dump truck carrying a load of gravel pulled right in front of him, forcing him to slow down even more. Robby cussed and fumed, knowing the loose gravel flying from the truck was going to put a hurting on his new paint.

If he stayed behind, he would continue to get sprayed with gravel, if he passed...well, that's the impossible dream. He decided to go for it and pass this monster truck on the hardest climb in Tennessee. He was already in second gear, going about 10 miles per hour when he pulled in the left lane. He heard the engine scream, sounding more like the turbine engine on the

Hueys in Nam. He quickly shifted into third gear and noticed the speedometer indicated he was going 50 MPH. 50 in second gear? No way!!! Maybe in a Mustang, but not in a '62 VW. He flew by the dump truck in third gear at 70 miles an hour in a van that wide open would go 59. He shifted into 4th gear, going yet faster, maybe 80 or more by now. Is the throttle stuck? At first this was a thrill, but now it's scary...not knowing what's going on, exactly. Robby decided he cannot go on any more like this...too fast...too unsafe for the bus, so he decided to pull onto the shoulder of the road and turn off the engine.

As he looked into the mirror behind him, he saw a rock slide that had thrown enormous boulders on the street right where he would have been if he had stayed behind that slow moving truck. There was a deafening thud as the series of rock and boulder crash down on the truck, leaving a large billow of dust that engulfed the entire dump truck.

Robby ran down hill to see if the driver survived. Holding his shirt over his nose and mouth so he could breathe, he saw that the dust had settled enough to see that the rock and dirt had landed on the bed of the truck and at the rear, almost all the way to the back; but thankfully, none of the debris landed on the cab, to the driver's good fortune.

"Goddamn, that was close!" the driver said as he jumped from his rig, his hands shaking and his eyes wide. "You know if you hadn't passed me, you woulda been under all that shit right now. I saw you in my mirrors and figured you'd never make it by me...with that little old Volkswagen, and all. But damn, you took off like a scalded dog! What kinda engine you got in that thing, buddy? Is it a 350 or something?"

Robby was too shaken up to give an intelligent answer, if there was one. He was amazed the driver was OK and equally taken back by his good fortune. Trying to stay calm, he said, "I'm not sure about the engine, but the main thing is, are you OK?"

"Yeah, I'm fine. Looks like there's a load of gravel that ain't gonna get delivered today. You OK?"

"Oh yeah, I'm fine...fine as a frog hair. If everything's cool, I'm heading back to my van and just sit for a spell. Do you need me to call someone?"

"Naw, I got a cell phone, I'm good to go."

They shook hands and parted company.

Sitting in the van, Robby had some thinking to do. Twice, the Microbus was in a situation with a large truck and he escaped with his life both times. This, in turn, made him think back of all the times in Nam he had a close brush with death. And then, the time with the van when he escaped death in a Mexican desert. How many more near death experiences are there going to be? Again the question of 'Why?' came into his head. Why had he survived when so many others died? It seemed the journey in the van had done little to nothing to answer that question. If it has, he thought maybe he was too stupid to realize it. But then, the trip isn't over...two more stops...the cemetery and then the pier. He remembered once a wise man said, "Don't make it happen, let it happen." So he decided not to force the issue, but to be patient, and allow the answers to come to him.

And, oh yeah...the bus. You know, the one that was running like a cheetah uphill, pretending it was the first NASCAR Microbus. He bumped the starter and...tic tic tic...back to normal. Robby did notice something different from his last near death experience in the van; there were no smells and sights of the old bus. Not the least bit of a flash back. And he heard no whispering voice say, "I gotcha back bro." He did notice the wind had picked up quite rapidly to the point where he did not want to sit in that spot any more. Any voices this time? He would not admit to hearing voices while in his Microbus. Oh hell, it was all coincidence blended with a good imagination anyway.

He learned from Deri that his phone would also play music. So, he found what he wanted, plugged his phone into the Kenwood, and listened to Lynyrd Skynyrd singing *Sweet Home*

Alabama. With the sound of southern rock he said, "Next stop, Jacksonville, North Carolina."

Chapter 36

. . . .

Coming Home

After a few stops at snack-filled service stations, and listening to a few more VW stories, he arrived at the cemetery. And there it was, the marker that read: *"Clarence Obadiah Forrester II."* He stood in silence, took to one knee, and said, "Hey bro. I didn't expect to find you here. I thought maybe in a nice house in the suburbs, or maybe in Florida on a fishing boat, or...shit...maybe even in rehab or jail, but not here. I brought you something." From a kneeling position, he placed a bottle of Dewar's Scotch and a bacon biscuit on the ground in front of the cross that beared his name...his two favorite things. He placed his right hand on his heart, then to his lips with a gentle kiss, and touched the marker with his fingers. He stood up, did a perfect about face. As he walked back to the bus, he stopped dead in his tracks because he heard the faintest whisper of his name. He even looked back over his shoulder and saw nothing...just the wind. We get a lot of wind in the spring.

It was about a half hour drive from the cemetery to Surf City, and Robby wanted to time it where he arrived about one hour before sunset. He planned to stand on the spot where Moose had drawn his last breath. He wanted to be still and listen while meditating as the sun set over the water.

Things must have really changed since Moose lived there. There were rows and rows of condos on the beach that gave evidence they had been built recently, within the past five to ten years. Everywhere you turned there were souvenir shops, and ice cream and candy for sale. Much of Surf City looked new and he doubted that any of what he saw was here in '69. The only things that were the same from Kim's description was the old draw bridge and the pier. As he walked toward the pier, he saw an old weather beaten building right at the edge of the pier that he assumed to be the place where Moose had been employed. A large white sign with red letters announced "FOR SALE". The old building looked out of place with all the new construction and he was sure whoever bought the place would bulldoze it and start over.

Kim was right about the pier trembling. The waves were large and powerful and shook the pier support system. He walked by an elderly couple with their grandson, who was taking lessons from Grandpa on how to cast into the ocean when you are only four feet tall. Another young man, in his late teens was jumping up and down in excitement as he showed his buddy the Stingray he had just caught...a small Stingray, but nevertheless, a very formidable adversary that he had conquered.

Robby was pleased that no one was at the end of the pier, which gave him the privacy he wanted. He stood straight, with his head up and his knees slightly bent and felt the salt air brush his face and move through his hair as the pier shook beneath his feet, letting his mind wander as if to another world. He stared motionless at the sun as it sent an array of colors across an ocean that appeared to go forever. The sounds around him: the pounding of the waves, the screeching of birds, the occasional sound of triumph when someone caught a fish, a bi-plane pulling an advertisement along the beach...all these sounds gradually disappeared as he fell deeper into his meditation. Suddenly, he snapped to, eyes wide. "I got it!! I got the why of the matter!!!"

Although it seemed like a brief moment to Robby, it was dark now, and much colder on the pier with the wind feeling quite sharp as it cut through his short sleeved Hawaiian shirt.

Robby almost ran back to the parking lot. Jumping into the

bus, he knew it was not going to be much warmer in there, but at least he would be protected from the wind. After throwing on his sweatshirt for a little warmth against the cool April evening, he called Deri. "Hey Deri, this is Robby."

"Yes, I can see that. Your name is on my Caller ID screen. So how've you been? Are you OK?"

"Oh yes, I've never been better. First, I need to apologize. I was going to call you and tell you I'm running behind schedule. I found Moose...he had passed away. I've been at his gravesite and I'll give you details later. Also, I need Kim's phone number...I lost it and was going to call him to get my number. Soooo....what's my number and what's Kim's number?"

"I'll be coming home for good, now, and I changed my mind about driving to Oregon. I'm parking the bus, and I will fly to see my son."

"And I'm so happy, I'm about to bust!!! Deri, I figured it all out. I know the why that I have searched for my whole life. And you know what? It was too easy. The answer all the time was right in front of me hidden within the experiences of my old buddies."

"That's great, Rob. What do you want to do now?"

"I'm glad you asked that question. I know exactly what I want to do now. I want to make you laugh every day. I want to help you with your chores and pull weeds out of your garden. I want to take care of you when you're sick, and protect you from all harm. I want to sit with you every morning, drink coffee, read the comics and do crossword puzzles. I want to hold you when you cry, hold you when you laugh...oh hell...I want to hold you all the time and not miss a day until I'm dead and gone. This is what I want to do. Deri, what I want to do is marry you and stay your loyal husband from now on. I know how you feel about marriage, but I'm saying it anyway: Deri, will you marry me? Would you please do me the honor of being my wife?"

* * *

"*Well now, as my ole daddy would say, "Dat wuz dat." What I mean is when Mr. Rob drove that little yellow Microbus home, he never took another trip in it again. When he came home from that trip, he was a changed man. He was happy all the time and always helping others less fortunate than he was. He helped me go from a garbage truck driver to the head of security of his development company and the proud owner of a two story house in a nice subdivision. He even helped me get an education and lose 60 pounds by working out in his gym, which he never used.*"

"*Sometimes, I'd catch him just standing and looking at that bus, or he would sit in it for a while and then go on about his business. He drove it enough to keep it running and took the best of care of it, but no more trips. I asked him one time why he never took that across the country trip, and all he said was, "No need to." After a while, he quit driving it altogether, and asked me to drive it...just enough to where it wouldn't freeze up or anything.*"

"*That ole bus just sat there for years, a testimony to days gone by. He never would part with it. Not long ago, someone offered him $50,000.00 for it and he said no. Then they offered $75,000.00 for it, and he said NO! Then they offered him $95,000.00 for that van...cash money, and he said FUCK NO! And that was that.*"

"*So you might think the Volkswagen story is over, but it isn't. A new story began ten years later, right when Mr. Rob turned 75.*"~Jimmy Johnson

Chapter 37

· · · · · · · · · · · · · ·

April 12, 2023, Ten Years Later

Today, Robby was going to treat himself to sleeping late, maybe to 6:00, because it was a special day. It was special for two reasons: today was his 75th birthday, and today he was to go the conference center to receive the Humanitarian of the Decade Award. He was to be recognized for his efforts in creating housing for many veterans of war, refugees, and people who otherwise could never afford decent housing.

He looked in the mirror at his long hair that had now gone from silver to white, but, as he had often said, "I'm glad I still have hair at all at this age." Then, in the quiet of the morning, he practiced his acceptance speech:

"I am grateful and humbled by this very great honor to be considered the Humanitarian of the Decade for the City of Atlanta. As with any worthwhile task, it is never accomplished alone. First of all, my "partner in crime," Roger Hilton. We sat down one day over coffee and decided that we did not want to be the richest men in the cemetery, so we sat out on a plan of making a difference in people's lives by giving them good, respectable housing. Roger, not only donated a great deal of time and money to this project, but he made sure everybody had plenty of water.

Then there was the issue of fund raising, and the best fundraiser I ever knew came on board...Kim Hernandez. I truly thank Kim. He is here today...who at 80 years old, is still a spark that ignites the world.

It would not be proper unless I thanked the man who directly oversaw every project we did, and that is Mr. Dan Holcomb. Dan not only had oversight of our new construction, but was directly involved in the refurbishing of many homes owned by the elderly who could not afford costly repairs and modern updates on their homes. I would like to ask for a minute of silence for Dan, who passed away last December. He was truly a hard worker for the cause for almost ten years.

I share this honor with Roger Hilton, Kim Hernandez, and Dan Holcomb."

After finishing his speech in front of the mirror he went on the roof to practice his tai chi, slowly taking one step at a time since the arthritis that now bedeviled him made his knees hurt to the point of distraction. He smelled the aroma of bacon mixed with Dogwood Flowers in bloom and cut his workout session short to 45 minutes instead of the usual one hour.

As he entered his condo, the intercom buzzed...it was Jimmy the Security Guard, "Mr. Rob, there's a man here to see you...said he wanted to meet you."

"Did you tell him I am busy today?"

"Yes sir, I did, but he insisted on seeing you anyway. He said he had been looking for you ever since he retired from the Marines. Uh...I wrote down his name...uh, hold on now, let me get my glasses...here it is. His name is Clarence Obadiah Forrester III. And I'm a tellin you, this man is as big as his name."

"Well, if that doesn't beat all! Send him up, Jimmy. No, better yet, you personally escort him to my door. Give him first class treatment."

Robby opened the door to see a man six feet six inches tall about 220 pounds, in perfect physical shape. From head to toe, he looked all military...from his grey hair that is cut short in a flat-top to his boots that have such a shine the girls are afraid to wear a skirt around him. He could swear that it was Moose standing here before him, not Clarence Forrester III. He had the same jaw line, the same smile, the same eyes, and as he spoke, he had the same low voice, "I'm glad to meet you sir. My name is Clarence Forrester, retired Sergeant Major from the USMC. I've been looking for you for a while. I believe you knew my father."

"Yes sir, I did. We called him Moose. That was the only name I knew him by."

"I know. My grandma always called me Little Moose...still does, in fact. She's 95 now and still going strong. I never knew my father, but grandma always said that he always had a lot of respect for you and talked about you often. He also spoke of a trip you guys took across country in a beat up Volkswagen van. He talked about that more than anything else, so says grandma. I do not mean to take up your time sir; I just wanted to meet you face to face and shake your hand. I have been through three wars in the Middle East and I can understand what you and my dad went through."

"Come on in...sit. I'll make some coffee. You do like coffee, don't you?"

"Yes sir!"

As the coffee was brewing, a tall, slim woman appeared in an intricately stitched Chinese kimono. A little puzzled, she said, "I thought I heard voices. Robby who's your friend?"

"This is Clarence. He's the son of Moose Forrester, my buddy in the Marines. Clarence, this is Deri, my wife...the woman I worship and adore. Next week will mark our 10th anniversary."

"Pleased to meet you, ma'am," Clarence said as he stepped forward to take Deri's hand. "Mr. McLeod is very fortunate to have such a pretty wife as you."

With a little laugh, Robby said, "I can certainly tell you're Moose's son. He always had a way with words. Sometime his words got him in trouble, but that's another story."

"I can only guess what he was like, since I never met him. All I had to go by was what my grandma said. My mama never told me much, and when she married, she didn't have much use for me, and I went to live with grandmama. She's the one that really raised me. What was he like, Mr. McLeod?"

"He was strong, hard, military, loyal, fun loving, and quite a ladies' man. We had each other's backs and he saved my life once, by carrying me to a Huey on his shoulder. I tell you, son, it's a miracle any of us survived...your father, or me. You said he spoke of the trip we took in that old VW bus?"

"Yes sir. My grandma told me that he said you guys got in more tight spots on that trip than you did in Vietnam. He talked quite often about the old van that cost $500.00 and was supposed to sell it, but never did. Is that true?"

"Ummm...yeah, seems like I remember something about that. Say Clarence, do you have a few minutes? There's something I want to show you in my storage room."

Deri reminded him before he got too sidetracked, "Robby dear, don't forget about your meeting today at 1:00."

"OK, sweetheart. I've never been late before...won't be late today. This will only take a few minutes."

The two men walked down the hallway toward the elevator appearing to be a bit of an odd couple. Clarence was tall, early 50s with a chiseled, lean appearance walking erect and full of confidence, whereas Robby was quite short walking with a slight limp and not quite as erect as he used to be...two warriors from two different eras.

The elevator took them to the ground floor, below to the parking deck, where the storage room was located. As he unlocked the storage room, Robby was reminded of a conversation he had in this very spot with Dan Holcomb ten years ago:

"Hey Dan, you come to pick up some supplies?"

"Uh yeah, I'm gonna put in a sink and cabinets today, if that's OK with you."

"Oh sure, take all you need. By the way, how much do you know about construction? I thought you were a VW mechanic."

"Well sir, I do pretty good when it comes to building houses.

My father was a builder and so was my grandfather, and his father before him. I started helping my dad when I was 13 and it was a learn as you go kinda thing. That house in Salemburg, my cousins and me did all the building and it passed all the inspections the first time. When I wasn't working on Volkswagens, I was working weekends with my family, building houses. "

"I'm asking because I need someone like you I can trust to supervise some building projects for me. My old buddy and I are going to build some houses for charity and repair houses for the poor and elderly. It'll be part time and you will not have to do any heavy work...just make sure the plans are followed and it is built right. Are you in?"

"Oh yes sir, I'm in. I like helping others and it'll give me something to do."

"See Deri and she'll do the paperwork and get you on the payroll."

Robby was jolted back to the present by the fact that all the building materials and scrap wood were gone now, and all that remained in that large storage room was the bus. Robby took the cover off a perfectly restored antique Volkswagen Microbus. Clarence was speechless as he walked around it and looked at every detail.

"Is this like the one you and my dad traveled in?"

"More than that, son, it is the same van, only it's been restored and got a color change."

"Oh holy Christ, sir. I've never seen anything like this, except in books. May I please sit in it? Uh...could we take it for a ride?"

"No, I have a better idea. Can you drive a four speed?

"Yes sir."

"Here's the keys, you can take it."

"Don't you want to go with me?"

"No need to. You can take it; I mean it's yours. It's yours to have, to keep, to call your own."

"Sir, I can't accept this...no way."

"Yes way. View it as a token of appreciation for the service you have done for our country. Deri can get all the paperwork together. Her office is on the first floor."

"I haven't driven it in a couple of years. My eyesight is getting bad, and my knee hurts so that it's hard to operate the clutch. Jimmy drives it once a month to keep everything working. I'm positive...it's all yours as soon as the paperwork is done."

"Sir, I don't know what to say."

"Say Semper Fi...do or die."

"Yes sir. Do or Die"

Deri did the paperwork without a word, knowing Robby had his reasons for giving it away. It was a relief to know that Clarence lived in Chattanooga, Tennessee so it wouldn't be too long a ride for him.

Chapter 38

· · · · · · · · · · · · ·

"Say Goodnight, Gracie"

Robby, Deri, and Clarence all said their goodbyes and promised to stay in touch. Then the two old sweethearts who still acted like teenagers in love, made ready for the awards banquet ...pinching and giggling as they dressed.

After the banquet, they went to Piedmont Park and walked, holding hands. They sat on a bench and looked at the lake, taking in all the sights a spring day had to offer. They caught a glimpse in the distance of a high-flying kite; giggled as two children chased a Beagle puppy, and tucked their feet in underneath the bench as a herd of inline skaters sped by. Robby broke the silence, "I'm getting tired of sitting...can we go home, now?"

"Sure, babe; we've been sitting here over an hour. I'm surprised you sat still this long."

Deri, in spite of her love and respect for Robby, sternly scolded him, "Mr. McLeod, who do you think you are kidding not bringing your cane today? It's not like your knee is going to get better if you keep abusing it...and it damn sure doesn't make anyone believe you are not old."

"Well, I'm NOT old, and my knee IS getting better every day. I'm not depending on a damn cane for anything!"

"Ok, OK, Mr. Macho." And then she squeezed his arm and bats her eyelashes, saying, "But you will bring your cane next time, just for me, won't you?"

"Sure gorgeous, anything for you."

As they exited the park, arm in arm, smiling, bumping and

giggling, someone said, "Aren't they adorable? Honey, I want to be just like that when we get old."

Robby heard that, and immediately turned around and sternly said, "We are not old...old is 97! We ain't even close to old. And another thing..."

But he was interrupted by Deri's sweet voice, "You know dear, they were trying to give us a compliment. How many other people do you know that are called adorable at our age?"

"You're right Deri...again. Let's go home. I'm getting really tired."

As they walked along the sidewalk that would take them back to Peachtree Street, walking toward them was a young couple, arm in arm, so very close to one another, so full of happiness. Robby quickly observed the Marine uniform the man was wearing, nodded as if to say hello, and did a quick salute to him as they passed on the sidewalk. He stopped, turned around to take in this sight one more time. For a moment, he was brought back to the time of his youth when everything was fresh and new...to a time when you stayed up late just for fun, and not because your joints ached...to a time when even the large tasks were easy, and bending over to pick up a pencil was something you didn't even think about. He called to mind his military days and thought of his buds...those who made it, those who didn't. Like an electric shock, it occurred to him that young Marine was about the age of his grandson and looked more like a little boy playing dress up, pretending to be a soldier, than a bona fide young adult soldier.

"You know Deri, maybe those people who called us an old couple were right. I just don't remember getting old. I guess I would rather be young on the inside and old on the outside, than be young on the outside and old on the inside." Again he stopped his walking and gave Deri a strong hug and a kiss on the neck, saying, "It is you that has kept me feeling young on the inside all these years. Now, let's go home and take a nap."

Back at the condo, Robby headed right to his old recliner and plopped down with a heavy sigh, "Man oh man, I'm really tired for some reason and I think I'm going to go to bed very soon. I mean, I can't express how tired I am."

With an understanding voice, Deri said, "I see. It has been an exciting day: you received a prestigious award, gave an inspiring speech, visited with Roger and Kim...where y'all drank and talked and joked around way too much. Then to top it all off, you gave away your Microbus to your friend's son. So today, it all came together...you were reunited with the fearsome foursome. Not to mention, you insisted we walk to the park and back today. No wonder you're tired. Do I have to tell you how old you are, Robby?"

"OK, OK, point well taken," He said, although slightly irritated, knowing she was right. In spite of all the pain, he never thinks of being 75.

"I'll join you as soon as I take off my make up."

He went to his roll top desk for a moment, shuffled and re-arranged some papers at the top of a pile, and then went straight to bed.

As always, they fell asleep in each other's arms, the feel of their warm, soft, nude bodies marking the perfect end to a perfect day. Then they did the same routine they had done every day since they first slept together. He kissed her on the neck and said, "I'll always kiss you goodnight." Then they would both roll over...Robby facing east, Deri facing west, and they would squirm until their butt cheeks touched and that's how they fell asleep. Never once did they tire of this; nor have they ever tired of laughing, cuddling, and shopping for crazy things, such as funny coffee cups, smart ass t-shirts and bargains at the Save-A-Lot store.

A strange thing happened at 5:30. Robby woke up full of energy, full of joy, and without any pain. This was so strange because since Nam, he always had some pain and as he got into his seventies, he endured so much knee and back pain. And, his hearing and eyesight....perfect. WOW!

Another strange thing was happening. It was as if he was at the ceiling, looking down on Deri, and he saw Deri shaking him and thumping his chest, yelling, "NO...NO... Robby please don't die...OH PLEASE DON'T." But it was too late. Robert H. McLeod passed away at 5:32AM.

Chapter 39

· · · · · · · · · · · · · ·

The final chapter

The next day, Deri couldn't really think. Everything was a blur and nothing seemed to make sense, nothing seemed real. She kept wandering from room to room, hoping that she would run into Robby but knowing deep down that she wouldn't.

She knew there were a hundred things that had to be done, but she couldn't concentrate on a damn thing... just yet.

Her wandering took her into Robby's office, where she sat in his chair and began going through Robby's roll top desk, trying to figure out what to do. At the front of a mindless clutter of miscellaneous papers, she saw an envelope with her name written in purple ink...her favorite color. The note inside read:

"Hey Sweetheart. I have really been feeling bad lately, but I didn't want to burden you with worrisome news. There are some things I want you to know. First of all, my will is in the bottom left drawer of my desk, with another copy at the lawyer's office. Here goes: My four children get the shopping centers, and you get everything else. I want you to give the Microbus to a deserving veteran because it may help someone who came back from war like it helped me.

The night I asked you to marry me, I never

told you I had figured out the why of things. It's easy...there is no why. Things are what they are and we need not worry about them. I do know why my life was spared so many times. That, too, is easy. Just look at my friends. Roger and Kim would have died in the desert had not Moose and I saved their life. All the good they did would have never happened: the clean water, the civil rights, all the work done for the poor and homeless would never have happened had they lost their life that night in Mexico. Moose would have never had a son who led many to victory in the wars in the Middle East, where we finally have peace. You see, all the good that has been done by these guys would have never happened had I not been spared. It all started with Jimmy. He saved my life first, then Moose, then the Microbus; and all this good was done because I was spared.

But my luck has run out, and by now I will have found out who was right about God... Kim or me. I will miss you and I look forward to seeing you again where we will once more laugh and love; where we will travel the universe together as one...forever. Who knows? You may get to meet Moose and lots of other buds of mine."

Love you always and forever,
Rob

As Deri was reading this note, there was a classic antique

yellow Microbus traveling I-75 North toward Chattanooga with cars zipping by on the left and right so fast the bus looked as though it was standing still. He pulled down the sun visor, and there he saw a picture of the fearsome foursome with a faded red VW behind them. Clarence was going through the channels on an original Blaupunkt radio, and said to himself, "Oh man, this old radio just gets AM stations. All I can get is News and Mexican music. I'll just turn it off for now. Maybe when I get home I'll put in a Kenwood."

In the silence of the van, with only the slight hum of the engine in the rear, Clarence swore he heard someone whisper, "Don't worry, Little Moose, we gotcha back..."

The End

"And that's Mr. Rob's Volkswagen story. Like he said, "Everybody's got a Volkswagen story." Here's a few VW stories from his friends:"

Other Volkswagen Stories:

I had a VW Bus, called it the One Room Condo... and a Super Beetle with 88 jugs that out ran a lot of so called Hot Rods ... running the roads &fields in the '70s.
>   – David Wood, "Woody" from Cherokee County,
>   Georgia

I'm an artist, lived in my VW camper for many, many years. ATL, Amelia Island, Tenn. Panama C.B., S.Ga....
Great times.
>   – David Brian Wasden- Jacksonville, Florida

True, they would float....they were air tight. In new VW's , you had to roll the window down a little to get the door to close. We called it the Tupperware car. Once during a flood, we drove into a creek and it floated across to safety.
>   – Ray Johnson, from Minnesota

We could always push start it. Pop that clutch!
>   – Joseph T from Arizona.

I learned to drive in a VW beetle. Lord, I gave that car hell!
>   – Bird LeCroy

My first car was a blue VW bug. The key broke off in the ignition and I had no money to fix it, so we pushed it to get it started everywhere we went. We always had to park on a hill.
>   – Kathy from Texas

My daddy bought one and it quit running. He was so angry, he left it on the side of the road and never went back to get it.

– Michelle Girage from Atlanta

Mine was red. It had an automatic transmission, first ever in a VW. I felt so cutting edge.

– Eddie Wells from Galveston Texas

My first car was '55 VW. 36 horsepower, white. The turn signals were a metal rod that flipped out the side of the car. This was during the time when everybody had a V-8 high performance car, and here I am with 36 HP.

– Jay Thompson from Orlando, Fl

When it snowed, my car was the only one on the road. During the ice and snow the VW's and the Jeeps would go to abandoned parking lots and show out.

– Joe from Virginia Beach

I remember as a child, getting in the compartment behind the back seat and falling asleep. It was my private space.

– Sarah from North Carolina

I put a Porsche engine kit in mine. In 1965, it would blow the doors off a '57 Chevy.

– Tommy James from Decatur, GA

My first car was a 1955 black bug. Back then, summer of 1966 a new bug was $1995.00! Easy to drive and a little underpowered, but I loved it. Cruising the drive-ins I felt under dressed as it was the age of the muscle car. Wish I had it today.

– Roger Hall from Toledo, OH

It was 1968, and I was riding in the car with my father. Dad was an unusual minister, for many reasons. I'll mention only one here: While other pastors drove big Buicks and other suitably American-made vehicles, Dad drove a Volkswagen Bug. It wasn't just a foreign car, which was looked down on enough in the American South. Some people still considered it the car of the enemy.

Dad didn't care. If someone voiced a complaint, he might have used one of his favorite cuss words: Fiddlesticks. Dad liked the affordable bugs with good gas mileage and that oh-so-distinctive interior smell. Engine in the back? Trunk in the front? Why not?

– Ray Robertson from Columbus, GA

"So now, what's your Volkswagen story?"

CPSIA information can be obtained
at www.ICGtesting.com
Printed in the USA
BVOW08s1700181217

503103BV00003B/349/P